THE CITY OF DEATH

SARWAT CHADDA

Arthur A. Levine Books
An Imprint of Scholastic Inc.

Library of Congress Cataloging-in-Publication Data

Chadda, Sarwat.
  The city of death / Sarwat Chadda. — First edition.
    pages cm
  Summary: British schoolboy Ash Mistry, the reincarnation of the great Indian hero Ashoka and an agent of the goddess of death, faces the evil Lord Savage again after the villain sends his minions to capture Gemma, Ash's unrequited crush.
  ISBN 978-0-545-38518-3 (hardcover : alk. paper) — ISBN 978-0-545-38519-0 (pbk.) — ISBN 978-0-545-57640-6 (ebook) [1. Demonology — Fiction. 2. Supernatural — Fiction. 3. East Indians — Great Britain — Fiction. 4. London (England) — Fiction. 5. England — Fiction. 6. India — Fiction.] I. Title.
  PZ7.C343Cit 2013
  [Fic] — dc23
                                                          2013006974

10 9 8 7 6 5 4 3 2 1   13 14 15 16 17
Printed in the U.S.A. 23
First U.S. edition, November 2013

To my parents

When the stars threw down their spears,
And watered heaven with their tears,
Did he smile his work to see?
Did he who made the Lamb make thee?
— "The Tyger" by William Blake

CHAPTER ONE

"I can't do it," said Ash. He'd beaten a demon king. He'd faced down an immortal sorcerer. He'd saved the world. He shouldn't be scared of *anything*. But now fear grabbed at his chest with icy fingers. "It's suicide."

"C'mon, Ash," said Akbar. "It's now or never."

Josh murmured in agreement.

"Fine. I'll do it." That's if he didn't die of heart failure first. "How do I look?"

Akbar grimaced. "Honestly? A bit sick."

"Yeah," added Josh. "Sweaty."

"That's so helpful," Ash snapped back. His friends should be backing him up, not digging his grave. He swallowed and waited for his legs to stop shaking. "I'm going to do it. Now."

Akbar swept his long, straggly black hair away from his face and peered past Ash. "Whenever you're ready," he said.

Josh did his tongue-wagging grin. Along with Sean, who was somewhere in the science block earning extra credit, the four of them were the Nerd Herd. The smartest, hardest working, most socially inept and physically clumsy students to grace the hallowed halls of West Dulwich High.

Josh slapped Ash's shoulder. "Just go."

"Right. Now," said Ash. "I'm off."

He looked across the vast space of the crowded school cafeteria.

What's the longest distance in the world?

That between you and your heart's desire.

Gemma sat with her friends. She was laughing at something Anne was saying, and Ash watched as she brushed her golden hair from her face. Was it his imagination, or was it especially shiny today?

"Stop that, Ash," said Josh. "You're sighing again."

"I'm not actually asking her out. You know that, don't you?" Ash took another sip of water. How could his throat be so dry? "I'm just asking if she's got plans for tonight."

"Nope. Not asking her out *at all*," said Josh.

"Though I hear she and Jack are no longer together. Jamie's best friend, Debbie, heard it from her sister's boyfriend," added Akbar.

"Then it must be true. The golden couple have split." Josh leaned closer, eyes darting across the cafeteria. "So, if you were asking her out, which you are not, now would be the time. Or wouldn't, if you weren't."

"Whatever." Ash stood up. The chair's metal legs screeched as they scraped across the floor. It was strange how something as automatic as, like, walking, could suddenly become so difficult. Left, right, don't trip over anything or crash into a table. Why were there so many tables in here? And chairs? And people? He'd never make it over there!

Oh, God, she's seen me.

Be cool. Remember who you are.

Ash Mistry. Eternal Warrior. The demons of hell wet their pants when they hear your name.

Gemma was still talking to Anne, but her head was half-turned and her eyes were on him. She gave a little laugh. Why was she laughing? Was it something Anne had said, or because of him? Even from here Ash saw the light sparkle in her hazel eyes. She had amazing eyes, sometimes gray, sometimes green, sometimes brown. Amazing eyes.

But why is she looking at me like that?

Oh, no. Have I got snot hanging from my nostril? Is my fly open?

He should have checked. Surely one of his friends would have told him?

No, the scumbags. He bet they were laughing their heads off, watching him stroll over with a booger dangling down his face. Or worse: with his *Doctor Who* boxers on full exposure. Maybe he could detour to the corridor and do a full body check.

"Hi, Ash," said Gemma.

"Er, hi, Gemma."

The table fell totally silent. All ten of Gemma's friends stopped eating, chatting, and texting, and turned their attention to him.

Why oh why hadn't he waited till after school? Caught her on the way home or something? Or in math? She sat next to him in math. Math would have been perfect.

"You okay?" she asked. "You're looking a bit pale."

Ash stared at her mouth. Her teeth were a row of perfect little pearls and her lips red and glossy. Two dimples appeared as her smile grew. He smelled the soft, flowery scent of her perfume, making him think of springtime and bright sunlight. Jeez, *she smelled of springtime and sunlight*? He needed to slap himself hard before he felt the overwhelming desire to write poetry. Again.

"I'm fine. Totally fine," he said. "How are you? Fine?"

Did I just say that? Beyond lame.

Gemma arched her eyebrows, waiting. "Was there something you wanted?"

Ask her out. Just ask her out.

"I was wondering," he began, pausing to lick his oh-so-dry lips. "Wondering about Bonfire Night. Y'know, it's Bonfire Night. Tonight."

Aaargh. So totally smooth.

"Yes?" She shifted around on her chair, her blonde curls bouncing as she looked up at him.

Oh, my God. Was that a hair flick? It was some sort of code. Hair flicks meant something; he'd read about it in one of his sister's magazines. But what? He was deep in unknown territory: the world of girls.

"If you're going?" he said. "To the big bonfire in Dulwich Park. Tonight."

Like she couldn't work that out herself.

"Why? Are you going?"

She's asking me? What does that mean?

"I was thinking —"

"Clear the way, loser."

Jack Owen dropped his bag on the floor and himself on an empty chair. He leaned the chair back on its rear legs and flipped his cell — the latest iPhone — from his Prada leather jacket. He glanced over his shoulder as he texted. "You still here?"

Jack Owen. Ash's archenemy. The archenemy of the entire Nerd Herd. Tanned, ridiculously handsome in that obvious "big muscles, perfect features, straight nose, and floppy hair" sort of way. Oh, yeah, and captain of the soccer, rugby, and

4

cricket teams too. A company-director dad with all the toys money could buy.

I am Ash Mistry. I've done things that would melt Jack's brain. I've fought Ravana, the greatest evil the world has ever known. I've defeated the demon nations.

Then why do I want to puke?

Ash moved half a step back. That was the old Ash, who would back down and hide. Then the new Ash rose like a black snake up through his belly, driving a sharp, flint-hard anger into his throat. "I was talking to Gemma."

"And now you're not." Slowly, Jack got to his feet and faced Ash.

Gemma put her hand on Jack's wrist. "C'mon, Jack, this is stupid."

Jack looked Ash up and down.

"I see you've lost some weight. Turned some of that lard into muscle." Jack leaned so close that he was whispering in Ash's ear. "Think you can take me? Is that it? You a tough guy now?"

Jack had no idea.

So many ways to kill you.

Two bright golden lights settled on Jack's neck — one just below his bulging Adam's apple, the other near the jaw.

Easy ways.

Ash closed his eyes. But he could see the bright points shining through his eyelids. He covered his face with his hands, but it did no good.

Jack laughed. "Look at him. He's going to cry." He prodded Ash in the chest. "Boohoo."

"Leave him alone, Jack. It's not nice."

"Jesus, Gemma, I'm just trying to toughen the boy up." There was a laugh from one of the others around the table.

"Everyone knows he's madly in *luurve* with you. Isn't that true, Ash?"

"Jack, I'm warning you," said Gemma.

Jack ignored her. "C'mon, Ash. We all know you fancy her. Be a man, just say it." He put his fingers on either side of Ash's chin, wiggling it up and down. "Say it. 'Gemma, I love you so much.'" He squeezed harder, burying his nails into Ash's skin. "Say it."

Ash opened his eyes and gazed at the brilliant lights that lay like a galaxy of stars over Jack. They glistened along his arteries. They shone upon his heart, his lungs. Joints sparkled. His eyes were golden bright.

The Chinese called it Dim Mak, the Death Touch. But to Ash it was *marma-adi*, the 108 kill points. He knew them all — the points of weakness all living things possessed — and he could exploit these points to injure, disable, or kill. They moved and varied in intensity depending on the person. The old, infirm, and very young had many more than the 108. Jack had fewer — he was young and strong and fit — but he had enough.

There was a spot glowing on the side of Jack's head. Ash just needed to touch it, not very hard. Enough to create a blood clot in the brain. Death would come in five seconds, maybe six.

It would look like an accident.

"I'd let go, Jack," said Ash. A warning. That was fair.

"Or what?"

Ash shivered. It wasn't fear that made his heart quicken; it was excitement. He slowly raised his right hand. He could just tap the spot with his finger. . . .

"That's it." Gemma got up and grabbed her bag. "C'mon, Anne."

"Whatever," said Jack, letting go of Ash. He grinned at the audience and got a smattering of embarrassed giggles for his performance.

Gemma gave Jack a withering look as she slung her backpack over her shoulder and strode off, almost knocking down some small kid. Jack turned to Ash and winked.

"Way out of your league." He picked up his own bag, making sure he tensed his biceps as he did so. "Leave the hot ones to guys like me. You stick to the farmyard animals." Then he left. The others around the table, the entertainment over, quickly gathered their own gear and began to break up. Anne gave Ash a half-shrug before scurrying off after Gemma.

Ash stood by the now-empty table. What was he thinking? He stared at his hand like it wasn't his. He'd almost killed Jack. Over what?

Josh joined Ash. "Well, that went down like the *Titanic*."

Ash looked at him. Lungs, heart . . . There were nodes of energy shining on Josh's throat, and on either side of his eyes too. So many . . . Ash retreated a step, afraid an accidental touch might kill his best friend.

"You all right?" Josh asked.

Ash braced himself against a table. "Just . . . catching my breath." The sensation passed. It felt like a cloud fading from his soul. The marma-adi visions were happening more and more often. He needed to be careful.

"That was banging," said Josh.

"Banging?"

"Where were you over the summer, Ash? I remember, out in India, bored out of your brain. Everyone's using it. *Banging.* Impressive. Of an epic nature."

"What? Really? That was impressive?" Ash blinked, more than a little surprised by the assessment. "I thought I looked like a moron."

"You did," said Josh. "I was talking about Jack. That was a great line, don't you think? The one about the farmyard animals. Couldn't have thought it up himself, but he's got the delivery."

"I just wish I'd had something smart and devastating to say back," said Ash.

Josh nodded. "Like 'In your fat face, Jack'? That's pretty cool."

"If you're seven." Ash gazed toward the cafeteria doors, half-hoping Gemma might turn around and come back. No such luck. "Why is it so hard to talk to girls?"

Josh slapped Ash's head. "Because we're nerds. Acting awkwardly around girls is our superpower. Anyway, forget about Gemma. You coming around next Tuesday?"

"Tuesday?" asked Ash.

"*Dungeons and Dragons*, old-school style. We're on the last level of the 'The Catacombs of Doom' and we need you, Ash."

Oh, yeah, *Dungeons and Dragons*. Josh's dad had banned him from any sort of computer gaming — any sort of computer access at all. Josh hadn't explained why, but Akbar reckoned he'd been caught visiting a few sites *way* inappropriate for his age. So they'd dusted off their old role-playing games and miniature figures, and Tuesday nights were *D&D*.

Josh put his arm over Ash's shoulder. "It will bang to the utmost. You'll be fighting the demon lord of hell."

"Done that already."

"What?"

"Never mind." Ash wriggled out from under Josh's heavy arm. "Remind me again why I hang out with you?"

Josh gave a mocking sob. "What? After all I've done for you? If it hadn't been for me, remember, Gemma wouldn't know you even exist. That poem you wrote her was banging."

"Uploading it onto the school blog wasn't what I had in mind."

"Then you should have a better password than *TARDIS*, shouldn't you?"

CHAPTER TWO

Ash kicked a full trash can on his way home. It must have weighed more than forty pounds, but it lofted into the air and spun in a high arc over a long line of oak trees, a block of houses, and the A205 road. He heard it splash down in a pond somewhere in Dulwich Park, half a mile away.

He could do that, but he couldn't ask a girl out. Anger surged within him, and Ash struggled to cool down.

But maybe he didn't want to cool down. Maybe he could show Jack and everyone what he was capable of. They'd look at him differently then.

Yeah, they'd look at him with horror.

Some days, it was as if nothing had ever happened, and Ash was just a normal fourteen-year-old boy trying to keep on the straight and narrow. Not exceptionally bright like Akbar, nor as cool as Jack, just kind of in the middle, not making any ripples.

But then the dreams came. Dreams of blood and death.

Then Ash remembered exactly what he was.

The Kali-aastra, the living weapon of the death goddess Kali. He'd slain the demon king Ravana and absorbed his preternatural energies. He could leap tall buildings in a single bound and do five impossible things before breakfast. Six on the weekend.

Had it only been last summer? It felt like a lifetime ago. It *had* been a lifetime ago. Ash touched the scar on his abdomen that he'd gotten when his old life had, literally, ended. Three months had passed since his rebirth, and the powers had lessened somewhat, but that was like saying K2 was smaller than Mount Everest. It was still a huge mountain and Ash was still somewhere high above normal.

He remembered going running one night in September, just after coming back from India. Ravana's strength surged through every atom of his body, and it was threatening to explode out of him, so he'd needed to burn it off. He ran. And ran and ran. He'd stopped when he got to Edinburgh, four hundred miles away. He'd climbed the old castle, then run all the way back. He'd still been home before dawn.

But raw power wasn't everything. There was no point in having the strength to knock out an elephant if you didn't have the skill to hit it where it hurt most. So every morning before the sun came up, Ash crept out to the park or the nearby Sydenham Woods and trained. He'd been taught the basics of kalaripayit, the ancient Indian martial art, and once he'd caught a glimpse of Kali herself and watched her fight. Somewhere in his DNA lay all the arts of combat. Kicks, high and low, sweeping arcs, punches, spear-strikes, blocks and grapples: He shifted from one move to another with instinctive grace. That rhythm, the dance of Kali, came to him more and more easily.

Would he ever be truly "normal"? No. The death energies he'd absorbed from Ravana would fade away over time, but when? It could be decades. Centuries. There were no scales that could measure the strength of the demon king. And when — *if* — Ravana's energies did fade, Ash would forever absorb more. Death was the one certainty, and death strengthened him.

Death was everywhere.

Now, in winter, the trees lining the road had lost their summer coats, and the gutters were filled with damp, golden leaves steadily rotting, steadily dying. A small trickle of power entered his fingertips as he passed along the decaying piles. At night Ash gazed at stars and wondered whether somewhere out in the universe there was a supernova happening, a star's life ending. A solar system becoming extinct, waves of energy radiating out across the cosmos. Were the heavens making him stronger too?

It felt too big sometimes, what he was and what it meant. So he liked to be normal at school. That was why he hid his powers. It was nice to pretend, to escape, even if it was just for a few hours a day.

He registered that it was cold, but it didn't bother him. He wore the sweater merely for show nowadays. It had just turned half-past four, and the long, late autumn shadows led him home.

Ash stopped by his garden gate and looked up and down the road. For what? Gemma following him home? Not bloody likely, given his pathetic performance in the lunch hall.

You blew it.

So much about him had changed and not changed. He still didn't understand math and he certainly couldn't get a date.

He turned into Croxted Road and saw a battered white van parked outside their drive. Must be to do with Number 43; they were having their house repainted. He'd ask them to move it before Dad got home. If they didn't, he could do it himself. It looked about three tons. No problem.

Lucky opened the door before Ash even knocked. His sister was still in her school uniform, green sweater and gray skirt, gray socks that came up to her knees. Her long black ponytail flicked across her face as she turned back and forth. "Ash —"

"Before you ask, the answer is no." Ash went in and threw his backpack into the corner. "I did not ask Gemma out."

"Ash —"

"Just give it a rest, will you? Who says I'm interested in her anyway?" He passed through the hall to the kitchen. He really needed some comfort food right now, and that packet of doughnuts up on the sweets shelf would do nicely. Lucky grabbed his sleeve as he turned the door handle.

"Ash!"

"What?"

Lucky was the only one who knew what he'd been through in India, but she didn't treat him any differently, which was why, even though she was eleven and way too smart for her own good, he would die for her.

Had died for her.

You would think that would count for something, wouldn't you? But right now she was being a typical younger sister. Which was irritating.

Lucky stared hard at him, as if she were trying to project her thoughts directly into his head. Alas, while he could kill with a touch, Ash couldn't read minds. Maybe that would come later.

"What is it?" he said. Then he paused and sniffed the air. "Is Dad smoking again? Mum will go mental if he's doing it in the house."

"This is nothing to do with Dad." Lucky frowned and crossed her arms. Not good. "You've got visitors." Then she spun on her heels and stomped upstairs to her room. The whole house shook as she slammed the door.

Gemma? Had she come over to see him? She did live just down the road. It had to be. He checked that his fly was up and quickly wiped his nose. Then he opened the kitchen door.

So not Gemma. A gaunt old woman leaned against the sink, blowing cigarette smoke out of the half-open window. Her hair would have suited a witch: wild, thick as a bush, and gray as slate. She dropped her stub into Ash's Yoda mug, where it died with a hiss.

The old woman smiled at Ash, her thin lips parting to reveal a row of yellow teeth. It wasn't pretty. She searched her baggy woolen cardigan and took out a packet of Marlboro Lights. She flicked her Zippo and within two puffs the fresh cigarette was glowing.

"You're not allowed to smoke in here," Ash said. He'd been brought up to respect his elders — it was the Indian way — but there was something thoroughly disrespectful about this woman.

"So you're Ash Mistry," she said. "The Kali-aastra."

Ash tensed. "Do I know you?"

"I'm Elaine."

"I don't know any Elaines."

"She's a friend of mine."

Ash spun around at the new voice, one he recognized.

An Indian girl stepped out from behind the fridge. That was why he hadn't seen her, but then she was very good at being invisible. She played with a silver locket as she gazed at him through her big black sunglasses. She wore a pair of dark green trousers and a black cotton shirt, its collar and cuffs embroidered with entwined serpents. Looking at her, a stranger would guess she was about fifteen. They'd only be off by about four thousand years.

She took off her glasses, and her pupils, vertical slits, dilated with sly amusement. The green irises filled out the rest of her eyes, leaving no whites at all. Her lips parted into a smile, and Ash glimpsed a pair of half-extended venomous fangs where her canines should have been.

She looked like a vampire, cold and with a terrible beauty. But no vampire could compare to her. She was the daughter of the demon king and born to end men's lives.

"*Namaste*," said Parvati.

CHAPTER THREE

They looked at each other, neither moving. Then Ash came forward and somewhat awkwardly hugged Parvati.

She stepped back and looked at him.

"You've changed," she said.

"For the better, right?"

"That remains to be seen."

Oh, nice to see you again too, Parvati.

"How have you been?" he asked. "It's been ages and I haven't heard anything."

"You missed me? How nice."

"I didn't say that. But I thought you might have dropped me an e-mail at least."

"I've been busy."

"Ouch, Parvati." He'd forgotten she didn't do sensitive. "I'm just saying, it's good to see you."

"So who's this Gemma?" she asked. "Found true love, have we?"

"What?" How did she know about Gemma? Ah, yes. Because he'd been shouting her name in the hallway. "Er, she's just a friend."

"Is she the one you wrote the poem about?"

Despite the cold air coming through the open window, Ash suddenly became very hot. And bothered. "You know about that?"

"I've been keeping up-to-date. Checking the blogs and boards. We do have the Internet in India, in case you didn't know."

"What did you think?" He had to ask. "Of the poem?"

Parvati tapped her chin in thought, brow furrowed in contemplation. "Deeply disturbing. On many levels."

"Thanks, Parvati. A lot." She obviously knew nothing about poetry. "I assume you're not here to discuss my literary endeavors, so why *are* you here?"

Parvati didn't answer. Her attention was on a photo on the wall. Ash knew exactly which one.

An Indian couple, in black-and-white, sat stiffly looking at the camera. The man's hair was glossy ebony with oil. If he'd used any more, it would have been declared an environmental disaster. His black plastic-framed glasses sat firm on his thin nose.

The woman wore a traditional sari and had a puja mark on her forehead. She had a large gold nose ring and thick kohl circled her deep black eyes.

Uncle Vik and Aunt Anita.

The photo had been taken years and years ago, when they were newlyweds. Had they imagined how their lives would go? How their lives would end?

It had happened in Varanasi, the holiest city in India. Uncle Vik had been an archaeologist, teaching at the university. But there they'd met Lord Alexander Savage. The English aristocrat had asked Uncle Vik to translate some ancient Harappan scrolls, translations that were crucial to Savage's plans to resurrect Ravana. When Vik ultimately refused, Savage had killed Ash's uncle and aunt.

Savage was over three hundred years old, and when Ash had first met him, he'd looked it. A living skeleton with skin flaking off his withered flesh, the man only kept going by his magic, and even that was beginning to fail. His plan had been to resurrect Ravana, the master of all ten sorceries, in the hope that the demon king would give him immortal youth in exchange for bringing him back from the dead. And it had all been going well for him until Ash had turned up and put his fist through Ravana's chest, ending him once and forever.

Ash could still picture the young, rejuvenated Savage, fleeing through the chaos that had followed Ravana's destruction. He had wanted to go after the English sorcerer, but in the end, he knew where his priorities lay. He had a sister, parents, and a home. This was where he belonged. It was Parvati's job to hunt down Savage — she had her own grudge against him. But Ash's anger was still there. He missed his aunt and uncle, and Savage needed to pay for what he'd done.

"Have you found him?" asked Ash.

"No. But I'm still looking." Parvati put her hand on Ash's shoulder. "I will find him. I promise you." She looked him up and down. "How are you, Ash?"

"Great. Better than great." That was true. He was in perfect health. Beyond perfect.

"You certainly look good."

Ash nodded. "Don't need to sleep, eat, anything like that. I can run hundreds of miles a day without feeling tired. Never get sick, not even a cold. There was a super-flu going around a month ago, and half the school stayed home."

"I heard about that," said Parvati. "Made the news back in India."

Ash slapped his chest. "Not even a sniffle." He sat down and picked up an apple.

"It will fade, over time," said Parvati. "You'll return to being . . . more human. But never quite all the way."

"It's kinda cool being a superhero."

Parvati arched her eyebrow. "Just don't start wearing your underpants outside your trousers. It's not a good look for you."

"Thanks for the fashion tip."

"So you're managing?" She toyed with her sunglasses. "Restraining yourself? Not letting people see exactly who you are? What you are, I should say."

"Is that why you're here? To make sure I haven't fallen to the dark side of the Force?"

"Probably too late for that." Parvati laughed, and Ash's heart quickened. He'd forgotten how her laughter was like the chiming of silver bells. "But no, that's not why I'm here. I need your help." She looked toward Elaine. "My friend had best explain."

Elaine rummaged around in her pocket and put a postcard on the table. The card was a cheap one that you could get in any tourist shop in London. It showed two bejeweled crowns, a scepter, and a golden orb, each one sitting regally on a red cushion.

"The Crown Jewels?" said Ash. He'd visited the Tower of London loads of times on school trips. Every school kid in Britain recognized them.

"You've heard of the Koh-I-Noor?" asked Parvati.

"Of course I have." He looked at the humongous diamond sparkling in the center of one of the crowns. "The Mountain of Light."

"Stolen by the British in the mid-nineteenth century from the maharajah of Lahore," Parvati said. "It was given to Queen Victoria. The original stone was much bigger than what it is now. The British cut it in half and put the largest piece in here." She tapped the central image. "The Queen Mother's Crown."

"Not anymore," said Elaine. "It was stolen five days ago."

"Impossible. It would have been in the news," said Ash.

Elaine shook her head. "No. This sort of news is kept very quiet. Why would the government want to admit a national heirloom has been stolen? You can count on the prime minister's office to cover up this sort of thing to avoid a scandal."

Ash sat down. "Why was it nicked? To sell it?"

"It is up for sale, that's for certain," said Elaine. "It's the buyer we're interested in."

"It is an *aastra*, Ash," Parvati replied.

"Ah," said Ash.

An aastra was anything made by a god — usually weapons. Ash had found one, a golden arrowhead, in an underground chamber in Varanasi, where a splinter of the aastra had entered his thumb. That minute piece of god-forged metal was the source of all his power and all the trouble that had followed: the death of his uncle and aunt, Lucky's kidnapping, and his own demise and return.

"Will it work? The British cut it in half, didn't they?" he asked.

"You only have a fraction of the Kali-aastra, far less than a half, and it's served you well," replied Parvati.

She had a point. Ash peered at his thumb, at the scar marking where the splinter had entered. The sliver of metal was long gone, bound to every atom of his body.

"Whose aastra is it?" he asked. Each aastra was different, depending on which god had forged it. The aastra of Agni, the fire god, gained power from heat and fire. Could the Koh-I-Noor be another Kali-aastra like his? That didn't bear thinking about.

Elaine looked down at her boots as she lit another cigarette and gave a slight shrug. "That we don't know."

Ash frowned. "Parvati? Any idea?"

"No," she declared. "The Koh-I-Noor is exceedingly ancient, but I've never known anyone to successfully awaken it."

"Awakened or not, we can't risk letting it fall into the wrong hands," said Elaine.

"And by the wrong hands, you mean Savage, don't you?"

Elaine nodded. "Savage has been a thorn in our side for a few hundred years."

"What do you mean, 'our side'?"

Elaine smiled. "I represent certain . . . interested parties. It's our job to know what's going on."

Ash leaned back in his chair. The Koh-I-Noor was perhaps the most famous diamond in the world, and the most cursed. Every Indian knew the story of how it had been passed down through the ages, how many of its owners had come to hideous deaths.

"How did it get nicked?" asked Ash. The security around the Crown Jewels would be intense.

"Swapped, somehow, while the jewels were being given their monthly polish." Parvati inspected the fruit bowl and picked out an apple. Ash couldn't help but notice how her canines, slightly longer than normal, sank into the flesh and two thin beads of juice ran off the punctures. "The jeweler turned around for a moment, and when he turned back, the Koh-I-Noor was gone and a piece of glass was there instead."

"No one else came in, was hiding behind the cupboard? Under the sink?"

"No."

"So we're not talking about a normal thief, are we?" said Ash. The stakes were getting higher every passing second.

"No, we're not."

"Any ideas who?"

"Name of Monty. He specializes in stealing such esoteric items. Word has got around that he's putting it on the market."

"We going to make him an offer?" said Ash.

Parvati smiled. It wasn't nice. "One he can't refuse."

Elaine picked up the postcard and tucked it away. "I've got feelers out and should have his address any time now."

Parvati spoke. "Such artifacts don't turn up every day. Savage will be after it."

"You think he might know how to use it?" asked Ash. Aastras were the Englishman's specialty. He'd spent years searching for the Kali-aastra before Ash found it accidentally, so it made sense that he'd be looking for others too.

"I really don't want to give him the opportunity. This is our chance to end this once and for all."

A tremor of excitement ran through him. "How?"

"With your help. If you're not too busy?"

"Can it wait until after *Doctor Who*?"

"Ash —"

"Joke."

Elaine buttoned up her cardigan. "We'd offer our services, but we've got some of our own business to take care of."

"What sort of business?" asked Ash.

"None of yours," interrupted Parvati. She put on her sunglasses. "Elaine will text us the address. We'll meet up later and visit this Monty."

Ash showed them to the door, where Elaine suddenly checked her pockets. "My cigarettes. I think I left them in the kitchen. You go wait in the van, Parvati, I'll only be a minute."

Parvati nodded, then, with a small bow and smile for Ash, left.

Elaine and Ash returned to the kitchen. She made a show of searching the table, the worktop.

"Try your left pocket," said Ash. He'd seen her put them away and knew she knew that too. This was a ruse to have a quiet moment without Parvati listening.

"Ah." Out came the packet. Elaine tapped it idly, her attention on Ash. "Rishi told me a lot about you."

"You knew him?" Rishi had been the first person to realize that Ash was the Eternal Warrior, the latest reincarnation of some of the greatest heroes the world had ever known. The old holy man had started Ash on his training, but had been killed by Savage's henchman before he could teach Ash more about his new nature, what he had become.

"Getting any urges? Beyond those normal for a hormonal teen boy?"

"What do you mean?"

"Rishi suspected you'd found the Kali-aastra and asked me to keep an eye on you if anything happened to him. He wanted you to continue your training."

"Don't take this the wrong way," Ash said, "but you really don't look like the sort of teacher I need." She was breathing heavily just unwrapping the cigarette packet.

Elaine drew out a business card and pushed it across the table. "Rishi gave me a list of contacts. Most are out in India. You call me if you need any help."

"I've got Parvati."

"There are things Parvati can't teach you. And her agenda may not be the same as yours."

"Meaning?" Ash didn't like what she was implying.

Elaine glanced toward the door, checking that Parvati was out of hearing. "As much as I respect Parvati, I don't trust her, and neither should you. While Rishi was around, he was able to keep her in check, but she's a demon princess, and Ravana was her father."

"She hated Ravana. She helped me kill him."

"And now the throne of the demon nations sits empty." Elaine shrugged. "Parvati is ambitious. It's in her nature."

Ash reluctantly picked up the card. " 'Elaine's Bazaar'?"

"It's a junk shop near Finsbury Park. Open all hours."

He looked at her a moment longer. He didn't need marma-adi to see Elaine's weaknesses; her smoking habit was enough for anyone to have a guess at what was killing her. The lungs glowed brightest, but her veins and arteries were clogged and thin, the blood circulation poor. Death covered her, a ready shroud. She didn't have long.

She went pale. "What do you see, lad?"

He shook his head. "Nothing. I see nothing."

She looked at the half-empty packet. "I suppose I should cut down. Maybe quit."

"It wouldn't make any difference."

Elaine cleared her throat and put the packet back in her pocket. "Just watch yourself. You read these stories about kids who get hold of their parents' guns and . . . bang, someone ends up very sorry and someone ends up very dead."

"Are you saying I'm a kid with my dad's revolver?"

"No, I'm saying you're a kid with a thermonuclear device, with a big red button saying PRESS ME." She tapped Ash's hand. "Keep out of trouble, lad."

CHAPTER FOUR

And just like that, Parvati was back in his life. Ash stood in the hallway, bewildered, well after the van had disappeared.

What should he do now?

He'd spent months wondering if he'd ever see her again, waiting every day for some message, getting none. First he'd been angry, then he'd tried to have a "quiet" life. And just when he thought it was all back to normal, there she was in his kitchen! His guts felt like they were on SPIN in a washing machine.

A pair of bright headlights lit up the driveway. His parents were home. Ash opened the door just as his mum was unbuttoning her coat.

"Hi, Ash," she said, ruffling his hair as she entered. Briefcase went alongside the small table beside the door as her raincoat went over the banister, and she brushed imaginary dust from her smart navy-blue suit jacket. She gave a weary sigh and took off her shoes, wiggling her toes for a moment. She tucked her glasses in her slipcase as she glanced at the answering machine for any messages. Then she turned slowly. "Anything wrong?" she asked. Ash was still by the door.

"Girl trouble, I bet," said Sanjay, Ash's father, as he followed his wife inside, his gaze on his BlackBerry. "That right, son?"

"Like you wouldn't believe," said Ash.

Ash's mum lifted the BlackBerry from her husband's hands. "That's enough, Sanjay."

"See what I mean?" Dad shrugged. "Girl trouble." Ash's mum was about to protest, but Sanjay took her hand and twirled her, clomping about in his boots. His own suit wasn't quite as neat or as smart as his wife's, but Sanjay worked as an engineer and spent half the week on building sites, making sure the walls stayed up and the roofs stayed on. He was at least eighteen inches taller and quite a bit wider than his wife, so when he pulled her toward him, Ash's mum was pressed against the globe of his belly.

"Is it Gemma?" asked Mum.

"The girl in the poem?" said Dad, and there was an irritating smirk across his face, the sort of smirk all parents get when they are about to mortally embarrass their children.

"Hold on. You know about that?" Ash said.

"I think it's very romantic," said Mum. "I would have been flattered if some boy had written me a poem."

Ash wanted to die, right there and then. Was there anyone in the Greater London area who didn't know about his stupid poem? It was meant to be private, and it had gone viral on the Internet. One day Josh was going to pay.

"How did it go, Bina?" Ash's dad dropped to one knee while still holding his wife's hand, cleared his throat, and began to recite. "'If I may be so bold, to say your hair is like fallen gold, and that when I see you smile, my heart flutters for a while. . . .'"

"Dad, just shut up. It's got nothing to do with Gemma."

Both looked at him with more than mild surprise. Dad lightly punched Ash's arm. "Another girl? That's my boy. Come on, do it." He held up his fist. Ash groaned as he gave his father a fist bump. Parents trying to be cool. Seriously, had he been swapped at birth or what? "Just make sure it doesn't affect your school work."

Ash left his dad in the hallway undoing his boots and went back into the kitchen with his mum. The tap went on and soon the kettle was bubbling. She paused by the open window and sniffed suspiciously. "Someone been smoking?"

"Smoking? Of course not." Ash grabbed the Yoda mug with the cigarette stubs. He really didn't want to explain what had just happened. Frankly, it would sound quite mental. "Let me help wash up."

"This girl, she's someone important, isn't she?"

Weird, wasn't it? Normal girls like Gemma left him sweating and tongue-tied, but Parvati, a half-demon assassin? No problem. There had been a moment when, well, if not exactly a girlfriend-and-boyfriend sort of setup — there *was* a significant age gap between them — they had been something a bit more than just "friends." She had kissed him, twice. Didn't that count for something? But once he'd left India, there hadn't been a word. She'd completely forgotten him. And now, just when Ash himself was moving on, here she was, and it felt like not a minute had passed since they'd last seen each other.

"Mum, I just don't know."

The doorbell rang. Must be Josh. He'd planned to come over early so the two of them could head out to Dulwich Park together for Bonfire Night. Ash would have to tell him his plans had changed and he couldn't come. Not that he'd want to go to the park anyway if it meant bumping into Gemma and having to relive the humiliation of what had happened in the cafeteria.

"Ash," his dad called from the hallway. "It's your friend."

Ash went to the hall, and his dad winked at him as he passed. What was that about? Jeez, maybe it was Elaine again. What had she forgotten now, her walker?

Ash opened the door. "Look —"

"Hi, Ash."

Oh, my God. Gemma.

"Er, hi. Er, Gemma." He looked around, wondering if she'd gotten lost or something. "Er, yes?"

He so wanted to punch his own face. Why oh why couldn't he just talk to her like a normal person rather than a cretin?

"Can I come in?"

"Here?" Yes, he should punch his own face repeatedly. "Of course."

Gemma stood in the hall. "Hi, Lucks."

Lucky sat at the top of the stairs, chin on her knees, watching. She waved back. "Hey, Gemma, my brother was —"

"Go away, Lucks," Ash said.

Lucky didn't move. She was totally immune to his threats.

"Please, Lucks?"

Lucky blinked. She didn't know how to respond to politeness. She blinked again, then left.

So. Gemma. Him. Standing in the hall. Well.

She'd tied back her hair but a few curls had slipped free, framing her face. She looked uneasy. "Listen, Ash. I just came to say I'm sorry about Jack. He's not usually —"

"Such a git?"

She smiled. Ash felt another poem coming on. "Git. Just the word I was going to use."

"Is that why you're here? To apologize for him?"

"No. I never answered your question."

"Question?"

"About Bonfire Night." She smiled at him. "I am going. What about you?"

"No. Plans have changed."

"Oh. All right then." She gave a shrug. "Well, I'll see you later. At school." She adjusted her backpack in an "I'm about to leave now and you've totally blown it" sort of motion.

Hold on. He rewound the last few seconds, trying to understand the complex subtext of that last conversation. Somewhere he'd gone wrong.

"What I meant to say was I . . . yes, I am going. Totally. I am."

"Great. What time?"

She was asking him. She was asking him. That hair flick in the cafeteria *had* meant something!

Time to play it cool. For once in your life.

Ash glanced at his watch. "I dunno, about eight?"

"I'm only down the road. Shall I pop over?" Then she laughed. "D'you remember when we were at primary school? I was here almost every day. Playing that board game —" Gemma frowned. "What was it called?"

"The Orpheus Quest."

She snapped her fingers. "Down into the underworld to rescue the princess, right? You still have it?"

Ash shrugged. "Went to the charity shop years ago, sorry."

"What happened? We used to hang all the time. I only live around the corner."

"I stayed in the Nerd Herd and you didn't, I suppose." Ash put his hands in his pockets. "We ended up in different crowds. High school's a big place."

"Do you think I've changed that much?" she asked.

"We all change, Gemma."

"That doesn't have to be a bad thing."

Ash's cell phone buzzed. It was Parvati, with an address. She wanted to meet at six thirty.

Typical. Of all the days since time began, why today?

Gemma glanced down at the glowing screen. "Problem?"

"No. There's just something I need to do, but it shouldn't take long. I'll meet you there. In case I'm late or something."

"Oh, okay." She paused by the door. "Bye, Ash."

"Bye, Gemma." He closed the front door behind her.

Ash's parents both fell silent as he entered the kitchen. They were each staring intently at their mugs.

Ash's mum turned to his dad. "That Gemma, I know her family well. Very respectable."

"Yes, her father is a dentist. Perfect teeth, both Gemma and her sister. Have you ever seen more beautiful smiles?" said his dad. "There is the dowry, him having two daughters. But no rush. We will wait until Ash has finished university, then the wedding."

"But can she cook curries?" asked his mum. "It is simple to fix. I will teach her once they are married."

"Just . . ." Ash backed out of the kitchen. "Oh, just shut up."

CHAPTER FIVE

The plan was simple. Ash would meet Parvati in Soho at six-thirty, get the Koh-I-Noor from this Monty fella, then head off to Dulwich Park at eight. And hang out with Gemma. Sorted.

This was turning out to be more fun than he'd thought.

Lucky shoved his clothes off the bed and threw herself on it. Resting her chin on a pillow, she surveyed the wardrobe scattered across the carpet. "How many T-shirts can one person need?" she asked. "And Mum told you to tidy up."

"This is tidy," Ash said. There were no clothes on the floor that didn't belong there, most of his books were up on the shelves, and the bed was made, sort of. You could even see some of the carpet. Disney wallpaper for a fourteen-year-old was social death, so it had to be covered up with posters, though poster selection was a minefield. The posters told any visitors who you were, what you were, your religious beliefs. Ash was going through a major superhero phase. Batman. The X-Men. Even a vintage James Bond from the 1960s. It informed the casual observer that Ash was either a dangerous outsider with superpowers, or a total geek. It just so happened he was both.

Ash sniffed his deodorant. According to the ads, this

particular brand would attract a whole planeload of European supermodels. He'd better use just a small amount.

He checked his hair in the mirror as he slid his gel-coated fingers through his thick black locks. He'd grown them out over the last few months and they were getting perilously long; the gel barely held his hair under any sort of control. "Pass me the Levi's T-shirt," he said. "The black one."

"They're all black." She picked up a random T-shirt. "What happened to all your other clothes?"

"Thought it was time for a new look. Anyway, a lot of my old stuff didn't fit anymore." After his time in India, he'd come back a different shape. The old Ash had been "cuddly"; this new Ash was as sharp as a razor.

"So you've decided to go all skintight and superhero-ish?"

"Something like that."

As Ash took off his shirt, he saw the scar — a pale white line locked in the dark skin, wedged between hard muscle at the top of his stomach. He drew his fingernail along it. That was where Savage had pushed the arrowhead in. Another Ash had died that night in the ancient capital of the demon king. Another boy had bled to death on the sand-covered flagstones before the Iron Gates. Now Ash was a dead man walking, brought back to life by Kali to be her weapon.

"Do you miss him?" he asked Lucky. "The old Ash?"

"You're still here. Same as you ever were."

Ash slid the T-shirt on. "We know that's not true."

"Where it matters, it is." She glanced at the mirror. Ash stood there, the T-shirt taut across his chest, clinging to the contours of his torso. He double-knotted his Converse All Stars. It wouldn't do to go tripping over a loose shoelace.

Ash pulled out his shirt drawer and dropped it on the floor. He stretched his arm to the back of the dresser and felt around. His fingers touched bare steel. The object was taped to the back panel of the cabinet. He ripped the tape off.

Hands tightening around the hilt, Ash pulled out his katar.

The Indian punch dagger was about a foot long, the blade almost half the length. Its handle was shaped like an H, gripped along the short, horizontal bar, with the wide triangular blade jutting forward, so the attack was delivered via a straight punch. The tip was diamond hard and designed for penetrating steel armor. It was like no other weapon in the world, unique to India.

Lucky drew in her breath. "I didn't know you still had it."

Ash checked the edges. Still razor sharp. "You approve?"

"No." She sat up. "I don't want you getting involved with Parvati."

Ash took out a folded piece of leather. He'd made the scabbard himself one evening at the school workshop, doing some after-hours work to earn more credits. He slipped his belt through the straps and then put it on. The katar went into the leather sheath, nestling against his lower back.

"Ash . . ."

"I'm just doing her a favor, that's all." Ash put his Victorian Army greatcoat on over the katar, a knee-length number, his "Sherlock Special." He checked himself in the mirror. The coat hid the katar perfectly, but with a flick he could instantly grab it. Lucky peered over his shoulder.

"You'll knock 'em dead," she said before grimacing. "But not in the literal sense. Okay?"

"Okay."

"And Gemma will be there." Lucky sniffed the deodorant

and wrinkled her nose. "Who knows, you might get your first real kiss tonight."

"I've kissed a girl before."

"Really? Who?"

There was a long pause. "Parvati."

"Parvati? As in daughter of Ravana? As in half-demon assassin?" Lucky leaned forward, resting her chin on her fists. "What was it like?"

"All I remember was the abject fear and the sense that I was about to suffer a slow and hideous death."

"I'm sure it'll be better next time around," Lucky said.

CHAPTER SIX

An hour later, Ash got off the bus at Piccadilly Circus. Despite the cold, London was buzzing. Tonight was the fifth of November, Guy Fawkes Night. Fireworks flared into the night sky, but a dingy fog was sinking over the city, steadily smothering all light and color.

Ash checked his cell phone. Parvati wanted to meet at the Royal Bengal restaurant. He went along Shaftesbury Avenue, with its theaters showing musicals and Shakespearean plays. The Lyric had a revival of *Faustus*, and a glaring red devil loomed over the passersby, his face split by a bloody grin. Ash turned down Windmill Street and away from the bright lights and bustling streets into a very different part of London. Soho.

Soho still had an edgy, forbidden atmosphere, especially for a boy with parental locks on his computer. His parents would go mental if they knew he was wandering around here at night. In spite of the gleaming towers and flashy shops, most of London still lay upon ancient streets and winding lanes, which made Soho a labyrinth of seedy, dark alleys where dimly seen figures lurked in the doorways and the encroaching fog seemed to choke all color, fading it to gray. Ash kept his eyes down.

"Nice coat," said Parvati as Ash entered the restaurant. The place was packed with diners and smelled of spices — fried onions, cardamom, and garlic. A waiter slipped past holding a sizzling balti tray. Molten butter shone on the fresh naan bread.

Ash's mouth watered. "Dinner first?"

"Just tea." Parvati pointed out the window. "Monty's flat is around the corner."

The neon lights from the bar opposite filled the front window with garish color, and it took Ash a second to realize there was someone waiting at the table for them.

"This is Khan," said Parvati, taking a seat.

Khan stood up and reached across to greet Ash. "Namaste." His voice was a deep, rumbling growl — the sort of sound that wouldn't be out of place in a jungle. Over six feet tall, the guy had bronze skin with cropped light brown hair, and the stitches on his dark purple shirt strained against the pressure of his muscles. He met Ash's gaze with confident amber eyes. Despite his size, he moved with feline grace.

Ash felt Khan's nails prick his skin as they shook hands. He sat down, acutely aware that everyone in the restaurant was watching him. No, they were watching Khan. The phrase "animal magnetism" sprang to mind.

Dark stripes marked Khan's arm. Ash didn't need any more clues to know what sort of rakshasa this guy was. "Tiger," Ash said. "Yes?"

Khan nodded. Once, and not that long ago, Ash hadn't believed in rakshasas. They were the bad guys in Indian mythology, immortal shapechangers who had fought humanity thousands of years ago over rulership of the world. The Ramayana was the story of that long ago war, recounting how

Prince Rama had defeated Ravana, the biggest and baddest of the rakshasas, and led humanity to victory.

Rakshasas were legends. Now here Ash was having tea with two of them.

Parvati put her hand on Khan's arm. Ash's blood boiled at the way she smiled at the tiger demon. "Khan and I go way back. He's here to help."

Khan grinned. "Sikander, wasn't it? You were leading the maharajah's infantry to the left, I was with the royal body-guard." He stretched out his arms and the grin grew even wider. "Now that was a fight. Nothing gets the blood going like an elephant charge. I don't care what the historians say — Sikander crapped his pants."

Sikander? Ash frowned. Wasn't that the Indian name for . . .

"You fought Alexander the Great? Seriously? What was he like?"

Khan put out his hand, holding it around shoulder height. "Shorter than you'd imagine and, on that day, in need of a change of underwear."

Ash stared at the two of them. Khan was showing off, name-dropping Alexander like that, but Ash had to admit the story was still pretty awesome. He was into history, thanks to Uncle Vik. What his uncle would have given to be here, sitting with a pair who had been part of all the history he could only read and guess about. But the two of them treated it so casually, barely acknowledging the legends they'd met. Maybe if you were a legend yourself, things like fighting Alexander the Great didn't seem like such a big deal.

Parvati laid her cell phone on the table and pointed at the map on the screen. "There's an easy way into Monty's place from the side alleyway. It's blocked off so no one goes down there."

"Any visitors we should know about?" asked Ash.

"Like Savage?" replied Parvati. "Let's ask Monty. Nicely."

"Nicely?" Ash grinned. "You're terror made flesh, Parvati."

Parvati stopped and looked at him in a particularly meaningful way. "That's an interesting phrase, Ash," she said. "Where did you hear it?"

"Dunno. Just made it up, I suppose." Ash couldn't miss the way she was looking at him now. Worried. "Why?"

Parvati shrugged. "I thought I'd heard it before. Some time ago."

A minute later they were climbing over a large trash bin that hid the alleyway from view. A greasy kitchen exhaust duct rattled and spat above their heads, and black plastic trash bags, stinking with rotten vegetables, lay scattered underfoot. A mangy dog tore at one of the bags and sniffed at the spilled garbage. Khan gave a throaty growl. The dog whimpered and fled.

"I don't like dogs," said Khan.

"It's high up," said Parvati, ignoring him.

She was right. There was a single window facing into the alley, but it was about twelve feet up and semiopaque.

Khan shrugged. "Will that be a problem?"

"No," said Ash. He stepped back and focused on the small window. Closing his eyes, he drew down within himself, feeling his mind, his senses, descending into a dark swirling maelstrom somewhere where his soul might be.

Ash shuddered and enjoyed the electric thrill as preternatural energy swelled within him. He felt the rush of a tidal wave. It was like riding a tsunami.

Ash opened his eyes and gazed about him.

Every sense buzzed on overload. He could see the very grains of the brickwork, each stroke of the brush on the paint that covered the walls. He smelled and separated every odor, however faint: the pungent, moist cabbage leaves that covered the floor; the gurgling drains with old, sooty rainwater; the sharp, sweet stink of gasoline.

He looked up at the window and merely reached for it. It wasn't much of a jump; he barely flexed his muscles, and then he flew upward. A moment later he touched down on the narrow window ledge, balancing on his toes twelve feet above the ground. He perched there for a moment, ear pressed against the window. Nothing.

Ash curled his fingers and drove his fist through the glass. He peered into the darkness beyond; to him it was as bright as day. A small, simple, smelly old bathroom. He climbed in.

There was a snarl from behind him and suddenly Khan was there. His nails were a few inches longer than before, and Ash saw the faint ripple of black-striped fur across his arms.

Parvati slipped in behind Khan, and suddenly the bathroom was awfully cramped.

"This is cozy," she said. "Shall we wait here for Monty to join us?"

Ash opened the bathroom door and entered Monty's flat.

Aged, yellowed wallpaper hung off the walls and patches of snot-green mold stained the ceiling. They went into the living room and found it covered with discarded books and tottering piles of newspapers that went back years, decades even. The furniture looked like it had been collected from Dumpsters. The table was missing one leg and rested on a pile of bricks. More books filled the shelves, stuffed in with no sense of order. Ash registered the number of titles specializing in Indian jewelry. Flies buzzed around an unfinished meal. Green mold covered the cups and the plates were encrusted with who knew what. And his mum complained about his room being untidy. She would have a heart attack if she saw this place.

"There's no one at home," said Ash. He picked up an old bowler hat. Strange, it was the only clean thing here. A set of clothes sat, neatly folded, beneath it.

"Thanks for stating the blindingly obvious," said Parvati.

"Disgusting," said Ash. "There are mouse droppings everywhere."

Parvati turned to him, finger to her lips.

Ash listened, not sure what for — something that didn't fit, something that was wrong.

There, behind the pile of magazines. He could hear a scratching. Too steady to be an accident. The noise stopped, as though something was aware it had been heard. There was even the delicate huff of a breath being held.

Parvati's hand shot out and a second later she had a rat dangling from her grip.

A rat. Great.

Ash frowned. "Sorry, I thought it was something."

Parvati took off her glasses and held the rodent tightly. It squealed as it stared into her cobra eyes. She flexed her jaw, widening it far beyond normal dimensions.

"For heaven's sake, Parvati, you need to eat it right now?" said Ash.

"Hear that?" asked Parvati. She was addressing the rat.

"Looks like you're dinner." Her jaws widened and her fangs sprang out, each slick with deadly poison. Her tongue, forked, flickered out across the rat's whiskers.

The rat scrabbled desperately but vainly. It twisted, head straining, and the tiny black eyes looked straight at Ash, imploring him for help.

"Please!" it squeaked in a tiny voice. "Don't let her eat me!"

CHAPTER SEVEN

Parvati held the rat upside down by its tail, swinging it slowly back and forth. "I'm going to let you go. Don't even think about fleeing, or the only hole you'll be running down will be my gullet. Understand?"

It looked like the rat was trying to nod. Not easy, being upside down.

"I'm sorry, but can we have a reality check?" said Ash. "That rat. It talked."

The rat fell, and in a second it was on its feet, nose and whiskers twitching. It rubbed its eyes and Ash swore it stamped its foot. Then it shook itself like a dog coming out of a pond. But instead of water, minute hairs tumbled off its body. The pink, oily skin pulsed and bubbled as the rat spasmed. Its squeak rose to a high, sharp violin screech as it blew up like some distorted balloon. Arms stuck out of the pink, swelling flesh and irregular patches of black hair spiraled out from its deformed head. The arms lengthened and the claws twisted into hands. Within seconds the rat was gone, and a pale, naked man stood before them.

The man grinned as he covered his privates with his hands and stood at an awkward, gawky angle. A stumpy pink tail still flicked back and forth. He glanced around. "You couldn't pass me my clothes, could you?" he said. "It's just a bit drafty."

Parvati tossed him his bowler hat.

"Who are you?" asked Ash.

"The name's Monty."

Parvati's own nose wrinkled up in a look of disgust. "A common rat demon."

"Now, there's no reason to be rude, your highness." Monty shifted his shoulders, trying to strike a more proud stance — not easy while holding a bowler over his private parts. "Common. Of all the cheek."

"Let's play with it," said Khan. His nails were two-inch claws. He tapped them on the table, dragging little grooves through the wood.

"Easy, tiger," said Parvati. But there was a malicious edge to her voice.

Monty registered the deadly looks. He backed away but just bumped against Ash. He sank to his knees, grabbing Ash's hands and dropping the bowler hat. "Sir, you look like a reasonable man. Surely we can come to some arrangement?"

Khan spoke. "Whatever he says, it'll be lies. The rats are the lowest caste of rakshasa. Hardly rakshasas at all."

Ash slowly slid his hand out and wiped it on his trousers. "An arrangement?"

"Your protection, sir. In exchange for information."

"Your information had better be top quality," said Parvati. She'd revealed more of her own demon form, with green scales clustered around her throat and her cobra eyes acutely slanted, large and hypnotic. Her tongue flicked the air, tasting Monty's fear.

Monty looked around at all three of them. "What do you want to know?"

"We're looking for the Koh-I-Noor. We understand you've just stolen it," said Ash.

"The Koh-I-Noor? You think I'd have something like that?" He shook his head. "Way out of my league. Try Sotheby's. They've got a special department for that sort of stuff."

Khan's roar shook the windowpanes as he pounced, crossing the room in an instant. He lifted Monty up by the throat, pushing the rat demon high into the air until his head was touching the ceiling. Khan's canines were long and much thicker than Parvati's. What they lacked in venom, they made up for in sharpness. They could tear Monty open with minimal effort.

"Wrong answer," Khan snarled.

"Oh, the Koh-I-Noor!" cried Monty. "I must have misheard. It's my ears; full of fur."

Khan dropped him. The rat demon lay on the floor, coughing.

Ash helped him up. "So you steal. Is that what rat demons do?"

"We've all got to earn a living, put some cheese on the table, as it were," said Monty. "I do a bit of this and a bit of that. It's not like the old days, when we were top dogs."

"The Plague Years," said Parvati.

Monty sighed. "Golden days. I miss them. Demons nowadays got no sense of pride, no sense of history."

"There still a lot of them in London?" asked Ash.

Monty snorted. "Working for those big banks in Canary Wharf."

Ash laughed. "There's profit in misery." It was the Savage family motto.

Monty put on a pair of trousers and a jacket. Then he

scooped up his bowler, tapped it into place, and sighed with satisfaction. "Now, to business."

Ash looked at the demon. *This* guy had stolen probably the most heavily guarded item in the entire country? He looked more like the kind of bloke you'd find on a street corner selling knockoff perfume. "How did you do it?"

"Ah, sir, we have our professional secrets."

Khan growled. Monty gulped. "Well, if you really want to know. The sewers."

"Sewers? The drainpipes? Wouldn't they have grilles and bars to prevent that sort of thing?"

"You're a very clever lad, if I may say so. That's what I've always said, brains always triumph over brawn." Monty gave Khan a look of superior disdain. "The sewer defenses are designed to prevent human-sized infiltration. Why, half my family lives down there. It was just a matter of time before we worked out which set of pipes led where."

Parvati smiled, maybe with just a touch of admiration. "So you just crawled into the room?"

"I won't say it was that simple, but fundamentally, yes, that's exactly what I did. The guard went out for a minute to answer a call of nature. I clamped the diamond in my teeth, which is harder than it sounds, then dived back down the drain. Four hours it took me to get back. Almost drowned in a sea of —"

"Yes, we've heard enough," said Khan. He uncurled his claws, holding out his palm. "Give us the Koh-I-Noor."

Monty looked from Khan, to Parvati, and finally to Ash. "Now let's not be hasty. Surely we can come to some arrangement?"

Parvati's eyes narrowed and a soft, dangerous hiss slipped from between her lips. She sat on the edge of the table, quite still — but in the stillness was a lethal pause. Beside her stood Khan, his predatory eyes on the rat. His claws clicked and clicked with anticipation, about to take feline-rodent relations to their usual bloody conclusion. This was a glimpse into the demon heart of Parvati, and Ash wasn't sure he liked it. His friends were dangerous people.

And what does that make me?

Monty put his hand to his throat and backed away. "A teeny-tiny arrangement?" He swallowed and sweat dripped off his long nose. "Fine. Have it your way." He went to an old cathode ray–style TV in the corner. He unscrewed the back with his nail. "You have the diamond and we're even, right?"

"We'll see," said Parvati.

The back cover fell off and Monty searched inside, coming out with a small brown cardboard box. Parvati took it off him and opened it up.

The diamond caught every speck of light and amplified it within the countless faces on its surface. According to Indian legend, all diamonds had their own sort of life, and seeing the Koh-I-Noor glowing within the dingy room, Ash believed it. There was power, ancient and even malevolent, within its flawless heart. Rumored to be cursed, it was said that he who possessed it would hold all the treasures of the world, and all its miseries.

Ash turned to Monty. "Has anyone else made an offer for this?"

Monty's eyebrows rose. "What do you mean?"

Ash's voice dropped with cold anger. "Did Savage want it?"

"Easy, Ash, I'll deal with this," said Parvati.

"Oh, my God." Monty backed away. "You're Ash Mistry, aren't you? The Kali-aastra?" There was true, deep fear in

Monty's voice. He cringed in the corner, eyes wide and breath coming in desperate pants.

Rakshasas died, like everyone else. But unlike humans, the demons were reincarnated with their memories and powers intact. It might take a few years for them to remember everything, but they didn't fear death the way mortals did.

Yet they feared Kali, the goddess of death and destruction. She was true annihilation. The end of existence. If a demon was killed by Kali or her weapon, there was no coming back. Ever.

And Ash was exactly that, the weapon of Kali.

Monty seemed to shrink. "Yes. He did. Savage wanted it."

"We've got company," interrupted Khan. He was peering through the curtains at the main street. Ash joined him.

A large white Humvee had rolled up onto the curb, and Ash watched as a tawny-haired woman in white stepped out. Jackie, Savage's right-hand woman. She was a jackal rakshasa and one of the two directly responsible for killing his uncle and aunt. Three men also got out of the big car, rakshasas for sure, but no one he recognized. With his enhanced senses, he knew Savage wasn't in the car.

Ash gripped the curtain. He wanted to tear it off and leap down and fight them. Kill them. The power inside of him stirred and swelled, urging him on.

"Not now, Ash," warned Parvati. "We don't want to give Savage any warning."

Ash spun around and grabbed Monty. "Where is he?"

"I don't know, honestly!"

Three points of light along Monty's neck, two on the left, one at the base of his throat. A couple on either side of his head. Activating his knowledge of the kill points, of marma-adi, was getting easier and easier. Ash tightened his right fist. Glowering at the petrified rat, he whispered, "I am going to count to three. Then, if the answer isn't the one I want, I will put my knuckles through what little brain you have. One . . ."

"Kolkata! He's in Kolkata!" Monty's gaze widened and his tail twitched in panic. "I only spoke to him today, check the area code on the cell phone if you don't believe me. He told me he was sending his servants over with the cash. It's true!"

"Where in Kolkata?" asked Parvati.

"Two . . ."

"Somewhere out of the Savage Foundation. That's all I know, I swear!"

The doorbell below rang.

"Well?" asked Khan. "Let's kill him and be gone."

"No, you promised," muttered Monty. "Please, I won't tell them anything."

Parvati sighed. "Sorry, but we know that's not true, don't we?" She looked at Ash. "Do you want to do it or shall I?"

Kali destroyed rakshasas. It was her holy duty. It was Ash's duty to serve her. Killing this rat demon was holy work. Ash would be cleansing the world. The desire to kill was like a fever, filling his head and heart. The black, swirling darkness urged him to do it: It struggled to take control of his body, to take over and then destroy.

But what would he become if he let that happen?

"No," Ash said. He wasn't going to kill anyone, even a demon, just because it was convenient. "Leave him." It was hard to make his fingers release their grip, but he did it. Suddenly he felt exhausted, soul weary. It had taken all his willpower to hold the darkness back, and the effort had drained him down to almost nothing. His senses dulled and he could feel the superhuman strength fading. The Kali-aastra was withdrawing its power.

He turned and tapped Monty's nose to get the rat's attention. "But see those other rakshasas outside, the ones Savage sent? Well, I've met Jackie before, and she'll be disappointed you don't have the Koh-I-Noor waiting for her. If I were you, I'd find a hole and bury myself deep down inside it for a year or two."

The doorbell rang again, and this time it was followed by banging. Monty chewed his lip, glancing at the door and then at them. Then he threw off his hat and wriggled. Limbs shrank and hair burst out over his skin in random patches. His nose stretched and whiskers sprouted on either side of the pink flesh. A moment later a rat stood on the dirty carpet. It stuck out its tongue and blew a faint, squeaking raspberry, then darted through a gap in the baseboard.

Khan leaped out of the bathroom window and hit the ground easily and silently. Jackie and Savage's other demons had disappeared into the building. Parvati somersaulted through the air, bouncing on the opposite wall before landing without stirring even the discarded paper. Ash slid down the drainpipe and joined them, and a few minutes later they were out on Charing Cross Road.

Parvati took Khan's arm. "We'll double back now. See if we can follow Jackie and her cronies back to wherever they're based."

"I'll come," said Ash. Seeing the jackal rakshasa in the flesh had brought it all back — all the rage and pain of what had happened in India and how she'd killed his uncle and aunt and threatened Lucky. He wanted to deal with her.

Parvati shook her head. "No. She doesn't know you're here, Ash; let's keep it that way. She could lead us to Savage, and starting a fight will accomplish nothing. This isn't just about you."

Ash understood. There was Lucks, his parents. He didn't want them getting involved. Keeping them safe was what mattered.

Khan backed away, leaving them alone. Parvati patted the lump of diamond in her pocket. "We did good, Ash."

"You're going already?"

"The sooner I get the Koh-I-Noor away, the better." She kissed him on the cheek lightly. It was barely a touch and over almost immediately.

It didn't feel like enough.

"Parvati . . ."

She smiled. "It was good seeing you again, Ash. You look after yourself."

She crossed the road to where Khan waited, and then the two of them disappeared into the London fog.

CHAPTER EIGHT

"Where on earth have you been?" asked Josh as Ash came through the park gates. "It's almost nine."

"You're lucky I'm here at all." Ash waved over his shoulder. "Errands to run." He'd planned to catch the bus back, but some accident due to the fog had the traffic at a standstill. He'd ended up walking all the way.

"Well, it's been an epic waste of time so far," muttered Akbar through the scarf that covered half his face. He stood, cold, shivering, and miserable in his duffle coat. "We're only here because of you, you know that?"

An impenetrable fog covered London, hiding everything beyond ten feet. It was like being lost in a world of ghosts.

Despite the weather, the fireworks display was going ahead. There was a whoosh in the darkness and some muffled burst from *somewhere*, but all you could see was dense mist, no colors, and certainly no firework explosions.

"Is anyone else here?" Ash asked.

Josh shrugged. "This is the most unbanging Guy Fawkes Night ever."

Small groups of spectators drifted in and out of the mists. Most were families with small kids waving their sparklers, but Ash recognized a few people from school.

"What's that?" He could hear something, a distant, dull roar.

"Up ahead." Josh pointed.

Through the haze of mist and smoke came a blurry orange glow. As Ash moved toward it, flickers of raw heat cut through the icy night air. Gloomy silhouettes began to solidify around them, ghosts emerging from the mist.

Ash stopped at the rope barrier.

The bonfire raged against the smothering fog. A tower of wooden debris blazed, over fifty feet tall, the flames intense and rising twice as high. Even at the perimeter ring, a good twenty feet from the bonfire, the heat made Ash's skin flush and sweaty. Monstrous clouds of smoke rose into the sky and millions of tiny, glowing embers swirled and danced like hellish imps in the fire-born drafts.

But the light the bonfire cast out did not extend much farther than the rope ring. Beyond, the darkness ruled, crowding around the living fire, waiting for the flames to go out so it could claim everything for itself. Oblivion.

"Did you . . . did you see Gemma around?" Ash said.

Josh slapped his forehead. "I knew there was something else. Yeah, she's been looking for you all evening."

"Where is she?"

"No idea. Could have gone home by now."

Great. He didn't have her cell phone number.

There was another pointless, invisible explosion as some fireworks went off. The crowd gave an ironic, half-hearted cheer.

A cold wind rippled through and the flames swayed. The radiant heat warmed only what faced the flames; Ash's back felt the chill.

"I'm getting a burger, want one?" asked Josh.

"I'll come with you," said Ash.

Dulwich Park had a small food hall attached to it, and tonight there would be burgers, baked potatoes, and drinks sold to the shivering crowd. As they made their way closer to the hall, the number of people increased. It seemed everyone was more interested in the food and drink than the fireworks display.

Ash smelled the crisp odor of burning meat and heard the sizzle of onions, his mouth watering. He weaved his way through the crowd, checking his pockets for cash.

"Hiya, Ash."

Gemma grinned at him, stamping her feet to keep some circulation going. Her hands were stuffed deep into her jeans and she had pulled her bobble hat low over her eyebrows.

She was here. Ash smiled back. The world seemed a brighter, happier place.

"Hi," he said. "You look frozen."

"It's not too bad by the bonfire, but this jumper's about as thick as tissue." She gestured to the hall. "Jack's gone off to get some food."

"So, Jack's still around." Now the world seemed much darker and colder.

"We're not going out or anything," said Gemma. "But, y'know how it is. . . ."

"No, not really."

"What's wrong?" asked Gemma. She seemed genuinely concerned. Why couldn't he have more friends like her? Instead he was hanging out with immortal assassins and demons. Maybe he needed to reevaluate his New Year's resolutions.

Fewer demons.

More Gemma.

He blushed. "Er, I've been thinking I've got the wrong sort of friends."

"Tell me about it." Gemma smiled, but her teeth chattered.

Ash whipped off his coat, adjusting his T-shirt to hide the punch dagger sheathed across his back. "Put this on."

"No. You're only wearing a T-shirt. You need it more than me."

"Trust me. I don't feel the cold much."

She laughed, but accepted the coat.

"What's so funny?"

"You, Ash. I remember seeing you slogging around the sports fields on cross-country runs, looking as miserable as a human being could. Muddy up to your knees, soaking wet, in last place."

"Always last. Yes, I remember those runs." Him last — Jack, as ever, first.

"But you kept on going. That was either incredibly stubborn or incredibly stupid."

"Probably equal amounts of both."

"But you stuck at it. I always thought that was great. Things never came that easy to you."

"Still don't."

Gemma's eyes narrowed. "That still true? You've changed a lot, Ash."

The way she said it made the hairs stand up on the back of his neck. Gemma spoke quietly, and her tone was edged with . . . what? *Interest.*

She put her hand in his. "You're right, you don't feel cold."

He looked into her eyes, and she didn't look away.

"Oh, Ash, I've been looking everywhere for you." Parvati was standing right next to him.

Ash couldn't believe it. "What are you doing here?"

Gemma dropped Ash's hand. "Who's this?"

Parvati ignored her. "We've got trouble."

Khan joined them. He looked Gemma up and down. "Namaste."

Parvati pulled Ash aside but Gemma followed. Parvati spun around. "Will you go away?"

Gemma glared, but Ash spoke up. "It's okay, Gemma. I'll be back in a minute."

Parvati arched her eyebrow. It was sharp and elegant and designed to be arched. "This is Gemma? The female you want to mate with?"

"What?" said Ash.

"What?" said Gemma.

Parvati continued. "You're not familiar with the term? Procreate? Make babies with?"

Why did the gods have it in for him? Ash turned to Gemma. "I won't be long."

"Fine. Take as long as you want," snapped Gemma before storming off.

"So that was Gemma?" asked Khan, grinning like a tiger having just spotted a limp deer. "Tasty."

"Leave her alone," said Ash. "I mean it."

Khan gave a melodramatic tremble. "I'm so scared."

How can tonight get any worse?

A high-pitched cackle rose out of the fog. It was brittle and cruel, and it descended into a hysterical laugh, echoing across the park. Children began to cry, and grown-ups stared around, bewildered and not a little frightened themselves.

That's how.

"Jackie," said Parvati. "I'm such a fool. She tracked you."

Jackie's mad, demonic cry had haunted Ash's nights many months after returning from India. Now, hearing it again, he remembered the depth of fear he'd felt the first time he'd heard it.

"How?" Ash asked.

"Scent. She must have picked it up at Monty's." Then she looked at Ash again, frowning. "Where's your coat?"

Oh, my God. My coat.

Jackie was following Ash's scent.

Which was all over his favorite Sherlock Holmes coat.

Which Gemma was wearing.

CHAPTER NINE

"I've got to find Gemma," said Ash.

People screamed as savage snarls and howls erupted all around them. A black shadow raced through the fog, hideously large with a massive head and shoulders, charging in and out of the mist on four legs.

Ash looked at Parvati, and the old understanding was there. She nodded and disappeared into the fog. He looked around. Where was Gemma? Then he saw someone who might know.

"Jack!" He ran up to the boy, who was balancing a tray of burgers and Cokes. "Where's Gemma?"

"You've got some nerve," he snarled. "Gemma's mine and she's not interested in a freak like you." He dropped the tray and put up his fists. "Time I taught you a lesson."

"I so don't have time for this," said Ash.

The howl broke in. A giant, dark shape raced toward them, its heavy paws slamming on the hard earth. Jack screamed and Ash pushed him behind him.

Kali's dark storm exploded within his soul, flooding him with supernatural energy. Ash roared and leaped.

He slammed into the beast. For a second he saw burning yellow eyes and long, crooked canines, a slavering tongue. The jaws widened.

Ash instinctively thrust his hand down the creature's throat. His fingers, locked into a spearpoint, tore through the soft tissue, sliced open the lungs, and then tightened around the pulsing heart. He ripped it out before the jaws could close around his arm.

The monster crashed, rolled, and came to a halt at the feet of the terrified Jack.

It was a huge hyena, more the size of a lion, with massive hunched shoulders and a misshapen head, snout fatter and shorter than a natural animal. Its pelt was bristling black and spotted and the claws long and curled. Blood spewed from its twitching jaws, washing the frozen earth.

Ash turned the pulsing sack of the monster's heart in his hand. It gave a feeble splutter as it discharged the last of its blood, then it stilled. He tossed it away.

"You were about to say something, Jack?"

Jack's legs shook as tears smeared his face. There was a wet stain running down his Levi's. "No . . . no . . . nothing."

"Good."

How many demons had Jackie brought with her? Ash remembered three others in the car, but here, lost in the fog, the sounds and cries and screams were all jumbled up and coming from everywhere. A rocket whizzed horizontally across the park, trailing bright multicolored sparks and smoke. It vanished into the swirling gray fog and exploded somewhere among the trees.

Ash ran along the wreckage of the display frames. The large scaffolds holding hundreds of fireworks had been toppled over. The timers tripped, and dozens of Catherine Wheels spun like fiery Frisbees across the ground. Missiles shot off in random directions or just exploded on their frames, setting the surrounding grass and nearby trees alight with rainbow-colored flames.

A small kid wandered alone, separated from his parents. He still held his sparkler, waving it dumbly while tears rolled down his fat cheeks. Then the fog rolled over him and he was gone. How could it have gone so wrong so quickly?

Where was Gemma?

Ash stared at the horrified faces of the people screaming and running in blind panic. Vaporous smog lay over the chaos. Then a bellowing roar shook the fog, making it tremble and ripple outward.

Ash ran toward the source of the ripples.

A tiger was fighting a huge dire hyena. A grotesque hunch-backed jackal stalked the outer ring of the battle, and behind them the towering bonfire tottered. The wooden struts cracked and the structure swayed side to side.

And behind the tiger stood Gemma.

She was staring around madly for an escape route but finding none. Behind her was the inferno, and before her were the rakshasas.

Dozens of wounds covered the tiger — *Khan* — some deep and bleeding with thick dark blood.

Khan saw Ash.

And so did Jackie.

The tiger charged the hyena, tearing into it. Khan forced the demon back, trying to open up a path between Ash and Gemma.

But Jackie was quicker. She sprang forty feet in an instant, even as Ash sprinted toward Gemma. Gemma screamed and stumbled back, ignoring the bonfire right behind her, more terrified of the slavering jaws of the demon than the unbearable heat.

"Gemma!" Ash screamed as a barrage of rockets shot over his head.

Like a thunderstorm, the fireworks smashed into the heart of the bonfire. Ash flung his arm over his eyes as the gunpowder exploded with a blinding white flash. He staggered back, dazed, as more and more firecrackers followed the smoky trail into the giant, blazing tower.

Jackie threw Gemma to the ground and stood over the cowering girl, her face a grotesque, unnatural blend of human and beast, long slavering jaws with human lips and eyes.

Parvati ran up to Ash. Ash stepped forward, but Jackie brought her fangs close to Gemma's throat. Gemma lay still and petrified.

"The Koh-I-Noor and the girl lives," Jackie growled. Spittle dripped off her canines onto Gemma's face.

They were maybe thirty feet apart, though it was hard to tell with the fog and smoke. Jackie's fangs were an inch from Gemma's bare neck. There was no way he'd make it.

Jackie's eyes blazed and her fur shivered across her shoulders. "The diamond, boy."

They had no choice. "Give it to her, Parvati."

"No."

"Give it to her!"

Parvati stepped back. "No." Her cold gaze didn't shift from the jackal rakshasa.

Ash reached to the back of his T-shirt, moving his hand ever so slowly. It was dark, the distance long, and the katar wasn't designed for throwing, but it was the only chance he had.

"Parvati, for God's sake . . ."

"No!"

Jackie howled and —

Ash grabbed the katar and hurled it at the rakshasa.

Gemma screamed as Jackie sank her fangs into her neck. She beat the demon with her fists, struggling under the massive, hairy monster. The katar punched into Jackie's shoulder, and Jackie released Gemma to howl again. She stumbled back, and Ash charged.

The rakshasa shook herself, trying to dislodge the katar wedged just below her lower neck. The blade refused to shift, so finally Jackie leaped into the fog, fangs and fur soaked with blood, her mad, howling laughter echoing in her wake. Parvati sprinted after her.

Ash fell to his knees beside Gemma.

"Gemma?"

Oh, God, her neck was covered in blood. He put his hands on the wound, feeling the muscles quiver and the breath hissing from her ruined throat, raising red bubbles that spluttered and popped.

"Someone get an ambulance!" he screamed. "Please!"

Gemma grabbed hold of his arm. She dug her fingers into his skin, hanging on to him as if she were sinking into a dark sea, focusing on him with frightening intensity. She tried to speak, but nothing came out.

The lights of death were spreading over her, multiplying second by second. She looked radiant, covered in gold, bright as an angel.

"Gemma, Gemma . . ."

Ash trembled as he began to absorb Gemma's death energies. "No. No."

He wanted to say more, to tell her it was okay, that she had to be brave and she would come back, but the words were bitter and dead on his tongue. This was Gemma and they'd played together since nursery school. Her sister was Lucky's best friend. He'd seen her almost every day of his life, and this was about to be her last.

Each bead of sweat on her shone brighter than any diamond, her skin pale as the most perfect marble. Each breath smelled sweeter than any rose. Gemma's grip weakened. Her eyes, ever changing in color, were wide and staring, her pupils swelling until they almost consumed her irises.

Ash heard sirens in the distance.

"Just hang on, Gemma. Hang on."

Heat burst within him, straight into his heart and flooding every atom of his being. The world shook around him as waves of energy pounded him, filling him with more and more power.

This was a Great Death.

CHAPTER TEN

Ash replayed the last moments of Gemma's life a thousand times, a hundred thousand times over the next few days. From the moment he woke, it haunted him. A fraction quicker, an inch truer with his aim, and it would have all been different.

He walked down the dark, lamp-lit street, head down and lost in memory.

The ambulance came, too late, and then the police found Ash covered in blood with a dead girl in his arms. Jack had been hysterical, shouting about him, and there were witnesses saying Ash had been with Gemma and then there'd been some argument with another girl. All these small, random details. A punch dagger had been found, smeared with blood, and the sheath strapped to his belt fit the blade perfectly. So the police and half the school added two and two and got five.

It had been a dark, lonely night in the police station before the fog had cleared in the morning and the police found a dead hyena. The wounds on Gemma proved to be from an animal bite — an escaped animal from some zoo, the police thought — and Ash finally went home with his parents.

Their silence had been awful. Lucky had looked at him with such cold hatred and disgust that though she had not said a word, he knew exactly what she was thinking. Gemma was dead because of him.

And she was right.

If only he'd stayed on the bus instead of walking back. Jackie wouldn't have been able to follow him. If only he hadn't given Gemma his coat. If only he'd been closer, he would have put the blade in Jackie's skull instead of her shoulder. If only he'd been quicker. If only he'd been faster, stronger, better.

If only . . .

Did Jackie bite Gemma before he'd thrown the katar, or after?

Why had Parvati said no when Jackie had demanded the diamond?

Why?

He stared at his left hand, at the small scar on his thumb. If it would do any good, he'd cut it off right now. But the Kali-aastra was all of him, and he was it. There was nothing heroic about what he'd become. Quite the opposite. He was a curse. Elaine had predicted this would happen. Someone had ended up dead, and he was so very sorry.

But what gripped his heart with fear was the certainty that this would never end. Who would be next? His parents? His other friends? Lucky?

Gemma's death had made him more powerful, and he hated himself for it. Parvati had explained, ages ago it seemed, that the more significant the death, the more power Ash gained. He hadn't realized what she meant until Gemma's energies had filled him: A Great Death. His strength, speed, agility, and senses had crept further up the scale, leaving "human" further behind. The shock of it left him dazed, far more than he'd expected.

Had his presence accelerated Gemma's death, even? Kali was a greedy, blood-drinking goddess. He felt sick to his guts whenever he heard his parents talking downstairs and Lucky crying. He picked up the looks and the fear from the other kids in class. His supernaturally acute hearing gathered the whispers and the quiet mutterings as he passed. The rumors about that awful night infected all of West Dulwich High. He missed seeing her in class. Her chair remained empty as if she'd gotten up, still warm with her presence, so he could fool himself, even just for a second, that Gemma was still there. Instead the shadow of the trees outside passed over it as the sun, winter low, crossed the sky east to west. How he wished he could make the shadows reverse their path. ·

Ash stared at his shadow now as it rose up against Josh's front door. He stood there, outside his best friend's house, and raised his fist. He could hear the others inside. There was Akbar's snorting laugh, and he could smell Sean's aftershave, and that they had salt and vinegar chips out, that there was hot chocolate brewing and their takeout pizza had cheese, olives, and anchovies on it, plus some curry powder. Josh burped after a mouthful of Sprite. Sean, Josh, and Akbar. His closest, oldest friends who'd known him for years and years. Ash had been just like them, and right now that was all he wanted. To be like them again. Normal, and none of this supernatural, superhuman crap.

Dice fell on the kitchen table and pencils scratched on notepaper. Akbar said something about the sorcerer casting a firestorm spell at the manticore. The game of *Dungeons and Dragons* was in full swing. Ash knocked.

Josh's laugh carried all the way to the door until he opened it and saw Ash. Then it froze on his face as he stood there, staring at him. He opened his mouth, but it took a few attempts before anything came out. "Ash?"

He's scared.

Josh's heartbeat accelerated, the rapid thumping as loud to Ash as a circus drum. Sweat formed across his forehead and upper lip, and the color faded from his face. His breath was short, shallow, and panicky; even his hand trembled on the door handle.

He's not scared, he's terrified. Of me.

Ash forced a smile, even though inside his heart was tearing in two. "It's Tuesday. 'The Catacombs of Doom,' remember?"

Josh's gaze shifted down to his feet. "Oh, right. It's just . . . we didn't think you'd come."

"I'm here now."

There was no move to let Ash in. But Josh's heart rate was over a hundred beats per minute. He looked up at Ash, biting his lower lip. He was struggling to speak, to say something, but couldn't.

Ash's gaze darkened. Josh shouldn't be treating him like this. "You going to let me in or what?"

"Or what, Ash? What are you going to do if I don't?"

"What?"

"What are you going to do?"

For a second, just a second, Ash let his anger, his rejection, show. He wanted to push past. He could do it so easily. Josh couldn't stop him, he was just a human. How dare Josh judge him, what right did he have? Didn't he know what Ash had done? Josh was pathetic. Ash raised his hand and —

— stepped back.

The look on Josh's face said it all. The fear practically dripped off him. He trembled. Ash lowered his hand, wishing he could take that last moment back. He smiled at Josh, but the smile was too harsh, too much like a grinning dead man.

"Look, Josh, there's nothing to be afraid of. You know me."

"Do I? Really?"

He couldn't believe it. Did Josh think he'd killed Gemma? How could he? "I've done nothing wrong, Josh. You have to believe me. I wouldn't hurt anyone. Christ, Josh, this is me."

"I saw you, Ash. I *saw* you." Josh winced and put his hand over his face. "I'm still not sure I believe it, but I saw what you did at the park the night Gemma died."

"And what was that?" asked Ash coldly. "You saw what, exactly?"

"I saw you push Jack out of the way and shove your arm down the throat of some insane monster. I saw you rip its heart out like you were picking apples from a tree. You moved so fast that you practically blurred. No one can move that fast. Not Usain Bolt pumped with rocket fuel. Nobody. It was mad, but I went over to the monster and saw it was real. Jack was screaming and crying and I didn't know what was going on, but there was some giant dead dog in the grass and beside it was its torn-out heart."

"It wasn't like —"

"I am not an idiot, Ash." Josh looked back at him, sad and lost. "Then I saw you with Gemma. With that thing with a human face and jackal's body. With a girl with scales and a forked tongue. I watched you throw the knife and watched you as Gemma died. I called the ambulance, did you know that?"

"Thanks." What else could he say? Deny it? Make his friend think he was insane to believe in monsters?

No, Josh believed. He had one standing right here in front of him.

"What are you, Ash?"

"I really don't know anymore."

"I think you'd better go."

Ash looked up at his mate. "You know I wouldn't let anything happen to you. Not to you or the other guys."

"Is that what you told Gemma?"

And Josh closed the door.

CHAPTER ELEVEN

Ashoka gazes down the hill. A few fires still burn within the village, edging out the cold desert night. Somewhere in the darkness a bullock grunts and a baby cries.

A dozen or so squat mud-brick dwellings. A fenced-off corral for the cattle. Chickens squawking within the sheds. Fields with dried-out gullies and meager crops. To the north squat the domed grain stores. How many such villages has he visited? How many fires has he lit? How many cries has he silenced?

Not enough. Not yet.

His band swells with each passing victory. Soon it will be an army. For Ashoka has dreams beyond village raids. This is how kingdoms begin.

He thinks about his father, a king, and his older brothers. They have grand palaces and dine off gold plates while he haunts the desert, eating with his band of brigands. His father laughed when Ashoka demanded his crown. How often was he laughed at, dismissed? Now they laugh no longer. They scream. If he cannot have their respect and love, he will have their fear.

Soon, the old palace will echo with wailing women, he thinks. That crown, and others, will be mine. *He wonders how the old man sleeps, knowing his son is out here, carving out a kingdom of his own.*

His men wait impatiently, like dogs eager for the hunt. They check their weapons, adjust their armor, ensuring helmets are fixed and there are no loose straps. But Ashoka expects little resistance. This will not be a battle — not against unarmed, unsuspecting villagers. This will be a slaughter.

His horse whinnies and stomps its hoof; it senses the coming bloodletting. Ashoka pats its thick neck. He himself wears a mail coat over his silk tunic and heavy cotton pantaloons. His boots, stiff leather, creak in the stirrups. A bright red sash lies across his waist, a jeweled dagger tucked into the cloth. Hanging from his saddle is his sword, a single-edged talwar with a gold-bound hilt. Which chieftain, which prince, did he slay to possess it? He cannot remember; there have been so many.

The jangle of reins and the snort of another steed snaps his attention back to his men.

A sleek mare with a high arching neck and white mane bound with silver and silk trots up beside him. The rider is clad in scales, and the saber on her hip is sheathed in green crocodile skin. She doffs her helmet and her emerald eyes shine in the moonlight.

"The men are ready," she says.

Ashoka observes her. She leans over the pommel, waiting in anticipation, her forked tongue flicking along her fangs. Her cobra eyes do not lower; she defies where others would bow and kneel. Perhaps that is why she has risen so rapidly in his command. And why should she bow? Is she not royalty herself? Was not her father a great king?

"You have done well," he says.

"My lord." She bows, almost. "I am but your servant."

"Ha! Servant? I doubt anyone could command you. You are terror made flesh, Parvati."

She smiles, a rare thing, then looks down the slope. "Why this particular village?"

"Their landlord defies me. He refuses to pay tribute and so must be punished."

"Shall I send a detachment to raid the stores?" She points toward the row of round huts some distance away. "They will be full of grain this time of year."

"No. Burn them. The message will be clear. Defy me and you will be annihilated."

"And the captives?"

"What captives?" Ashoka draws his own sword. "I want no survivors."

"Slaves could be sold, my lord."

Ashoka stands up in his stirrups and turns to his warriors. "Listen to me," he shouts. He sweeps the blade down toward the village. "You are my jackals. We feed on blood and the dead. No survivors. Kill them all!"

Howls fill the night. Then the line of horsemen descends the slope, drawing their weapons, and suddenly the night is filled with the thunder of hooves and battle cries. The moon shines on swords and spears and axes, each one sharp and notched with heavy use. Chariots — light wicker contraptions drawn by pairs of steeds — rattle and bounce over the uneven, rocky terrain. A driver weaves his team through a gap between two sandstone boulders as his passenger notches an arrow. The cavalry formation fragments as each man races his companion, eager to be the first to kill. Ashoka whips his horse and it froths at the bit, neighing with savage delight. He grins and his heart soars, a passion too primitive for words, so he merely howls as the wind rushes in his ears.

The village stirs. Men stumble from their doors, bewildered and still half-asleep. A dog races up to him but is crushed under the *hooves of his horse. The steed vaults over the low defensive wall and Ashoka catches the open-mouthed shock of a villager's face before he drives the tip of his sword into it. He twists his wrist and the sword tears free. He does not even turn to look back.*

Women run out, clutching screaming children and babes in their arms. They flee into the darkness. They will not escape. With a nod, three of his horsemen break off in pursuit.

He sees Parvati leap from her steed as it takes a spear in its chest. She turns in the air and her sword flashes. A head leaps off a pair of shoulders, trailing a ribbon of blood. She has not yet touched the ground. Her eyes burn with demonic light. Men fall beneath her blade like wheat beneath a reaper's scythe. She does what she does best: end men's lives.

Ashoka drops from his horse and sweeps his weapon across a man's throat without pause. He rams his shield into the face of another as he charges into the melee.

A hammer slams into his wrist, knocking his sword away. He spins and sees a huge, oak-chested man wielding a heavy wooden mattock. The man is covered in minor cuts but swings the hammer with bone-shattering power. A soldier runs to Ashoka's defense, then collapses as a single blow flattens his skull.

He discards his shield and leaps at the villager. Both fall and scrabble in the blood-soaked dust. Ashoka digs his fingers into the man's neck, squeezing —

"Ash!"

Ash squeezes the throat of his enemy as other soldiers grab his arms to try and haul him back. The big villager's face turns red and his eyes bulge.

"Ash!" a girl screamed as she hung on to his arm. She wept and screamed again. *Is she the man's daughter? She is nothing. She is —*

"Lucky?"

Ash dropped his grip and his dad gasped. There was a bruise over his cheek and he lay there, coughing and clutching his ribs. Had Ash punched him?

"Oh, God. Dad, I'm so sorry."

His mum switched on the light. Ash's bedroom was wrecked. His books had been thrown everywhere, the chair legs were snapped, and there was a fist-sized hole in the closet door.

Had he done that in his sleep? Ash stumbled back onto his bed. "I'm so sorry."

But no one listened. Mum was kneeling with Lucky beside Dad as his father struggled to breathe. Purple finger marks surrounded his neck.

Ash stared at his family and met Lucky's gaze. She stared back at him with horror and disgust. Her eyes were red with tears, but her face was hard and pale. All she could do was shake her head.

He couldn't bear to look. Instead he covered his face with his hands and sank down with a groan. What was happening to him?

CHAPTER TWELVE

"Ash?" His mum tapped his door. "There's a friend to see you."

"I don't want to see anyone."

"Ash, I think —"

"I said I don't want to see anyone!"

The door opened. He didn't need to turn to know exactly who it was. Ash remained where he was, looking at the wall, in the dark, his back to the door. "I especially don't want to see you, Parvati."

The light came on. Ash slowly swiveled around.

Parvati closed the door, sat down on the corner of his unmade bed, and, taking off her glasses, looked around.

"Is that dent meant to be in the door?" she asked.

The worst of the damage had been fixed or tidied away. Ash had straightened up the shelves and, with his dad, repaired the broken table and replaced the chair. He'd talked with his parents about it and they'd put it down to the trauma of Gemma's death. His dad now wore a cravat to hide the bruises.

"What do you want?" Ash snapped.

"To see how you're doing. We've not spoken since that night your friend died."

"Since you let her die, you mean."

When Parvati didn't respond, Ash peered at her. She'd changed. Her hair was a mess — dried out, brittle, and knotted — and her skin, usually smooth and clear, bore lines and a sickly yellow tinge.

"You're sick," Ash said. "I didn't know demons got sick."

She smiled weakly. "Everyone gets sick."

"And what's happened to your eyes?" The green irises almost filled her eyes, leaving hardly any white at all. The pupils dilated in the semidarkness to huge black disks.

"My demon heritage grows stronger as I age. The eyes are just the beginning. Sometimes it's hard to remember that I'm human at all."

"I'm sure I don't care." Ash stood up and walked to the door. "Well, you've seen me. You can go."

"Ash . . ."

"She's dead because of you," he said ever so quietly. It had to be quiet because if he let out what was really inside, he'd tear down the house. "You could have saved her."

"You think Jackie would have let her go?" Parvati looked up at him. "She would have killed her whatever we did."

"Why? Because rakshasas have no honor? Because they can't be trusted?" He opened the door for her. "You should know."

Parvati stood up. "What's the point? You're just a foolish boy. You have no idea what's at stake. You think some mortal girl's important in this? Grow up, Ash."

Ash grabbed Parvati around her throat and slammed her against the wall. His fist went back, tightened so his knuckles were white and shaking with rage.

Parvati gazed back at him without emotion. But her fangs were fully extended, each one coated with her fatal venom. This close, her large, serpentine eyes dominated her face and the curving green scales shimmered. "You want to kill me, Ash? Is that it?"

Kill the rakshasa. Wasn't that his duty? Wasn't that his reason for existing?

"You are a monster," he said, looking at her as if for the first time. "How could I have been so blind?"

"You want me to say I'm sorry?" Parvati hissed. "Beg for forgiveness? Sit in the dark and feel sorry for myself? Do you know who I am?" She shoved Ash back. "I am the daughter of Ravana. I do not beg."

She looked at him, the defiance fading with a sigh. "I am not sorry for what I did, though I am sorry your friend is dead." Parvati reached out to touch him, then stopped herself. "But do you think you're the only one who's suffered? I've lost friends, people more than friends, so many that I can't even begin to remember them all. But each one, Ash, each one left a hole here." She pointed at her heart. "That's the true curse of immortality. Each success is so fleeting you wonder why you bother, yet each failure weighs down your soul with lead. That's why rakshasas are such monsters. We must cut out that part that feels. Better to be cold, hard, become immune to pain."

Ash lowered his fist. What was he doing? In spite of Gemma, Parvati was the closest friend he had. He owed her his life. "I just wish there was something I could do," he said. "Gemma didn't deserve to die."

"Ash —"

Of course. It was so obvious. "I came back from the dead. Why not Gemma? There has to be a way."

Parvati's gaze darkened. "Kali brought you back. She reawakened your heart." Her words came out cold and hard. "What you're talking about is something only gods can do. And it is a decision best left to them. Who is worthy, who is not."

"Are you saying Gemma's not worthy?"

"What I'm saying is who are we to choose?"

"Gemma is worthy. She was a good person."

Parvati's response, a bitter laugh, stabbed him deep. "Oh, I did not realize you could see into people's souls and know whether they are good or evil. You *have* become powerful."

"That's not what I mean and you know it."

"Please, Ash . . ." It was almost a plea. "The girl you knew is gone."

Now that the thought was in his head, he couldn't let it go. Was there some way to fix the mistakes of the past? Rishi would have known what was possible and what was not. Get Gemma back. A vain delusion or a real hope? His head told him one thing, his heart another. Ash looked at Parvati as she inspected his bookshelves. Why wouldn't she want Gemma to return? Was Elaine right? Did Parvati have her own agenda?

Don't be stupid. If you can't trust Parvati, then who can you trust?

Ash fell back onto his bed. "Parvati, I don't know what's going on."

Parvati's fingers paused over a history book, one Ash knew well: *The Life of Ashoka*, a biography of the first emperor of India. The West might have Alexander the Great, but as far as Ash was concerned, no one came close to Ashoka, a violent brigand who'd ended up ruling one of the largest empires of the ancient world, back in the third century BC. Parvati tapped the book, her brow knotted, then picked another one off the shelf.

The Ramayana. What else?

She smirked. "They've given him ten heads, as usual."

It was an old children's book. The cover was torn and scribbled on, but standing in the center was Ravana, the demon king. Parvati's dad. He was resplendent in golden armor and had, indeed, ten heads, all glaring in red-faced fury. Prince Rama, the hero, stood to the side, his skin blue, arrow notched in his bow. The arrow had flames surrounding it.

A magic arrow to destroy the demon king. An aastra.

Ash remembered the smell of the battlefield, the tension in the bowstring as he drew the arrow back, the fury in Ravana's gaze. The memories were so fresh and so close he could almost reach out and touch them.

Parvati had talked about meeting him in previous incarnations. The thought still freaked him out. She said he was an Eternal Warrior, destined to be reborn again and again. How many people had he been? Rama? Ashoka? Who else? He'd visited museums and looked at the ancient armor and the rusting weapons in the glass cabinets, and his hands had curled, remembering how they'd once held axes and swords and spears and shields. The weight of armor, the narrow, restricted view through a helmet. He'd seen cities burn; he'd known little peace. A perpetual state of war. That was his destiny. But it had never been as vivid as the memory of Ashoka last night. He looked at the demon girl. "I need your help." He rubbed his temples. "I had a dream last night. I was the original Ashoka, the one who became the first emperor of India. I dreamed I was fighting and I woke up just as I was about to kill my dad."

"The past lives are taking control? Rishi warned me this might happen. The Kali-aastra, it feeds on violence and death. It wants more power, and your rage, your guilt, will only feed it."

"How can I stop it?"

Parvati smiled softly and sat down beside him. "I wish I knew, Ash, I really do. But that was something Rishi was meant to teach you."

"Isn't there anyone else?"

Her eyelids lowered and a hiss escaped her. She frowned. "No."

She was lying, he knew it. Why? "Are you sure? Elaine said —"

"I'm sure she did, but Elaine's no Rishi. There was no one like him."

"Then what am I going to do?"

"It's my fault. I came back into your life and stirred everything up. That's why I'm here, Ash. To tell you that I'm going and I won't be coming back. The farther away I am, the better for both of us."

"You're going after Savage?"

Parvati raised her hand to her chest and Ash noticed a lump, a pouch, under her tunic. "He'll come after the Koh-I-Noor." She laughed. "Like a rat after cheese, my favorite type of prey."

"Savage is dangerous, Parvati."

"And so am I. Still, I won't be facing him alone."

"You've got Khan, right?"

"Yes, I have Khan. But I am also Ravana's daughter. All Savage knows ultimately came from my father. Either from the scrolls he stole from me, or from that night he resurrected Ravana. I've studied those scrolls and learned a few tricks, and they'd counter most of what Savage can throw at me."

"Like that thing you did with your eyes?" Back in Varanasi she'd almost succeeded in hypnotizing him. That eerie emerald glow coming from her eyes wasn't easy to forget.

"Mesmerism. It's part of one of the sorceries, and we serpents are especially good at it."

"Maybe, but Savage is in another league, Parvati. Let me come." The thought was in his head and out his mouth the same instant. But why not? "I can't stay here."

"Ash, they are your family. Your place is with them."

"No. Not when I'm like this. Don't you get it? I was *this close* to killing my own father. Bloody hell, if I'd used marma-adi, he'd be dead. I can't stay around them."

"What about things like school?"

"You think I'll be missed? I reckon it'll be a lot easier for everyone if I'm gone for a few weeks. None of my friends talk to me and everyone whispers about me behind my back." There was even a display about Gemma at the school entrance with a photo of her, cards, and small gifts other pupils had left for her. She'd been popular. He glanced at his textbooks stacked up on the shelves over his desk. "And how can I concentrate on French verbs knowing Savage is out there? That Jackie's still around?"

"And going after Savage will help? No, it'll only make things worse. Killing Savage will not bring you peace, Ash, it'll only accelerate your descent into darkness. Don't give into the Kali-aastra. Don't feed it with more death."

"There is no peace while Savage is alive."

"Let me deal with the Englishman," said Parvati.

"You've had two hundred years to deal with him and how far have you got? Nowhere."

Parvati bristled under the insult but didn't rise to it. Maybe it was a bit below the belt, but Ash didn't care. He couldn't stay here where he might lose control. He'd been lucky that he'd snapped out of it before he'd done something terrible and that his dad had come in first; he was big and could take it. What if it had been Lucky? He could have broken her neck. "I can't stay, Parvati. Not like this."

Parvati said nothing. Her lips were fixed in a thin line and her green eyes glistened. She didn't look very happy, but she nodded. "Fine. Come."

Ash stood up. Yes, this was for the best. He'd be safely away from his family and with Parvati; they'd deal with Savage. An electric thrill ran up his spine at the thought of returning to India. He'd never been to the city of Kolkata, on the far eastern side of the subcontinent. He looked around his room. What should he pack? There was hardly anything he wanted to take.

His gaze fell on a small portrait he'd downloaded off the Web a couple of months ago. Lord Alexander Savage, wearing the uniform of the East India Company, his blue-eyed gaze cold and aloof. In his hand he held a bulbous poppy, symbol of the opium trade that had made part of the family fortune, and on a table in the background, in among the shadows, was a set of manacles. As well as trading in drugs, Savage had also been a slaver.

Drug dealer. Slave trader. Murderer, and the most powerful sorcerer in the world. Ash was going to kill him.

For the first time since Gemma died, Ash smiled.

CHAPTER THIRTEEN

"You're a stupid idiot," said Lucky.

"It's got to be done, Lucks." Ash rolled up another pair of jeans and shoved them into his backpack.

"You're going to get yourself killed."

"Being dead didn't stop me the first time."

Lucky hurled a pillow at him. "Don't joke about this, Ash!"

The pillow bounced off his head, but it was good things were back to normal between them following the arctic coldness right after Gemma's death. That was the thing about families: no one could stay mad for long.

"If this works out, we'll be rid of Savage once and for all. I need to do this." He squeezed in a few of his T-shirts. "Gemma deserves revenge."

"Gemma's dead, Ash," Lucky said quietly. "I was at her funeral."

He hadn't been invited. Even though the police confirmed he had nothing to do with Gemma's death, he had her blood on his hands, literally. So Ash stayed away. Gemma's family had enough to deal with without him being there. "How was it?"

"How do you think? Sad."

Ash shoved some more clothes into his bag.

"Why don't you tell them the truth? Mum and Dad should know about the rakshasas."

"The truth?" said Ash. "Has knowing what's out there made it any easier for you?"

As soon as he said it, he wished he hadn't. Lucky's face drained of all color and suddenly she looked very small, very frail, and very frightened. She knew the truth better than most. Lucky had been captured by Lord Savage and held hostage by the rakshasas for days, knowing that any one of them would be happy to tear her to pieces. Lord Savage had promised her to them, and Ash remembered how Lucky had woken up screaming every night for weeks. Their mum and dad couldn't help. They said there were no such thing as monsters, but they were so terribly wrong.

Ash took Lucky's hand. "I didn't know you still had those nightmares. You know I'd never let anyone hurt you."

Lucky bit her lip. "It's not the demons that frighten me."

"Oh? What then?"

She looked away from him, dropping her gaze. "It's not important."

"Tell me."

There was a deep, bone-weary sigh, and then, looking anxiously at him, Lucky told him the truth. "It's you. You are in my nightmares."

"But I saved you."

"Ash, you came back from the dead. I saw what you were, how you looked. You punched straight through Mayar. You charged straight through his body. I saw you standing there, drenched in his blood, only it was your eyes . . ."

Ash stared at his sister. "You never said anything. Why didn't you —"

"They were so full of rage, I couldn't believe it was you. The blood was so black and slimy on you. You looked so gaunt, I could count the ribs and the bones through your skin. Ash, you have no idea what you were when you came back. Really, you don't."

More terrible than the monsters. He'd been warned that was what he might become as the Kali-aastra, but it broke something inside him to see the fear in Lucky's eyes. That horrific night had changed them both. He'd lost more than his life. Ash held his sister's hand. "I'm sorry, Lucks. I'll make it up to you."

"Then stay, Ash. Let Parvati deal with Savage."

"Parvati's my friend. I have to help her."

Lucky shook her head. "I don't like her, Ash. And I don't know if she's your friend at all."

"What d'you mean?"

"She let Gemma die. Can't you see that?"

He went to his drawer, half-pulling it out before remembering his punch dagger had been confiscated by the police. He'd get a replacement as soon as he landed in India. Suddenly he didn't want to be talking about any of this. "She explained. She couldn't risk Jackie getting the diamond."

"Would you have done the same? No, not in a million years." Lucky pulled him around so they were face-to-face. "When Savage wanted the Kali-aastra in exchange for me, you didn't hesitate."

"That was different." But Lucky's comment made him uncomfortable. Parvati had been willing to leave Lucky, to abandon her in Savage's fortress. Her lives had been lonely and surrounded by bloodshed. Did she have any real feelings toward anyone? How much of her was human and how much of her was demon? How could anyone be remotely normal having Ravana for a dad?

"What about Mum and Dad?" Lucky added. "They won't let you go. You're only fourteen. You can't just leave school and everything."

Ash frowned. "Parvati's taking care of that too."

"How?" Lucky's voice had more than fear in it.

He made a spiraling motion in front of his eyes. "One of her Jedi mind tricks."

"She's hypnotizing them? To think what?"

"Do you remember Robert and Susan, Dad's old university friends?" Ash said. "The story is I'm too traumatized by Gemma's death to go to school, so I'm staying with them in Manchester. Just for a week or two. Until everything's sorted."

Lucky began to cry. Her little chin wrinkled up and she sat there, tears rolling down her face. "Don't go, Ash."

He hugged her. "You look after Mum and Dad." Ash grabbed his backpack. "It'll be fine. I promise."

"You can't promise those things," said Lucky.

Ash's mum squeezed him hard. "You say hello to Rob and Sue from us."

"You sure you want to take the train up, son? I could drive you." His dad checked the display on the station. The train was due in about three minutes.

Ash shook his head. "No, it'll be quicker by train. I'll be all right."

Lucky hadn't wanted to come. She said her good-byes at home before running upstairs and crying.

Ash looked at his parents. Should he tell them the truth? Didn't they deserve to know? But then what? Even if he could persuade them to let him go, they'd spend every minute worrying.

There were only a few people at the West Dulwich train station. Ash wore his winter coat and had his backpack on. He wanted them to leave, but wanted them to stay too. When he said good-bye to them last summer, it had been different. Then he and Lucky were staying with Uncle Vik and Aunt Anita, swapping one set of parents for another, almost. What was he getting himself into now? Hunting down demons, sorcerers, and who knew what other weirdness?

The rails rattled as the train came into view. This was it.

Ash hugged his dad. "I'm going to miss you." That was all that he needed to say.

"Call us when you get there, all right?" His mum wiped her face and gave him a smile. "All right?"

"I'll text. As often as possible."

Ash got on the train and waved to his mum and dad. He waved even when the doors closed and the train rolled off. He waved until he couldn't see the platform.

Then, three minutes later, he got off at the next stop, Herne Hill. The taxi was waiting. He nodded at Parvati and Khan, both in the backseat, then threw his backpack in the trunk. He pushed all thoughts of his parents and his sister and his home deep down and away as he got in the front. There would be no room for any of that from now on. From now on he was the Kali-aastra and nothing more.

It was time to kill.

*   *   *

Heathrow Airport was an hour's drive away. Parvati and Khan whispered to each other at the beginning, then fell into silence. Khan actually slept.

Ash watched Parvati via the side mirror. She didn't look good. Her movements were sluggish and uncoordinated. Something was off — she'd looked ill in his room, but this was way worse. "What's wrong?"

She ran her tongue over her dry, cracked lips. "Just tired. It'll pass."

Ash gazed at her. What wasn't she telling him?

The taxi drove to the cargo terminal off the South Perimeter Road. Parvati handed some papers over to the guard, and a few minutes later they were in, rolling slowly along the road that ran toward the cargo bays. Sharp aircraft fumes soaked the air and washed the evening sky with bright reds and golds and oranges. The ground trembled as a British Airways jumbo jet landed on a distant runway, the engine noise, even from here, shaking the minicab.

"This is our lift," said Khan, pointing to a plane out on the tarmac. The taxi rolled up to it and they got out.

An old, four-propeller Dakota stood in front of one of the smaller hangars. A crown had been freshly painted on the side and underneath it were the words *Maharajah Air*. The passenger door opened and an Indian man stepped out. Plump and wearing a pair of aviator Ray-Bans, he adjusted his two-sizes-too-small captain's jacket as he gazed out across the tarmac. He stroked his mustache, softly twisting the tips.

"Jimmy?" said Ash.

The man smiled broadly as he jumped down the steps and wrapped his arms around Ash, lifting him off his feet. "My

English friend! Such a pleasure to be seeing you again. How is your good self?"

"Been better. And you?"

Jimmy took off his Ray-Bans and looked back at the plane. "We are a three-plane company now, sahib."

"Yes, but only this one has wings," added Parvati as she walked past.

Jimmy had flown Ash and Parvati out to Ravana's tomb and had been paid handsomely for it with a bag of diamonds. It seemed he'd invested well. This new plane looked in far better shape than the rattling antique they'd last been in. Ash brushed his hand against the underside of the wing. "Rivets instead of cellotape. Which is nice."

The interior was basic, but comfortable. A small chandelier jangled above Ash, and the cabin smelled of incense and warmed-up curry. Instead of standard airplane seats, there were a couple of sofas, an armchair, and even a chaise lounge, all bolted to the floor.

"Still no seat belts?" Ash asked.

"I have better." Jimmy pointed to the small shrine in the front. Streams of smoke wove around a statue of Ganesha, the plump elephant-headed god of travel. Well, if the gods themselves were looking out for them, what could possibly go wrong? Ash just hoped Ganesha paid especially close attention to this particular plane.

Jimmy went to the bathroom at the back and banged on the door. "We have passengers. Get out!" He smiled weakly. "I am training new cabin crew."

"You've got a steward?" asked Ash. "That's . . ." What he wanted to say was "absolutely stupid of whichever lunatic decided to sign up with you," but for some reason it came out as ". . . interesting."

There was a moan from within the bathroom, then the sound of a flush. The tap ran for a long time with much sighing and sobbing. Jimmy pounded the door harder. "Hurry up! I pay you for pouring out tea, not vomit!"

The door opened and a small Indian boy wearing a dark blue jacket at least three sizes too large stumbled out. His hair was stuck across his forehead and he hung on to the door grimly. "Ash?"

"John?" Ash leaped up and grabbed John in a crushing embrace. He couldn't believe it. John had been his only friend back in Varanasi. "What are you doing here?"

John swayed even though the plane wasn't even moving. "Ujba didn't want me around. I helped you escape, remember?"

"So you work for Jimmy?"

Jimmy grunted. "An act of charity I am much regretting." He put his cap on, screwing it low over his head, and went into the cockpit. There was another guy in the copilot seat and the two of them chatted their way through the preflight checks.

Khan looked around the floor and stretched out on a piece of carpet. He patted his backpack into a pillow and yawned. "Wake me when you see the Ganges."

Ash glanced around himself, then took the armchair. Parvati lay down on a sofa and pulled the blanket up to her chin. She let out a long sigh and closed her eyes.

The engines rumbled and the propellers flicked around slowly, then powered up and buzzed into full life. John gulped. He covered his mouth and ran, stumbling, straight back into the bathroom.

First the cabin juddered. Then it shook violently, almost throwing Ash from his seat. The chandelier swung back and forth, jingling. Something rattled within the fuselage. Ash hoped it wasn't anything critical in the "staying in the air and not crashing in flames" sense.

"I'd forgotten this bit," he said, clamping his fingers onto the armrests.

CHAPTER FOURTEEN

Why was it he could fall asleep on a bus, on a train, and even on a bicycle but not on a plane? Ash shifted on the armchair, the blanket tucked under his chin, and tried to balance his cheek on the pillow. Not working. The steady drone of the propellers filled the tin can of the cabin. Ash looked around. It was dark beyond the small, round windows. He wondered where they were.

John lay on the floor, snoring softly. Khan was up, legs crossed and teeth sunk deep into a large piece of lamb. The juices, red and very raw, dribbled down his chin as the bones crunched. He peeled off a strip with his nail and offered it to Ash.

Ash shook his head.

Parvati slept on. The chandelier chimed overhead and the few lights cast her face in a sickly yellow tone. Or maybe it wasn't the lights. Her scales were flaking off her face, and the skin was drawn and tight over her bones. Her eyelids opened, just a razor's width, and a feverish green fire burned in her gaze.

"Parvati, what's wrong?"

Parvati struggled to sit up. She straightened the blankets and Ash glimpsed the bony body beneath it. How could she have lost so much weight so quickly? When she coughed, the air rattled within her withered lungs. She sank back into her seat, too tired even to speak. Ash saw the golden lights of death shining all over her.

Khan put his hand on Ash's shoulder. "She'll be better when we get back to India."

The two of them moved to the back of the plane, away from Parvati's hearing.

"What's happening to her?" asked Ash.

Khan frowned. "I thought you'd know. It's the Koh-I-Noor."

"The aastra?"

"Of course. Rakshasas cannot possess the tools of the gods. They were crafted to be used against us. The Koh-I-Noor robs her of her life because she was not meant to carry it. It's only because of her human heritage she's lasted this long."

"Where is it?"

"Around her neck."

"I'll get it off her, then." But as Ash stepped toward her, Khan placed his hand on his shoulder.

"No, I can't let you do that." Khan scowled. "I'm not so sure she would want you to have it. Aren't things hard enough already with you being the Kali-aastra?"

Ash didn't meet the tiger demon's gaze. "I don't know what you mean."

"Just because I'm ridiculously handsome does not make me stupid," said Khan.

Ash snorted. "Who says you're handsome?"

Khan crossed his arms. "I hear you've been having bad dreams."

"Nothing strange about that. Everyone has them from time to time."

Khan shook his head. "No. Parvati told me this might happen. It'll get worse as time progresses. The past will become more and more real until you cannot separate it from the present. What you are, Ash Mistry, will vanish under the waves of stronger, deeper souls. Especially those like Ashoka."

"Wait," said John as he joined them in one of his rare ventures beyond the bathroom. "You were Ashoka? The emperor Ashoka?"

Ash nodded.

John sat down opposite him, fascinated. "Cool."

"Wasn't as great as all that," Ash admitted.

Khan picked up a bottle of water and with a sharp swipe of his claw took off the top. He gulped it all down. "You know what his name means?"

"No. Never really thought about it."

" 'Without sorrow.' " Khan smacked his lips and tossed the bottle away. "I've met some bloodthirsty humans in my time, but Ashoka was in a class of his own."

"No. He was a great man. He was an emperor," said John. "Everyone knows that."

"Oh, I'm not denying he was great, but there's only one way to forge an empire, little man," said Khan. "And that's by killing absolutely everyone who stands in your way. Genghis Khan told me that, and he should know." Khan paused. "Or was it Napoleon? Short fellow on a horse. Wore a funny hat."

Khan was telling the truth, Ash had to admit. He had never felt such coldness and cruel ambition as when he'd dreamed he was Ashoka. He'd relished the death and the terror he'd brought to that nameless village. Reveled in it.

"How can I stop the memories from affecting me?" Ash asked.

Khan shrugged. "You can't. Kali brought you back. Did you never think there would be a price?"

CHAPTER FIFTEEN

There was nothing more surreal than arriving in a strange city, in a strange country, at three in the morning.

The streetlights glowed vague and insubstantial through the dense mist that covered Kolkata. Lone cars crept along the silent streets, and Ash looked out at the beggars and homeless families lying under thin cotton sheets on the pavement, with nothing but flattened cardboard boxes as mattresses. Mangy dogs sniffed at the rubbish piled in the alleyways, and skeletal cows roamed everywhere, nibbling at trash.

Khan snored in the backseat of their taxi. Parvati still looked terrible, bordering on hideous. She had a shawl over her head and was more demon than human now. Her skull had mutated into a flat, serpentine wedge, and a cobra hood spread out on either side of her neck. The venomous fangs glistened, and her tongue constantly flicked out, tasting the air. Scales covered her hands, and each nail was a long, slender needle.

John shifted, stuck as he was with Khan to his left and Parvati to his right. He'd decided to tag along with them after they'd landed. A life of flying didn't suit him, and Jimmy hadn't been sad to see him go. His eyes stared at the unfamiliar city. "And I thought Varanasi was gloomy," he said.

"You want to go back there?"

"Not likely." He smiled at Ash. "I owe you."

It was good to have John around. When Ash and Lucky had been hunted by Savage and his demons, he had turned out to be their only friend. The boy had lived in the Lalgur as one of the many half-starved urchins that haunted every big city in India, stealing food and trinkets and tourist gear for Ujba, who was a major player in Varanasi's criminal underworld.

Ujba. Ash scowled as he remembered the crime lord. Ujba had been given the task of training Ash in kalaripayit, the ancient Indian martial art. It had meant weeks of brutal beatings by Ujba's best students. Ujba believed in the school of extremely hard knocks.

John had helped Ash and Lucky escape Ujba's den. He'd also helped them get in touch with their parents. So Ash's dad had sent John money to help find his mother, who'd abandoned John in Varanasi when she hadn't been able to cope.

Ash knew John had found his mum, but wondered why he wasn't with her now. Had something gone wrong? He'd asked, but John had been evasive, moving the subject onto something else. Perhaps his mother hadn't wanted him back after all. Ash would find a better time to talk about it. Maybe his dad could send some more cash to help.

Kolkata had been the capital of British India for two centuries, and as the taxi rolled on through the city, Ash got a sense of its faded grandeur. Old, elegant Victorian buildings stood cloaked in regal squalor, their walls haphazardly repaired, windows broken or boarded up, cracks emerald-fringed and moist with mold. The taxi splashed through ocean-sized puddles, and every weed or strip of green was blooming thanks to the recent monsoon rains.

"There," said Parvati. "Stop there."

Khan yawned, displaying a fine set of canines. "Home at last."

Home? Ash got out of the front passenger seat and looked around. "Where's the hotel?"

Parvati opened the taxi door. "We're not staying at a hotel."

Why did Ash suddenly get the feeling this was going to be no fun at all?

A high wall stretched along a run-down street. Palm trees creaked along the road, which was filled with potholes and exposed drains. Rats, big rats, scrabbled up loose wiring that hung down from the electricity poles. They followed Parvati along the wall to a large, ivy-covered gate. The air was dense with musk and mold.

Ash read the carved sign above the gate, heart sinking even lower. "The English Cemetery?" He gazed past the rusty iron railings. The place looked like a jungle. "Don't tell me we're staying here."

"Okay, I won't tell you we're staying here." Parvati tossed her backpack over the railings. The gates were held closed with a heavy chain, but there was enough slack for her to slip through. Khan growled and vaulted over the gate, clearing the uppermost spikes with feet to spare. He looked back, grinning.

"Think there'll be snakes?" asked Ash. The grass was over six feet high.

"Plenty," said John. "But I've stayed in worse places."

"The Lalgur was better than this," said Ash.

John flinched. "I wasn't talking about the Lalgur."

"Where, then?"

But John just twitched his head, evidently not wanting to talk about it, and followed Parvati through the gap.

"I know I'm going to regret this. A lot," Ash said to no one in particular, but feeling it needed to be noted, as he'd bring it up later when it all went wrong under the heading "I told you so." He chucked his own backpack over, grabbed the rusty railings, and climbed up.

Crumbling limestone tombs and headstones lay obscured in the overflowing foliage. Creepers hung down from banyan trees and huge palm leaves littered the winding, weed-choked path.

"What is this place?" Ash asked. He'd taken out his flashlight and shone it on a nearby headstone. "'Sergeant Thomas Compton. Died 1802.'"

"Calcutta was just a small cluster of villages until the East India Company set it out as one of their headquarters," said Parvati, using Kolkata's old English name. "It became one of their three presidencies in India. It was from here, Madras, and Bombay that they ruled the country."

"And this is where they buried their dead?"

"There's a Scottish one farther down the road," Parvati said. "Even in death they did not want to mix with the locals."

"Or with the Scots, obviously," said Ash.

The grass shook beside him and a sharp bark burst out as two dogs leaped onto the path. Their fur was torn and patchy, tight against their ribs. Spittle hung from their yellow teeth.

"Leave them," said Parvati. "They're harmless."

"They're rabid," said Ash, wondering if all his injections were up-to-date.

The dogs glowered, guarding their patch of grass, and Ash gave them a wide berth, with John keeping Ash between himself and the pair of feral beasts.

Ash was soon hopelessly lost. Parvati guided them around and around. There were mausoleums to entire families slain by disease or war, broken stone angels weeping over dead soldiers, and vast marble tombs of the great and good.

John squeezed Ash's shoulder. Small lights shone up ahead.

Slowly, figures came into view. Dressed in cast-off clothes, they sat hunched over small cooking fires and passed around tin plates of food. Crude tents assembled out of rags and plastic sheets lined the side of the path.

"Wait," said Ash. "There's something wrong."

The figures moved toward them. But some crept on all fours, their skins bristling with thick hair. Others stood straighter, but the fire shone off skin made of scales or armored carapaces. One, a child, shook his head and snorted through tusks jutting from his lower jaw.

Rakshasas.

Ash pushed John behind him. "Get ready to run." He moved into a ready stance, weight evenly spread out on the balls of his feet, arms loose as whips.

The tree bough above him creaked and eight red eyes gazed down. A huge, eight-limbed woman slid down a silver rope of spider silk.

Parvati stopped in front of them.

"Parvati . . ." said Ash.

She didn't move.

Then, one after the other, the demons stepped forward. They bowed and touched Parvati's feet, a sign of deep respect. Even the spider-woman scuttled forward and crouched before the demon princess, her mandibles clicking. She looked like Makdi, the spider-woman who'd served Savage back in the Savage Fortress, but while Makdi had been arrogant and cruelly beautiful, this one was spindly and wretched.

Rakshasas were meant to be terrifying and powerful, not

pitiful. This lot were a motley group, riddled with deformities, totally unlike the sleek human-animal hybrids in Savage's crew.

"Who are they?" Ash whispered to Khan.

"The lost and the damned," he growled.

A huge, gray-skinned man made his way through the crowd, each step shaking the ground and making the tall grass quiver. He was easily the most gigantic person Ash had ever seen. Big ears flapped on either side of his head, and a pair of thick tusks jutted from his upper jaw. He groaned as he bent down to the ground and put his head to Parvati's feet, the ultimate submission.

"Your Royal Highness," he said. "We bid you welcome."

CHAPTER SIXTEEN

"They look like they want to eat us," whispered John.

"You?" said Khan. "You're not even an appetizer."

Ash sat with them on a gravestone as Parvati consulted the big elephant rakshasa, Mahout. One of the demons passed them a bowl of rice and spicy vegetable curry, but otherwise they kept separate. Only Khan seemed relaxed, but then he always did. He sniffed at the curry.

"Could do with a bit of beef," he said. "Goat would be nice. It's been a while since I've had some goat. Or human. Nothing beats a soft bit of man flesh."

John gulped and shifted farther along the fallen gravestone.

"Leave him alone," said Ash. He looked over at Parvati. A couple of lamps had been set up inside a large mausoleum. Ash noticed the old East India Company initials and a scroll with the name *Lord Cornwall* on the mausoleum, almost obscured by the vines creeping across the roof. "This guy must have been a player. His tomb's twice the size of everyone else's."

"Old president," said Khan. "Once, all of the province of Bengal was his."

Parvati was deep in conversation, leaning over some maps with Mahout and two other rakshasas. A small silk bag lay between them — the one with the Koh-I-Noor inside.

"Where did they come from?" Ash asked. "These rakshasas?"

Khan shrugged. "Not all demons followed Ravana."

"That include you?"

"Tiger rakshasas follow no one. We do what we please." Khan pointed a long nail at a group of small demons gathered around a pot. "Cockroaches. Scorpions. There." He gestured to two perched on the roof. "Crows. They're untouchables, lower caste demons. Ravana and the other royals would not have them, so they've turned to Parvati."

Ash understood. Parvati's mother had been human, so Parvati wasn't considered a true "royal" rakshasa. It seemed that those who could find no one else to lead them had decided to follow her. India was a country built, and divided, by caste — much like the old English class system, but a thousand times more complicated and a thousand times older. There were Brahmins, the priests, at the top. Next came the warrior caste, called the Kshatriya. After that were the merchants and farmers and then the lower castes. Finally there were the untouchables. He'd never thought the rakshasas would be similarly split.

"And what are you?" said John.

"Warrior caste, of course," said Khan. "Like all other predators."

"And Parvati. She must be a Brahmin," said John. "They're the highest caste, after all."

Khan shook his head. "No, rulers come from the warrior caste. Brahmins aren't allowed to bear arms. They are usually advisers, the power behind the throne, as it were."

"So who are the Brahmins in the rakshasa world?" said Ash.

"There is, was, a race of serpents, called *nagas*. Ravana was descended from them, hence Parvati's cobra heritage."

"Ravana was a Brahmin?"

"Originally, yes. But Ravana, instead of following the Brahmin path, chose to become a warrior. Moving from one caste to another is exceedingly rare, but then Ravana was an exception to most rules." Khan licked his fingers clean. "The nagas were the wisest of us all, but they disappeared soon after Ravana's defeat at the hands of Rama. I've not seen one since. Probably extinct by now."

Ash looked around the group. "How many of you are there? There must have been thousands at Ravana's rebirth. What happened to them? Those who survived, that is."

Khan pointed up at the sky. "See those stars? Every one of them is a rakshasa soul."

"That's a lot."

Khan smiled and his eyes, amber as fire, shone with wicked amusement. "Afraid?"

"I'd be stupid not to be."

Khan slapped Ash's back with a roar of a laugh, nearly knocking Ash over. He had to take a second to recover his breath.

"Don't worry, mortal," said Khan. "Most were killed in the great war with Rama. The sky burned with the fire of the gods. Aastras blazed down from the clouds and from the bow of Rama and his generals. Countless rakshasas were slaughtered. They won't be reincarnated in a hurry, if ever."

"But only the Kali-aastra truly destroys," said Ash. "Isn't there a chance that they may come back?"

"All at once? How? No. In a small, thin stream, perhaps. Not enough to be a threat to humanity, alas." Khan looked up at the star-filled night and sighed. "Perhaps Ravana could have done it with his sorcery, brought down all those wandering spirits. But there is no Ravana now and there never will be."

Ash looked at Parvati. She and Mahout were deep in discussion in the empty mausoleum a distance away. The rest of the motley band of rakshasas were camped around the larger tombs for shelter. There was something he needed to know and didn't want Parvati or the others hearing. "It must be nice, knowing you'll come back."

"I suppose. Never really thought about it."

"It's different for us mortals."

"You get reincarnated, don't you? Hardly different at all."

Ash frowned. "We don't remember our pasts. But there must be a way, a spell or sorcery or something that allows us to come back, the way we were?"

He couldn't shake it from his mind, the idea of bringing Gemma back somehow. But there was no point discussing it with Parvati. Khan was as old as she was. He'd lived as many lives. He might know something that could help.

Khan peered at Ash, eyebrow arched suspiciously. "What did Parvati say about this?"

"She said that when we're gone we're gone, forever."

"Then you have my answer."

"But —"

Khan raised his hand. "Enough." He stood up. "Now, I've been cooped up in a plane for a day and would like to stretch my legs. Good night, Ash."

Well, that conversation had been a big fat failure. Frustrated and too agitated to sleep, Ash put his bowl aside and joined Parvati.

"You're looking better," he said. She wasn't back to normal, but her skin had returned to its smooth, unblemished tone and her hair, instead of looking brittle and dull, was again as sleek and black as a raven's wing. "What's going on?"

A map of the city laid spread over a sarcophagus. Mahout was busy marking the map with red dots, holding the thick marker pen with his trunk.

Parvati indicated the red dots. "Savage is in one of these places, if my information is correct."

"There must be a hundred."

"A hundred and fifty-three," said Mahout. "Libraries, military establishments, hospitals. Financial houses. A few factories. All connected with the Savage Foundation. If we look thoroughly, we'll find Savage."

"You're sure you haven't missed any?" Ash asked.

"I never forget."

"How long's that going to take?"

"As long as necessary," said Parvati. "Fifteen million people live in this city, Ash. We need to be patient."

"And what about the Koh-I-Noor? Where is it?" The small silk bag had disappeared.

"Under here." Parvati tapped her nails on the stone lid of the tomb.

"Wait a minute," said Ash. He looked up at the big elephant. "Do you know what type of aastra the Koh-I-Noor is? Does anyone around here know?"

Mahout shook his big head, his ears flapping back and forth across his face.

"Nobody? At all?"

"Sorry, Ash," said Parvati. "Look, the Koh-I-Noor is nothing but bait. Bait to get Savage. That's what you want, isn't it?"

It just didn't make sense that no one knew what the aastra could do. The Koh-I-Noor was the most famous diamond in the world, and the rakshasas must have come across it in one of their past lives. "Didn't you serve with the maharajah of the Punjab? Didn't he own this?"

"No one knows how to awaken the diamond, Ash. Why can't you let it go?"

"Isn't it worth trying to find out what it does? It could help."

"What's the point? That's not important."

"Not important? Gemma died for it."

"If you want me to say I'm sorry again, then listen: I am sorry," Parvati said. "But there's nothing anyone can do about her death. Don't distract yourself, and get over your guilt and failure. We all fail, but we need to move on. Forget her."

Forget her? Of all the wrong things to say, that was the most wrong. "Yes, and I know it means nothing to you but this is *Gemma* we're talking about. She had family, she had people who loved her. She wasn't like you."

The temperature dropped about twenty degrees. Parvati threw Ash an exceedingly dirty look and marched off with Mahout right behind.

Khan let out a long puff. Ash hadn't noticed him lounging at the entrance. "Beautifully handled, Ash."

"I thought you'd gone off for a walk."

Khan grinned. "And miss all the fun? I've rarely seen Parvati this upset."

"Why's she so upset?" Ash punched the stone. "*I'm* upset. I've come all the way out here and there's something she's not telling me."

"About what?"

"The Koh-I-Noor." It was an itch he couldn't reach. Why did no one know what sort of aastra it was? Why did no one want to find out? Savage was after it, so it had to be important. "I don't know what's got into Parvati."

"At some point replay that conversation in your head and you'll know. Despite being a killer, a demon princess, and the heir to Ravana's throne, Parvati, you may be surprised to hear, is rather sensitive. I suppose it's her human half."

"She's four thousand years old. She's seen kingdoms come and go. Time means nothing to her."

"The years pass just as slowly for us as they do for you. She's been lonely for most of those four millennia. Lonely and homeless."

"She's never had a home? Why not?"

"What palace could equal that of Lanka?" said Khan. "The courts of the Moghul emperors were no better than cow sheds compared to the kingdom of her father. Never bothered me, because I've always preferred the jungle, but I think Parvati still misses it."

"What happened to it?"

Khan shrugged. "What else? It was destroyed. If you humans are good at one thing, it's wiping out civilizations. It's amazing you've lasted this long, given your passion for genocide."

"She hated Gemma, that's for certain."

"She envied her," replied Khan. "For all the reasons you so indelicately pointed out. Family. Being missed. Being loved. No one's said that of Parvati. Her reputation prohibits that sort of thing."

"What about you? You're as old as she is."

"Me? Firstly, tigers are solitary creatures. Secondly, hey, look at me." He puffed out his chest and flexed his biceps. "Do you honestly think I have problems getting company?"

Ash laughed. "You really are totally in love with yourself, aren't you?"

"You'd better believe it."

"Think I should say something?" Ash asked. "To Parvati, I mean?"

"She'd do anything for you, you know that, don't you?"

"I didn't ask her to."

"Friends shouldn't need to ask."

Ash came up and sat down beside Parvati at an overgrown, weed-filled fountain somewhere in the heart of the graveyard. Heavenly nymphs — *apsaras* — forged from bronze held out empty jugs and cups, their empty nozzles choked with foliage and rust.

Ash smiled. Parvati did not.

Ah, not going to be as easy as all that, he thought. *This is what you call your classic "awkward moment."* Ash needed something to break the arctic levels of ice. Facing a demon horde or dealing with some "fate of the world in the balance" scenario would be easier than trying to apologize to Parvati. Where to begin? With the truth.

"I'm such an idiot," he said.

"Yes. You are."

"You weren't supposed to agree so immediately."

"What was I meant to do, then?" said Parvati.

"Listen, Parvati. I'm sorry about what I said earlier. You know I didn't mean it. It's just, Gemma's dead because of me. That's not what it was meant to be like. Y'know, being a hero and everything. Heroes don't fail."

"Then you've got a lot to learn about being a hero. Heroes fail more than everyone else."

"That doesn't make sense. At all."

"You fail. You try again. And again and again. Keep on failing until you finally succeed. That's what being a hero is. But some things can't be fixed, and you need to learn to live with them and move on."

"It's Friday," said Ash suddenly. "This time last week I was standing in the cafeteria, sweating buckets and asking Gemma out. How can so much have changed in a week?" He shook his head. "Jeez, if I knew what was going to happen I would never have even spoken to her, let alone asked her out to Bonfire Night."

Parvati sighed. "That's the advantage of being mortal. You only need to learn to live with the mistakes of your current life. Rakshasas remember their past lives. We're never free of our guilt."

"Things like giving Savage your father's scrolls?"

"Yes, I think that would be in the top ten of 'my bad.'" Parvati shifted uncomfortably. "He'd promised to make me wholly human, something I thought I desired."

They'd talked about it once, how she'd wanted to be mortal, to feel what it was to belong and to be loved, something no rakshasa could ever have.

She smiled wryly. "That said, I remember some of the stupid things you did too."

"What? Where?"

"You really want to know?"

"Of course not, but you've started now, so how can I not know?" Ash paused. "How bad was it? The 'Oops, Captain, but I didn't see that iceberg, and are you sure we've got enough lifeboats?' sort of bad?"

Parvati gazed up at the stars. "I was serving Penthesilea, Queen of the Amazons. We'd been summoned by Prince Paris to defend Troy against the Greeks."

"You fought at Troy?"

"So did you. You were one of King Priam's sons — I can't recall which, he had fifty. Anyway, it looked like it was over. Achilles was dead and the Greeks were feeling pretty hopeless. One day we looked out across the city walls and the entire army was gone. All that was left was a huge wooden horse. An offering to Poseidon, god of the sea, for a safe journey home."

"I've a bad feeling about this," said Ash.

Parvati tapped her chin. "What was it that you said? Let me remember. . . ." She snapped her fingers. "Ah, yes. You said, 'How pretty! Let's get it. It'll look lovely in the city square.'"

"We've been through a lot together," said Ash.

Parvati nodded and took his hand, squeezing it. "And we've always made it, in the end." She summoned one of the rakshasas. The demon, a small whiskered boy with twitching ears, rushed forward and touched her feet. "Now get some sleep, we've a busy time ahead. Bhavit will show you to your room."

CHAPTER SEVENTEEN

The days passed with no sign of Savage. Parvati didn't only have her rakshasas out searching; there were others helping her as well, beggars, rickshaw drivers, stall keepers. The downtrodden of the city were the ignored — and therefore the best spies. Ash watched how they came up to Parvati, touched her feet, and offered her gifts. This was a side of Parvati Ash hadn't seen before. The noble. The commander. The worshipped. But in spite of all these eyes and ears looking out for him, there was nothing on Savage.

Had Monty lied? Maybe Savage was a thousand miles away in another country, making his plans while they rotted in the damp, moldy heat of Kolkata.

But Ash did learn more about the Englishman. How he'd come with the East India Company in the late eighteenth century and how he'd robbed and murdered his way up and up the company's hierarchy until he eventually met Parvati. He'd gotten her father's scrolls from her, starting his career in sorcery.

Some of the rakshasas could do a little magic. Mahout, the big elephant, had two masteries, and from him and a few of the other rakshasas, Ash gained a basic understanding of the ten sorceries.

The classical elements, Earth, Air, Fire, and Water, accounted for four. Mastery of Air, for example, allowed a sorcerer to fly, communicate with the birds, and, if skillful enough, even control the weather. Then there were the next four sorceries, the humors: Blood, Yellow Bile, Black Bile, and Phlegm. Codified back in ancient Mesopotamia, they controlled the mind, body, and emotions of all living creatures. Parvati was an expert in a few of those, hence her ability to hypnotize. The final two were Space and Time. A master of Space could teleport, which Ash thought would be pretty amazing. Never late for school ever again. No one could agree if you had to learn them in any order, but all concurred that Time was the most powerful, and the most dangerous.

"Has anyone ever mastered Time?" Ash had asked Mahout. "Actually used it?"

"How would we know?" Mahout replied. "How can you know if the past has been changed? Impossible, because we are trapped within the time stream of that changed past. Only someone outside of the stream would see the difference, be able to compare what is to what had been before the change. They would know there had been an alternative history that had happened, even though it had been deleted. But the wise do not meddle with Time. Ravana never used that sorcery, although he had mastered it."

"Why didn't he go back in time and change things? Make sure he beat Rama? It would be easy."

Mahout shook his head. "You might change one event, but that would lead to a whole new series of outcomes, potentially even worse than the ones you sought to correct. Whatever you do, destiny is inescapable, young Ash. Ravana was doomed to fail. Are you not the proof of that?"

"What about Savage? What masteries does he have?"

Another argument followed. Mahout was convinced Savage had to know the humors, balancing them within himself to extend his life span. The spider-woman thought he had some knowledge of the elements, learned while in the Far East. But no one knew for sure — neither what he was capable of, nor where he was.

Ash joined in the search for Savage, using it as an excuse to get out of the cemetery and discover this new city. Kolkata couldn't be more different from Varanasi. Varanasi was a place of temples and steeped in deep, ancient Indian religion. The narrow streets teemed with holy men and pilgrims. Kolkata, meanwhile, was a memorial to the British Empire, the capital of the Raj until 1917. Whitewashed Anglican churches and stately grand government buildings lined the wide boulevards.

The first stop on his tour was the Victoria Memorial with John. The memorial symbolized Britain's two-hundred-year rule over India. At dawn the vast domed roof of the memorial hall shone with a soft eggshell glow, and the gardens surrounding it filled swiftly with day-trippers and picnics and tourists and touts. Kites rose up among the trees, crowding the sky with multicolored diamonds made of tissue paper and bamboo.

Ash took a viewpoint up on the shoulder of a huge lion statue, watching the multitude come and go, vainly hoping he would catch a glimpse of Savage. He must have been here once. This was his sort of place, a center of power. The building looked a lot like the Capitol building in the United States: huge dome, wide wings, a colonnade, and statues of the great and the good everywhere. When Ash said this out loud, John scoffed and spat some nutshells at the feet of a statue of the governor. The statues were all of English, he said. From their point of view, Indians could be neither "great" nor "good."

The rest of the day was spent hopping on and off the rattling tin trams that still served as the main mode of public transport. The vehicles were invariably packed with people hanging off the railings and handles by their fingertips, scuttling on or dropping off whether the tram was moving or not. At first, Ash was amazed there weren't mangled bodies on every street, but by evening he was doing the same, swinging onto the back of any passing carriage, then leaping off as it slowed around the corners.

The next day of searching was similar: heat, astounding sights, and no Savage. And so it went. Ash's days were spent exploring the city, and his nights were . . .

His nights were haunted by dreams. Each morning he awoke exhausted. Unlike before, when the dreams had been a single memory, now they came in their broken hundreds: snatches and glimpses of his past lives, lasting a few seconds before rushing to another with no sense or order. He lived them, smelling the corpses, tasting the blood, relishing the slaughter. The dark dreams filled his sleeping hours, then fled like cowards by sunrise. He overflowed with bloodlust. Once he woke up from a dream so clear, so vivid, that he rushed out, expecting to see dead rakshasas scattered all around. He washed his hands afterward, desperate to rid himself of the blood that was only spilled in his nightmares.

He needed help, that was for sure.

Maybe he shouldn't have come. Kolkata was Kali's city. Legend had it she had been dismembered and her toe had fallen in the river here, at a place called Kali-ghat in honor of the story. From Kali-ghat came the name Kolkata.

The worship of Kali soaked the bones of the city. Her image was everywhere, with plenty of statues and temples dedicated to her. Ash had passed by the nineteenth-century main temple of her cult, where a goat was beheaded over her shrine daily, washing the statue of Kali in blood. A century ago they'd sacrificed humans in the same spot.

So, on the fourth day in Kolkata, Ash woke in a bad mood. He slipped on his sandals as he got out of his hammock and gulped his water bottle down to empty.

"John?" he called. They'd planned to head down to Fort William today and search another cluster of red dots on Mahout's map.

"Not here," said Parvati. "I don't think he likes sleeping among us rakshasas. Can't imagine why." She sat atop the mausoleum Ash used as a bedroom.

"How long have you been up there?"

She jumped down and frowned as she approached him. "You do not look well."

"Thanks," Ash replied. Parvati was different too, more demonic with her body covered in light green scales and her eyes huge, her fangs clearly visible. Maybe she was letting her hair down, in the demonic sense. "It's getting harder," he admitted. "Can't sleep at night."

"Your past lives, yes? What is it like?" Parvati shifted up close and put her hand on his.

"It's like I'm standing in the rain," he started. "A total downpour. I'm getting drenched, but each drop that hits me is another memory. There are so many I can't make sense of them. I see castles and cities that are now just dust in history. Some are my homes, places I've grown up in and fight to protect. Others I burn. Then the faces. Faces of people I've fought and defended. Of people I've tried to save and didn't. Parvati, I wish I could cut it all out of my head. I've done terrible things."

"Anyone you recognize?"

"Rishi, a couple of times. It's as though he's been after me throughout history. Him, and you."

"You see me?"

"Your age changes, but there can't be too many half-human, half-cobra girls in the world. Sometimes we're friends and sometimes . . . we're not." Ash sighed. "I wish Rishi were here. He'd know what to do."

Parvati sat for a long time, doing nothing but holding his hand. Then she took a deep breath, like she had made some decision. "He did. That is why he sent you to train with Ujba."

"Yeah, not one of Rishi's better ideas. I don't think I learned anything with Ujba except how to get punched. A lot, and very hard. What sort of teacher is that?"

"He taught you how to fight. That involves taking hits as well as giving them out."

"Some days I was beaten up so badly I could hardly walk. He let his cronies terrorize everyone else, he made John's life hell, and he *hated* you. Ujba was nothing but a thug." He remembered those days, trapped in the stifling heat of the training hall of the Lalgur, deep underground.

"An interesting term to use for Ujba, but most correct," she said.

"I called Elaine last night," said Ash. He held out his cell phone. "I had to. She told me Rishi had spoken to her and given her the names of people who could help me, if things got bad."

Parvati let a scowl slip, then her gaze narrowed with curiosity. "And what did she say?"

"Nothing, it went straight to voice mail. But I got a text this morning. An address. You know it?"

She looked at the screen and nodded. "It's not far from here."

"I feel like I'm losing myself. There are so many people in here" — he tapped his head — "all shouting. The dreams are so real, so violent. They're getting worse and I'm worried I'm going to wake up one day and find out I've done something . . . extremely homicidal."

Parvati shivered and the scales sank under her skin. Her fangs retreated and she drew out a pair of sunglasses, returning to her human guise. She took his hand. "Let's go."

CHAPTER EIGHTEEN

Beyond the quiet seclusion of the graveyard, Kolkata was up, awake and busy. They crossed the road, filled with honking cars and even human-powered rickshaws — two-wheeled vehicles pulled along the street by a single man, no horse or bicycle. It looked like a horrible lifestyle, the men thin, their passengers heavy.

But as Ash walked along the streets, his feet seemed to find their own path. He looked up at buildings around him. A cold dread filled him, and for a moment he wondered if this was still a dream. He'd been here before. He was sure of it.

"What is it?" Parvati asked.

"Déjà vu," said Ash. He stared ahead. "There's a place around that corner. Wait here."

Parvati said nothing.

Ash waved down the traffic to give him space and crossed the road, leaving Parvati behind him. He passed by a blind beggar who squatted under a torn umbrella, plastic cup in hand. Smoke drifted out of the darkness. The walls tilted and almost touched together a couple of floors up. Only a crude assembly of wooden supports kept them from collapsing. Ash ducked under them and crept down the alleyway.

"Hello?"

Whatever this place had been, now it was a crumbling shack. No door, walls lopsided, and window frames warped and covered in tangled weeds.

Ash stepped in, putting his foot on the marble threshold.

An old temple. There was a brass hook above him from which a bell would once have chimed. Plain white marble tiles, crushed and uneven, covered the floor. Litter, blown in by the wind, filled the corners, and the dust drew strange patterns upon the ground. Cobweb curtains hung off the wooden cross-beams, and Ash brushed them aside as he approached the altar and the statue upon it.

Kali stood above the cringing form of a demon, her ten arms fanned out. In one hand she carried a severed head by its long hair, its eyes half-closed and tongue hanging out, limp and dumb. In the other hands were weapons ranging from spears to swords to a noose. The paint had flaked off the statue, exposing the bare stone beneath, but that only made her more terrifying, as though she were sloughing off her own skin. Murals decorated the wall behind her, but in the poor light, Ash couldn't really see what they were.

A cold wind, a whisper of breath, caressed his neck. Ash spun around.

"Parvati?"

There was no one there.

No one.

"Hello?"

Another Kali temple. But why did this one feel so different? Kolkata was an alien city. He'd never walked its streets or seen its sights till a few days ago. But this temple was like . . . coming home.

He'd trodden these tiles before. He felt familiar dips and grooves, as though his toes had once rested in them during a time past. He touched the altar and searched the stone for nicks and marks. Instinctively his nail ran into a long shallow groove, something left by a blade. There were others.

People have died here.

Kali loves death best. Wasn't he proof of that? He became more powerful the more he killed. Kali blessed him. He ran his fingertips over the scored stone, shivering as old memories swirled in the dark places of his mind — memories from a previous life, maybe, of holding down a struggling victim and drawing a blade across his throat, the blade leaving a light scratch on the stone. Even now he felt the victim squirming against the altar. Ash's hand tightened as it remembered wrapping itself around the man's hair, gripping his head steady for the knife.

A hand touched his back.

Parvati gasped as he spun around and stopped his punch an inch from her face. Ash stepped back, his heart tripping with panic. "I'm sorry, Parvati, I don't know what happened."

"It's your past lives. They're guiding you now, subconsciously." She looked worried and put her hand on his cheek. "They were afraid this would happen."

"They?"

"They as in Rishi and I." A man sat in the darkness, by the doorway. Somehow Ash had walked straight past without seeing him. He was hunched over a small plate, and he wore a loose tunic and baggy trousers, a yellow scarf dangling around his thick neck. He put the plate aside and stood up, stretching until his head almost brushed the underside of the temple ceiling. His fingers smoothed down his black mustache.

"Ujba," Ash whispered.

"I prefer 'guru.'"

"What are you doing here?"

"Elaine sent for me. There is much more for you to learn, boy," said Ujba. "Especially now that you are the Kali-aastra."

"You?" said Parvati as she saw Ujba, and her fangs lengthened on instinct.

"Only I know how to deal with the Kali-aastra," said Ujba. "You are one of us, boy."

"And what is that, exactly?" Ash said.

"A devotee of Kali." Parvati glanced around the small chamber.

"Well, forget it. I'm not training with you anymore." Ash nodded to the doorway. "Let's go, Parvati."

"It was Rishi's wish," said Ujba, "that if anything happened to him, I would continue your training."

That made both of them, Ash and Parvati, stop. If Rishi had wished it, how could they say no?

Parvati narrowed her eyes as she gazed suspiciously at Ujba, but her fangs retreated back behind her lips. "I don't like this any more than you do, Ash, but he's right. He's a Brahmin of Kali."

"I thought Brahmins weren't allowed weapons."

"There are many things that do not apply to the worshippers of the black goddess," said Ujba. He looked at Parvati. "Leave us."

Parvati hesitated, looking not at all happy, then gave a short nod. "I'll be back at nightfall, Ash." She left.

Ash wanted to go too, to turn on his heels and follow her

out. But then what? More nightmares he couldn't handle? Another attack when he was asleep? He was getting out of control.

But Ujba? Why Ujba?

"So what do you want me to do?" he said.

Ujba reached behind a column and took out a broom and tossed it to Ash. "Clean."

"Clean?" Ash answered. "How's that going to help?"

"I am your guru. You do as I tell you."

"I've come a long way from the Lalgur, Ujba." The big man was a brutal teacher, his lessons harsh. Even now Ash could remember every punch and kick he'd suffered, every bruise and cut he'd got training with Ujba. But that was then, when he'd been slow and unfit and human. Now he was the Kali-aastra.

"You think there's nothing left to teach you?" said Ujba.

"Something like that."

"Perhaps you can show me some of this extraordinary skill? I would be most pleased to watch a true master at work. Perhaps I might learn from you?"

Ash bristled. Ujba clearly didn't believe him.

"You hesitate?" said Ujba. He slapped his chest. "Do you need an opponent? Use me. Don't be afraid of hurting me. I certainly won't be afraid of hurting you. Come, then."

"I don't think —"

Ujba moved. His punch caught Ash square in the chest and launched him off his feet. Ash landed and then flung himself aside just as Ujba's foot smashed into the wall, barely missing his face. Ash swung his fist, but Ujba jabbed his fingers into Ash's armpit, and his arm went limp.

Marma-adi. He knows —

The next blow was a light tap under his ribs, but it felt like a cannonball. Ash couldn't breathe. He stumbled back, his legs wobbling, then fell.

Ujba walked over to the broom and picked it up. He returned and stood over Ash.

"Feeling will return in ten minutes." He dropped the broom on Ash. "Then you clean."

CHAPTER NINETEEN

So Ash cleaned. He brushed the worst of the cobwebs away, swept the floor, arranged candleholders around the shrine, and put fresh garlands of marigolds around Kali's neck. Ujba watched, immobile but for the occasional twitch of the stick in his hand.

Eventually the guru clapped his hands. "Enough. Let us see what you remember. Honor Kali."

It was late morning and shafts of sunlight illuminated the temple, piercing through the cracks and holes in the roof. The day's heat, moist with the oncoming rains, weighed the air down, and sweat shone upon Ash's bare torso. He took three steps back and faced the statue. He hadn't done this since he'd left the Lalgur. He put his palms together. He began his salutations to the black goddess.

The moves came slowly, old memories reemerging under the gaze of guru and goddess. Ash unleashed blows, sunk into dives, and rose up with high-arching kicks. The old strength surged through him, accelerating his moves, multiplying the power of his strikes. This was what the Kali-aastra wanted. He twisted aside from imaginary attacks and reacted with bone-shattering punches of his own. The final move was the low stance before the goddess, touching the floor before her. Honoring her.

Sweat poured off his back. Ash stood up and ran his hand through his hair, away from his eyes.

Ujba scowled. "I thought you were the Kali-aastra. The weapon of the divine."

"What? Did I make a mistake?" He knew he hadn't. "I did that perfectly."

"Perfection is the least of my expectations." Ujba stood up and slapped the wall with his palm. "The Kali-aastra should demolish walls with his kicks. He should slay armies with his bare fists. Your attacks should shake mountains."

"That's impossible."

"I demand impossible things, then." He watched Ash with his small black eyes. "Rishi was a fool."

"Don't you dare say that."

Ujba scoffed. "Did you know him? At all?"

"He saved my life and my sister's. He was one of the good guys. He rescued me from the Savage Fortress. Don't remember seeing you there."

"He should have told me about the Kali-aastra. Perhaps then he would still be alive. That's the trouble with clever men — they sometimes outwit themselves."

"What do you want from me?" said Ash. "If I'm so useless?"

Ujba shrugged. "I thought I could train you, help you unlock the powers of the Kali-aastra. Teach you how to manage your past lives."

"You can do that?"

"Teach you? That depends on your willingness to learn. Your respect for your guru."

"Isn't respect earned?"

"Do you want to learn or not, boy?" Ujba looked at him with barely disguised contempt. "You have these gifts, but you squander them. Worse, you reject them. No wonder each waking moment is pain. Look in the mirror, boy. You're being eaten from within."

"The Kali-aastra gives me strength."

"It is the only thing keeping you alive. And poorly, it seems."

Ash stared hard at the dark man. Was it that bad? He touched the scar on his stomach. The nightmares, the waxing and waning of power, all because of who he was, what he was. The Kali-aastra. Could Ujba teach him to control it? If there was even a small chance, he had to take it. He couldn't carry on like this.

Reluctantly, Ash made a decision.

"Teach me, then," he said. "I want to learn."

Ujba put his hands to Ash's face and peered closely into his eyes. "You dream? Of your past incarnations?"

"Yes."

The guru nodded slowly. "You must learn when to fight and when to yield. A warrior must combine flexibility with rigidness. You fight against the others, your past selves, instead of bending. Look for a path of least resistance and attach yourself to that."

"How will I spot it?"

"Your previous incarnations do not come at random. There is a purpose to them wanting your attention. By yielding, you make them allies. Consider them guides. At different times, as your needs change, different personalities will come to your aid. You just need to recognize them among the multitude."

"How?"

"That wisdom is not easily acquired." Ujba picked up the broom and turned it in his fingers. "You will dream tonight, most likely. Do as I say and we will talk again tomorrow. But I do have one other piece of wisdom, one which is well meant, though I know you'll ignore it."

"Tell me."

"Do not trust the rakshasa. Her kind and ours are eternal enemies. I am your guru."

Ash laughed. "Parvati? In what alternate universe would I trust you instead of her? She's always been on my side."

"As have I, boy, though you've been too blind to see."

"Ash?"

They turned and there, in the doorway, was Parvati.

"Am I early?" she asked.

Ujba addressed Ash. "Tomorrow." Then, with one last dark look at Parvati, he left.

"He so doesn't like you, does he?" said Ash as he wiped the sweat off his face.

"He has reason." Parvati approached the shrine. She slid her fingers over the cracked altar stone, feeling the grooves and indentations. "Let's go. This place is evil."

"That's almost funny coming from a demon."

"Didn't Ujba tell you? About who worshipped here?"

Her voice quivered as she spoke. Ash's heart skipped a beat. Parvati was frightened. He hadn't thought that possible. But that cold, dreadful breeze haunted the edges of the temple, and Ash flexed his fingers, thinking of the man, the sacrificial victim, whom he'd held against the altar once upon a time.

"Who?" he asked.

"Kali's most devoted and deadly servants." She met his gaze and there was old terror in her eyes. "The Thugs."

CHAPTER TWENTY

"You mean like out of *Indiana Jones and the Temple of Doom*? The Thuggee?" asked Ash. They'd gone to a café for dinner and found a quiet corner away from the small crowd of men watching and cheering the cricket game on the old crackling TV.

"I forget most of your education comes from Hollywood," said Parvati. "What do you know about them?"

Ash tried to remember the film. There was something about chilled monkey brains and Indians being badass until the white hero came along and spoiled all the fun. "They strangled people quite a lot."

"Yes. It was the old way. They killed their victims without spilling blood. Have you ever strangled a man?"

"No." But he'd come close, hadn't he? Ash blushed with shame, thinking of how he'd almost strangled his dad when he'd dreamed of being the first Ashoka.

Parvati unwrapped her light cotton scarf and wound the ends around her fists. "It's hard work. The victim struggles, and unless you get the cloth in exactly the right place, knot under the Adam's apple, you waste a lot of energy achieving not very much."

"Sounds like you've done it."

"You think I'd need a scarf?"

No, of course not. Parvati's venom was lethal to man, demon, and probably god. One bite would do the job. Not for the first time Ash wondered exactly how many people she had killed in her long, long life.

"Do you know the legend of how the Thugs were made?" she asked.

"Not something that comes up in the National Curriculum."

"Kali was fighting a terrible demon. A demon as powerful as Ravana, and she was alone. All the other gods had fled." Parvati had a faraway look. It wasn't as though she was telling a story, something she'd read or been told by another person. It was as if she was remembering it from her past.

She continued. "So there she is, stabbing and slashing at this rakshasa. But she can't defeat him. From every drop of blood she spills, out grows another rakshasa. Soon she'll be overwhelmed."

"What does she do?"

Parvati ran her palm over her arm. "The goddess takes sweat from her body and creates two men. She rips a strip of cloth from her skirt and gives it to them. They kill each and every rakshasa." Parvati made a twisting movement with her fists. "Strangling them."

"Killing them without spilling any blood."

Parvati nodded. "The Thugs were created to be demon killers. To follow the path of Kali. Over the centuries they became greedy, petty-minded, and corrupt, using their skills for highway robbery and murder. But you're missing the bigger picture."

"What's that?"

"The first men she made, they were Kali-aastras." Parvati sighed. "The Thugs believed that if they killed enough, performed the correct rituals and observed the right omens, they would gain supernatural powers. They believed that by murder they might become Kali-aastras themselves. Like the first of Kali's creations. Like you."

Kali loves death. He'd been told that, ages ago. He gained power through death, so why wouldn't the Thugs believe the same thing? Weren't they, the Thugs and him, all servants of Kali?

"I'm not a Thug," said Ash.

"But you are, Ash. Kali made you to kill demons, like the first two Thugs. You are her weapon, her right hand. The hand that slays."

"I may have these powers, but that doesn't mean I'll use them."

She smiled weakly. "I know, Ash. But the Kali-aastra might not give you a choice. The more powerful you grow, the more it will demand of you."

"And Ujba? Is he a Thug?"

"In a manner of speaking. He knows all the old rituals and skills. He understands what the Kali-aastra is capable of better than anyone else. But his goals are not your goals. He worships Kali in a way that's rather antisocial."

"He's a killer?"

"He kills for what he believes in." She looked at him over her sunglasses. "And in that he's not alone, is he?"

"Then how is he going to help me?"

"By teaching you to channel your past, your other lives. Think about it." She tapped Ash's temple. "Think what knowledge lurks in there. What skills. If you could access your former selves in a controlled manner, you could use their abilities, what they know. You say Ashoka's one of your previous incarnations. Don't let him control you. *You* control him, instead. If you could use all his military wisdom and warcraft, you would be unstoppable."

Ash sank back into his chair. "It's never going to end, is it?"

Parvati smiled softly, but shook her head. "Not in this lifetime, nor any other."

CHAPTER TWENTY-ONE

And again they come. Ash screams as the images tumble through his mind, memories and emotions and dreams of countless people he has been since the beginning.

He is a red-robed soldier standing in a shield line as the sky darkens with arrows.

He urges his horse to a gallop as he raises his spear for the —

Hands tied, he takes steps to the scaffold. The sun shines on the headman's ax as he lifts it and the birds caw from —

More and more they assault him, and Ash feels as if he's drowning. He struggles against the endless torrent and —

Ashoka sits upon a horse, hand resting on his hilt. Beside him is a young woman in scaled armor —

He sits upon a horse, hand on his sword hilt. Beside him is Parvati.

He is with Parvati.

Ash pushes the others away, letting the spirits wash over him, and he guides himself toward this one moment, this one life.

Ashoka sits upon his horse, watching another city burn. The ash, even from here, is hot and the night sky boils over with dense clouds of smoke, lit by the roaring flames of temples, of palaces, of homes and shops and people. Sparks of tinder float in the darkness like the eyes of a million demons.

The soldiers drag the slaves, each one chained to the one in front, the lines stretching back to the horizon. Most are dumb with despair, dirty, some bloody and dressed in rags as they proceed along the road, a mute, living line of misery. Somewhere in the darkness there rises a long, wailing lamentation as the women find the corpses of their husbands and sons among the slaughtered.

The sound pleases Ashoka. It sounds like victory.

"They will call you emperor after this," says Parvati. The rakshasa princess rests upon a corpse, takes off her boot, and shakes out the dust. The man, breathing but hours ago, full of life, hope, joy, and dreams, is nothing more than part of the scenery now. With a sharp tug, Parvati pulls off his turban and begins to clean her sword with the long cloth.

Ashoka looks down from his saddle. "Emperor Ashoka. I like it."

"And then what?" Blood shines upon her armor, and her hair, braided and wrapped around her head to prevent it being grabbed in battle, is speckled with gore. She wipes her face and leaves a trail of red across her pale cheeks. The green, serpentine eyes glow. "More war?"

"Do you tire of it, sweet Parvati?"

She scoffs. "Mortal, I have seen such sights that would haunt even you. This" — she sweeps her hand over the burning city — "was but an hour's work for my father."

"Your father was the lord of the demon nations. I am but a man."

"A man. Cruel, vain, and petty." Parvati bows mockingly. "My father would have enjoyed your company. You and he would have had a lot in common."

"More than you think." Ashoka smiles at the confusion in the demon princess's eyes. He nods to his bodyguard. *"Bring him."*

His men drag an old man forward and throw him to the blood-soaked ground. It is the priest. His face is bruised and his clothes torn and bloodied, and he clutches a silver box to his chest. He kneels on the ground, head bowed. *"My great lord,"* he croaks.

Ashoka swings down from his saddle and stands in front of the man. He rests his hands upon the hilt of his sword. *"Tell me, Parvati. They say your noble father was the greatest sorcerer the world has ever known."*

"No other being has ever mastered the ten sorceries," says the rakshasa girl.

Ashoka snaps his fingers. *"The box, old man."*

"My lord, you do not understand —"

Ashoka grabs it and kicks the man back into the dirt.

The box is small, delicately engraved with ancient symbols and sigils of power. It is warm to the touch and heavier than it should be. The object within has weight.

"They say Ravana could transform himself into anything, or anyone. They say he could cross from one side of the world to the other in an eyeblink. Is what they say true, Parvati?"

"It is."

"Could he raise the dead?" challenges Ashoka.

"That no one can do."

He opens the box and takes out the object within.

Parvati gasped. *"The Koh-I-Noor."*

Ashoka grins. *"The Brahma-aastra, yes. They call it the Life Giver."* He leans closer to the man. *"Have you awoken it?"*

"Yes, my lord."

With one hand holding the massive, glowing gem, Ashoka draws out his sword with the other. Parvati says nothing, but her eyes narrow.

"Hold him," orders Ashoka.

The old man cries out as the guards grab him. Ashoka tightens his grip upon his hilt and lays the blade against the man's thin body. The Koh-I-Noor pulses within Ashoka's grasp, and beams of light rise out of its faces. The colors change and brighten and the stone begins to burn.

Ashoka grins. "Now, the test."

The blade enters the old man's chest. A thick fountain of blood bursts from the wound, spraying the guards and Ashoka. The old man's screams rise to a feverish pitch, and he thrashes in the grip of the guards, his scrawny body filled with a hideous, desperate strength. But eventually he slumps, his skin glistening with dark blood.

Ashoka draws out the sword and hands it to one of his men. He raises the limp head by its white hair and stares at the closed eyes and the slack jaw. More blood dribbles from the dead man's mouth and his tongue hangs dumbly.

Ashoka holds the glowing jewel and moves it back and forth so the light blazes upon the pale flesh.

The limbs, dead and bloodless, twitch.

Ashoka gazes intently at the dead man.

The dead man's eyes open and gaze back.

CHAPTER TWENTY-TWO

"It's a Brahma-aastra," said Ash. "It's the Life Giver. It raises the dead. And you *knew*."

He still couldn't quite believe it — that Ujba had been right about Parvati, that she couldn't be trusted. His guts churned in turmoil with anger, disappointment, and betrayal.

"Maybe we should discuss this privately, Ash," said Parvati.

The other rakshasas were just waking up in their soggy camp. Last night's downpour was now a fine falling mist, with water dripping off the huge, shiny green leaves into dirty brown puddles. A few small campfires flickered, fed with rubbish and semidry twigs. The ragtag demon followers of Parvati set about cooking breakfast as they shifted through the graveyard under wet blankets and tatty old coats. Mahout glanced at Ash, a hint of sadness in his little eyes, but Ash snarled back. Mahout had known also, and hadn't told him. Had they all known about the Koh-I-Noor?

"Why not here?" Ash's knuckles and finger joints clicked as he locked them into fists. "Or are you worried everyone will find out what a liar and traitor you really are?"

Parvati's fangs lengthened. Even in the gloom of dawn her eyes shone murderously bright. "Because you are my friend, Ash, I'll forgive you this once. But never presume to speak to me like that again, ever."

"You let Gemma die, and all the while we've had the power to bring her back." Ash shook his head and could barely keep the tears back. "We could bring her back, Parvati. Somehow."

"That's not possible."

"It is, I saw it happen. Ashoka took the Koh-I-Noor and made a dead man live. I was there."

"And so was I, Ash. It wasn't like that."

"I saw —"

"I don't care what you think you saw."

"What about Savage? He's been after the diamond from the beginning. Maybe he knows how to use it."

Parvati looked at him as if he'd gone absolutely monkey-loony insane. Then she laughed. Once, when she laughed, it had lifted Ash's heart and there was no better sound. Now it was pitiless and mocking. "Savage? Well, why don't you ask him when you find him? I'm sure he'll be happy to help."

"That's not what I mean. There might be others who can do it. Other sorcerers, good guys like Rishi."

"There's no one like Rishi. If there were, I would have found him by now."

"You don't understand," said Ash.

"No, *you* don't. Listen, Ash, I'll explain this again, slowly, so it gets into your stubborn head. The Koh-I-Noor cannot raise the dead. Savage is our enemy. That's it. Just follow my orders and we'll get through this. You start having your own ideas and it'll go badly for all of us, especially you."

How could she be so arrogant? Who did she think she was? "Is that a threat, Parvati? I've just as much right —"

"Will you just shut up for once?" Parvati folded her arms. "You have to let her go, Ash. Let Gemma rest in peace."

"Why?" he asked. Simply that.

"Fate, Ash, fate." Parvati sighed. "Gemma was fated to die. Because of you."

"Lies," Ash snarled. "You're just full of them. I never knew how much of a snake you really were — even your mind's all twisted." He gazed around at the gathered crowd. "All these people, they're here because they want to believe in you. But they don't know you like I do. Don't know how you'll use them, get close just so you can stab them in the back, like you did me. Like you did your own father. I thought it was because you believed in something better, but now I realize it's just your nature. To lie to those close to you. To betray the ones loyal to you. Treachery, it's all you know, isn't it?"

"Shut up, Ash, if you know what's good for you."

But he couldn't. The anger needed to get out and Ash wanted her to hurt as badly as he did. "You wonder why you have no friends. Why in over four thousand years no one's cared for you and why you've been so alone. The answer's right there. You just need to look in the mirror."

Parvati hissed, her cheeks flushed, her eyes filled with anger and humiliation, Ash knew he'd just destroyed all the friendship they'd had.

The other rakshasas watched in utter silence. No one moved except Khan. Slowly he stood and slowly he moved through the long grass, eyes never leaving Ash, until he was standing beside Parvati in a warrior stance.

Parvati glared at Ash, matching his rage with a dark fury of her own. "Go, before I kill you," she whispered.

CHAPTER TWENTY-THREE

Ash stalked away into the darkest reaches of the cemetery, chopping and swiping at the undergrowth. He kicked a tree trunk, watching the leaves quiver and shake. He kicked it again, harder.

It was all wrong! He didn't understand what was happening. Gemma was dead, his friends back home were scared of him, he'd attacked his dad, and now this — Parvati hated him.

He slumped down on a fallen gravestone. He didn't know what to do.

Why had she lied? Did Parvati hate Gemma that much? It didn't make sense. More likely she just didn't care, or understand. How could she? She was a demon, daughter of Ravana. What did the life of one girl mean to her? Nothing.

Parvati wanted Savage dead, and that was all the Koh-I-Noor was to her, bait to attract the Englishman.

A chill went through him. Did Savage know how to use the Brahma-astra? Was that why he was after it? He had mastered seven of the ten sorceries; mightn't he know the secret to this as well?

If he did, and got hold of it, then he could bring Gemma back from the dead. The Life Giver — that was what Ashoka had called the Koh-I-Noor. Yet who knew what other powers it might possess? Could he risk Savage getting even a sniff of the diamond?

But Parvati wanted to kill Savage the moment he came looking for it. The world would then be rid of an extremely bad, bad guy, but he wouldn't be able to save Gemma. How could Ash allow that? Gemma hadn't deserved to die, and if there was a single chance, no matter how small, how insane, to have her back, he had to take it.

Ash grabbed hold of a thick branch, too frustrated to do anything but try to twist and rip it off. He bent the bough as far as he could and glared at the creaking limb, determined to break it.

"What are you doing?" said John. He sat on top of one of the hundreds of tombs with a banana leaf in his hand, eating some stewed vegetables with his fingers.

Ash released the branch. "Where have you been?"

"Staying out of trouble. Unlike you." He scrunched up the leaf and tossed it. "You just seem to attract it."

Ash picked up a stick and swung it limply at the unyielding tree. "Tell me about it. Everything's gone epically wrong. Parvati's been lying to me from the very beginning. She's so caught up in avenging herself on Savage that she doesn't care who else gets hurt."

"What happened?"

Ash told him about the dream, the Koh-I-Noor, and how it could bring life back to the dead. That there was a way, a real way, to save Gemma. Repeating it out loud made Parvati's betrayal all the more painful. But John didn't seem surprised.

"She's a demon, what did you expect?" he said. "You can't trust anyone."

John sounded so bitter. It wasn't like him. "What's wrong?" Ash asked.

John stared at him.

"Out with it, John."

John hopped down. "Forget it. I'm all right." He tapped the tree. "So what are you going to do now?"

"See Ujba, I suppose."

"He's in Kolkata?" John gaped. "What . . . what does he want?"

"He's not after you, if that's what you're worried about. He wants to train me. I'm meant to be over there now. Apparently he agreed to continue my training if anything happened to Rishi." He scratched his thumb. "There are more powers within the Kali-aastra. He wants me to learn them."

"But you killed Ravana," said John. "Isn't that enough?"

Ash looked up at the tree. "Apparently not."

John glanced around him, agitated. Talking about Ujba had obviously scared him badly. He jumped at the sound of a bird breaking cover. Ash laughed.

"It's not funny, Ash," John said. "Don't trust Ujba. He's evil."

"Come on. I know he's hard, but Rishi thought —"

"Don't be an idiot!" John shouted. He held his fists up and gritted his teeth, almost boiling with rage. Ash had never seen him so angry. "Ujba will hurt you; it's what he does. Do you think he's forgiven you for running from him? A man like that holds grudges, believe me. I know." He said the last two words with quiet despair, shuddering as he said them.

"What happened? After we left?"

"What do you think happened?"

"My dad gave you money. To help find your mum. Didn't you —"

"Oh, a couple of hundred pounds. Thanks so much. We poor Indians are *soooo* grateful to the English sahib." John put his palms together and gave a low, mocking bow. "You come and give us your spare change, then go. Bye-bye, India."

"It wasn't like that, John. You know it wasn't."

"Ujba took the money off me. He . . . wasn't happy about what had happened. I helped you escape, remember? He didn't like that at all." John shook his head. "He beat me. I could barely walk after he and Hakim had finished. Then he kicked me out onto the streets. No one would help me, not after Ujba spread the word. You know what it's like to be starving when all around you are restaurants? When you can smell food sizzling in the pans? I tried to steal, but that just got me beaten up again. More."

"Oh, God. John, I'm so sorry. I never knew."

"Of course you didn't. All your problems were behind you."

"But you found your mum, you told me."

"I had a few friends. They helped me look. She's being taken care of now."

"Friends like Jimmy?"

John didn't meet Ash's gaze, but nodded. "He was one."

Ash took his friend's hand. "John, I can't fix what's happened. But I promise, I *promise* I'll make it up to you."

John drew his hand away. "I know you will, Ash." But he didn't sound at all happy about it.

CHAPTER TWENTY-FOUR

"You are late," said Ujba.

"How observant of you," said Ash.

"Then we must work twice as hard." Ujba pointed at the statue of Kali. "You know what to do. Honor the goddess."

Ash didn't move. He stared at Ujba, thinking about how he'd treated John, and he felt his fury build inside him. His hands shook until he pressed them against his legs; otherwise, he didn't know what he'd do. Smash Ujba to pieces, most likely.

"Well?" said Ujba, utterly unaware of Ash's desires.

Gold lights sprung up on Ujba's skin. Not many, not many at all. Most were dim — disabling points rather than fatal.

"You are angry. Why?" said Ujba, his back turned to Ash as he leaned over something in the corner.

Where to begin? "For a lot of things, but right here, right now? For what you did to John."

Now Ujba turned around. If Ash didn't know better, he'd have said the guru looked surprised.

"John? The little thief? What exactly did I do to him?"

"Beat him, starved him. Cast him out and stole his money. The money I gave him."

Ujba stroked his mustache. "The money, yes, I took it. Why not? But those other crimes? I will tell you this. I am hard, but

I am not cruel. John left the same day you went with your father. Poorer for certain, but unharmed by me or any of my house."

"But he told me —"

"The boy is a thief. He was perhaps working your Western sympathies for more rupees. He has a weak and pitiful face. I've told him more than once it will make his fortune. He is easy to pity. Easy to believe."

"Why would he lie to me?"

"Why indeed? This is a good question to ask yourself."

"John is my friend," said Ash. His only friend, it seemed. "He helped me escape your prison. That's why you did those things to him."

"Prison? You mean the Lalgur? You think you were in a prison? What happened when your so-called friend helped you escape my school? Were you not captured by Savage? Were you not forced to hand over the Kali-aastra to him? Was not your sister threatened with death, to be fed to Savage's demons? Was this the help John provided?" Ujba laughed, and his amusement was brutal. "I think you could do with fewer of these types of friends."

"What, and more friends like you?"

"I am your guru. That is far more important." He brushed the dust off his palms. "Now, we have work to do."

Ujba took a wooden box and brought it over. It was about the size of a shoe box, made of old, dark wood, smooth and shiny with age. Elaborate Sanskrit writing covered the lid, once inlaid with gold leaf, but the letters were too worn to be read and most of the gold was gone. The guru knelt down, silently motioning for Ash to do the same opposite him.

What was going on? John had told him that Ujba had been brutal, and Ash believed him. But as Ash searched the guru's face, he couldn't be sure. Rishi trusted Ujba; he'd made arrangements for Ash's training with him. Ujba might be evil, but he was a priest of Kali. Ash was a servant of Kali. He didn't know what to believe.

Lost in confusion, he sat down.

The smell of herbs, bitter and sweet, spilled out as Ujba gently raised the lid on the box. He took out a small silver bowl — little larger than an eggcup — a folded paper packet, and a razor. He shook black powder into the bowl. "Hold out your hand."

Ash did. The razor slipped over his palm.

"Ow!" Ash shouted. He stared at the thin red line. "What'd you do that for?"

Ujba grabbed Ash's bleeding hand and let the blood drip into the bowl. He muttered prayers to himself as he swirled the mixture. Then he held it up. "Drink."

Ash sniffed the oily black liquid within and almost gagged up breakfast. The smell was sickeningly sweet, but putrid, like meat left out too long in the hot sun. "What is it?"

"*Soma*," said Ujba. "It's to bring you closer to Kali."

"Really? One whiff of that almost killed me."

"It might. Most of the ingredients are poisonous." Ujba smirked. "But you've been dead before and that didn't stop you, did it?"

"What'll happen to me if I drink it?"

"Your senses will ascend to a higher plane. You will see Kali. You will understand what she has planned for you. If you are worthy, she will unlock further powers from the Kali-aastra. If you are unworthy, you will die."

"In which case you'd better pour it down the drain."

Ujba pushed the bowl into Ash's hand. "Drink it. It's what Kali wants. You will become a true Kali-aastra, able to use all the power of Kali. You will be purged of any . . . weakness."

"What sort of weakness?"

"Doubt. Fear. Compassion. You are destined to do great and terrible things, boy."

"I'll be a Thug, that's it, isn't it?"

"And so much more. Once you rid yourself of your humanity you will be unstoppable. The perfect weapon of Kali."

Ujba wanted Ash to be some remorseless killing machine. A psychopath. He looked at the guru, wondering what sort of teacher Rishi had sent him. This was the price for more power? Hadn't Parvati said something about this, ages ago, when he'd first assumed the powers of the Kali-aastra? *Power corrupts, and absolute power corrupts absolutely.* She had also said Gemma was dead because of him, and the more he embraced the powers of the Kali-aastra, the more death would surround him. Who would be next? John? Josh? His dad? Lucky? He didn't want such power if that was the price. It had to stop.

"No," he said.

Ujba's voice hardened. "Don't you want to be more powerful?"

"I . . . don't want to become a monster," he said. "I've had enough."

Ujba pushed the bowl against Ash's chest and Ash flicked it away. The contents splashed over the clean tiles, leaving a black, oily trail. The bowl rang as it bounced across the floor.

"This lesson is over," said Ash as he stood. For the first time in ages he felt a sense of relief. This one decision he knew was right.

Ujba glowered. "You are a fool."

Ash left.

CHAPTER TWENTY-FIVE

Everyone ignored Ash when he got back to the cemetery. The other rakshasas didn't even look in his direction, and there was no place by the campfire for him when they gathered around it for supper. All their backs were turned to him, and the only looks he got were scowls. John just shrugged when Ash found him, and then went off to get some food from one of the street vendors, while Ash parked himself away from the main party.

Parvati had lied to him, and he didn't see how he was in the wrong. How could he ignore what he'd seen in his vision?

Still, they needed to clear the air. He should speak to her, apologize for the things he'd said, to get on with what was important. Finding Savage.

Ash went looking for Parvati without success. She and Mahout were gone. But he did find Khan, not far away, snoozing under a crude lean-to made of palm leaves. The tiger rakshasa lay flat on his back, arms behind his head with a scarf covering his eyes. The thin, light cloth fluttered with his soft snores.

"Khan? You awake?"

Khan peeled the cloth away and blinked the sleep dust out of his eyes. "What have you done now?"

"Where's Parvati?"

"No idea." He rolled over, turning his back to Ash. "I'm busy."

"You've been sleeping all day. Get up."

With a melodramatic groan and a lot of scratching and stretching, Khan stood up. "What's the problem?"

"Parvati. You think I should say something?"

"Haven't you said enough? Still, it proves one thing. She must really, *really* like you."

"How so?"

"You're still alive. The old Parvati would have had her fangs in your neck for humiliating her in front of everyone like that. It must be hanging out with mortals, it's made her mellow."

Mellow? That wasn't a word Ash associated with Parvati. "She makes it so hard — she's become totally stuck-up. Look at the way everyone bows and scrapes in front of her."

Khan gave a low whistle. "Oh, and you're not stuck up at all, Mr. Ash 'Kali-aastra' Mistry? You're just as bad. And Parvati's got a lot of responsibility now that Ravana's dead."

"Meaning what? She wants to take over the demon nations?"

"Better her than Savage, don't you think?" Khan picked at a canine tooth with his long forefinger nail. "Was that why you woke me, to talk politics?"

"She knew the Koh-I-Noor was a Brahma-aastra. Why didn't she tell me?"

"You want to know about the Brahma-aastra, is that it?"

"You knew too?" They'd all been keeping secrets from him. Why? It didn't matter, as long as he found out about it now. "Can it raise the dead?"

Khan leaned against a tree trunk. "It's better we start at the beginning. Let me tell you about the Koh-I-Noor. I first saw it in Lanka, back when Ravana was still alive and before all that trouble with Rama. He'd got it off some prince or king, I forget who."

"But rakshasas can't use aastras."

"That didn't stop him from trying. We're talking about Ravana, the demon king. Most of the rules didn't apply to him. Remember I told you he'd once been a Brahmin? He was devoted to all the gods and he gained all his magic from them, but he became so powerful that he started to think he was better than they were. He had learned all the mantras, the spells, of Brahma, the Creator, and he thought he could awaken the Koh-I-Noor using one such spell."

"Did he?"

"Not as far as I know. But soon after that, stories started spreading that the diamond was cursed. Following Ravana's defeat, the diamond became part of the booty handed over to Rama, and since then it has passed from one human king to another."

"But what about the mantras? Someone surely knew how to awaken the aastra?"

"I reckon some imperfect understanding of the awakening mantra is all that exists now. The spell was passed down from one generation to the next, copied from scroll to scroll or recited from master to student. Over the centuries, errors crept in and the spell changed. Your friend, Savage, probably *thinks* he knows how to activate the Koh-I-Noor, though I seriously doubt it. But what he does know will cause a huge amount of trouble."

"Trouble? How can raising the dead be trouble?"

Khan smiled, and instead of his usual self-confident arrogance this smile was softer, almost sympathetic. "The ones who come back are never the ones who left, Ash. Gemma, the girl you knew — she is gone and gone forever. Do not be tempted by false hopes. Look at Savage, what he is, what he does, all in his quest for life beyond his natural span. His search for immortality is a fool's one. He's trying to catch a cloud. You mortals have just one life, and that is for a reason. It is that knowledge that drives you to do the things you do, both good and evil. Humans excel because they know the limits of their time here. Remember the dead, honor them, but let them be. And that pain you feel, that loss, hold on to it."

Ash shook his head. Thinking about Gemma brought the pain back: a cold blade high in his chest and ice that crushed his lungs. "I don't want to feel it."

"To feel it is human. The day that agony goes, the day you care nothing about death, that is the day you become a monster, Ash."

Rain began to fall — first a few heavy drops, then it was as if the entire sky opened up and sheets of water descended. Ash stood under the cover of a mausoleum doorway, soaked through within seconds. He waved as John appeared, carrying two wrapped packets.

"Try this," said John as he joined Ash. "Fresh and hot."

Ash opened the paper and held a samosa with his fingertips. The triangular deep-fried pastry smelled delicious. He bit into it and savored the spiced vegetable filling. John smiled as Ash gave a thumbs-up. "Thanks, John." At least he had one friend he could depend on.

"Well? How did it go with Ujba?"

Ash shrugged. "Badly. I don't know what Rishi was thinking when he agreed for me to train with him."

"That deal was made when Rishi was alive. Ujba wouldn't have dared try anything while the old *sadhu* was around."

"You think Ujba was scared of Rishi?"

"Rishi was the master of the mantras of the gods. Ujba is just a big, ugly bruiser. No contest."

"I wish Rishi *were* around right now. He'd sort it all out." Ash finished the samosa, licking the crumbs off his fingertips. "That was most excellent."

"No luck with finding Savage, then?" said John.

"We're getting nowhere with anything. We've only the word of a rat rakshasa to go on, and maybe Monty was lying." Ash looked out across the jungle. "Savage could be anywhere. I don't think he's even in Kolkata."

"I've an idea," said John. "I've been thinking about that map of Parvati's."

"Yeah?"

John picked up a long, drooping palm leaf and held it over them like an umbrella. "Come on."

The downpour was in full torrential mode as they hit the streets, which had transformed into small rivers. Dirty tan streams ran across the pavements, and the drainpipes, unable to cope with the immense flow, spouted water from every joint. Ash could see a group of rickshaws with their brightly polished fenders and decorated canopies parked along the front of one of the grander hotels. The drivers sat hunched on the wall, heads tucked into their shoulders, sharing cigarettes. No one wanted to be out in this drenching rain.

"A lot of bookshops here, have you noticed?" said John in a meaningful tone, gazing into a shop window.

"Maybe Amazon doesn't deliver this far east."

"Kolkata's built on books."

Now that John mentioned it, Ash realized it was true. There *were* a lot of bookshops. They were standing in front of one, in .fact. Ash looked up at the shop sign, written in English and Hindi.

Education Center.

Kolkata was a famous intellectual center, he knew that, with lots of big universities. And universities needed bookshops. He peered into the window himself, barely able to see the store within; the glass was semiopaque with dust. A few books on display had gone yellow with age and sun exposure, their pages crinkled in the corners.

"Looks like it hasn't changed in two hundred years," said Ash. "I bet Savage probably shopped here for his first Hindi-English dictionary."

"Exactly," said John with a smile. He opened the door. "C'mon."

The shop smelled damp and moldy. All this paper and all this rain wasn't a great combination. There were a few bestsellers on the table nearest the counter, all neatly wrapped in plastic to keep them pristine.

The shelves were made of dark wood and absolutely stuffed with books. A local turned a squeaking rack, inspecting political pamphlets. A student hummed and hahhed as he flicked through some heavy engineering textbook.

"What are we looking for?" asked Ash.

John went to the counter. A woman in an orange sari sat behind an old-fashioned cash register, a copy of some black-and-red-covered paranormal romance in her hand.

"Begging your pardon, miss, but do you have any maps? Old maps?" John asked.

"Of where?"

"Of British Calcutta."

The assistant tucked a strip of ribbon into the book before closing it. She headed for the back, John and Ash a few paces behind her.

"You've lost me," said Ash.

"When was Savage first here?"

"Mid-nineteenth century. Back when the East India Company was in charge."

"Don't you get it, Ash?"

"Let's assume I have no idea what you're talking about. It'll be easier."

The assistant touched a stack of papers. "Here you are."

John began rearranging the items on the table, moving books off it so he could work through the pile of maps carefully. "Savage doesn't know modern Kolkata. Does he?"

"No, he's only recently come back to India. He's spent the last century out in the Far East."

"So doesn't it make sense he'd base himself somewhere he knew?" John was turning over the maps quicker and quicker.

"A place that existed back then?"

"Yes." John stopped at one of the maps, leaning over it to read the faint copperplate calligraphy. "We need to compare a map from the 1850s with ours. We need a map of old Calcutta, not modern Kolkata. Find out which locations appear on both."

Ash quickly unfolded the modern map they'd been using. They'd marked all the 153 potential locations on it with red felt pen. Only half had been checked so far.

"We want this one," said John.

The map he held had been printed in 1849. Calcutta was a fraction of its present size then, but Ash recognized the snaking path of the Hooghly River, the octagonal Fort William, the neatly arranged Botanical Gardens and the main Kali Temple. Palaces of local rulers were also outlined, as were the various military compounds that housed the East India Company's troops, there to keep an eye on their mercantile and political interests.

The maps had been drawn to different scales, and the earlier one lacked the satellite accuracy of the modern one Ash had, but by using the river, the fort, and the temple as reference points, they could quickly tick off which locations were common to both. Some had already been checked, others dismissed as blatantly inappropriate for Savage, being too public and exposed. But there was one . . .

"The cantonment." Ash pointed to a large rectangle on the outskirts of the city. "Here."

The word *cantonment* was still used in India for a large, enclosed compound. It usually referred to civil servant accommodations, with offices and facilities like hospitals and shops within the walls. A city within a city, originally set up by foreign armies to house their troops.

"It's isolated, large, and judging by the main building, suitably palatial," said Ash.

"Perfect for Savage, don't you think?" John couldn't help but smile.

"Totally." Ash checked his wallet. The map wasn't cheap, but he had enough. "Let's get this and take it to the others."

"Don't you think we should check the cantonment out first?" said John. "If we go in loud and noisy, Savage will just run away and we're back to the beginning. Anyway, this is only an idea. He may not be there. Let's just snoop and make sure."

What better way to make it up with Parvati than to find Savage? Ash grinned. "You've changed a lot, John."

John looked at him. "I just follow your example."

CHAPTER TWENTY-SIX

The last time Ash had visited India, it had been during the height of summer. He'd spent the days dripping in sweat, living in an oven. The rivers had been dry and the landscape a sea of bone-white dust. But now — after the monsoons — the countryside overflowed with life. Tall fields of green grass swayed at the roadsides and the trees were hung with sagging vines bearing massive, polished leaves.

John and Ash sat in the back of a motor rickshaw. The three-wheeled cross between a scooter and a taxi zipped in and out of traffic, taking them away from Kolkata across the Howrah Bridge. That massive cathedral of steel, twenty-three hundred feet long and a hundred wide, was the main crossing over the Hooghly River. Gigantic steel arches, pummeled with fist-sized rivets, stretched across from one bank to the other. It reminded Ash that when India did something, it did it supersized.

The entire frame crawled with traffic, wheeled and on foot, motorized and bullock- or donkey-driven. It felt as if the entire city was on the move. Stall owners offering snacks and drinks and trinkets lined the railings, some perilously perched on the beams above, crying out for customers. Kids weaved between the gridlocked cars, selling newspapers and cigarettes. Ash and John's rickshaw joined this sluggish river of life and machinery until they finally broke free of the city into the surrounding countryside. Night was falling, and cloying smells rose from the blooming flowers, filling the air along with musk and whining insects.

"The cantonment, sahib," said the rickshaw driver.

The rickshaw's single bright headlamp lit a path across a thicket to a cracked, vine-covered wall. The original plaster had long since crumbled away and was covered in plant growth and moss, creating a curtain of green. Tree roots broke up the short drive to the front gates, which themselves were rusty iron and bound with ivy.

Ash jumped out and approached the gates. He pulled out a small flashlight and shone it through the gap in the railings. The light didn't reach far, but he could make out a row of derelict bungalows, almost lost within the overgrowth. Trees rose and spread over the central path, overwhelming it in darkness. Cicadas chirped their nightly songs from the trees and bushes.

John tugged at the gates. They were held fast by the vines. The place looked like it hadn't been used in a century. It might have once been all neat lawns and cozy verandas, but now the jungle had reclaimed it, quashing all signs of civilization under a sea of tangled roots and leaves.

Ash looked up and down the long wall. No lights, no signs of anything or anyone.

"I don't think this is the place," he said. There was nothing here but jungle and insects.

"There could be another way in," said John. He tested one of the thick vines clinging to the wall. "We could get over easily. If you're up for it."

"Shall we go back, sahib?" The rickshaw driver was already wheeling his vehicle around.

"We've come all the way out here," said John. "We might as well take a look."

"You wait here," said Ash as he handed the driver a fistful of rupees. The man looked at them, clearly confused about why they'd want to be out here at this time of night, then shrugged and switched off his engine. He held up both hands.

"Ten minutes, no more," he said.

"Fine. Ten minutes." That should be more than enough time for a snoop around.

John put one foot up and swiftly climbed to the top of the wall. "Come on," he said.

Ash took hold of a sticky, sap-coated vine and a few moments later crossed over the wall and dropped down into the darkness within the compound.

They hid among the tall grass, watching and listening. The nearest bungalow was about forty feet away, now half-submerged under heavy leaves and tree roots.

And then Ash saw someone.

The figure was resting his hand on his chin, looking at something on the ground. All Ash could see was the moonlight shining on his curved back. Ash put his finger to his lips and waved that John should wait where he was.

In spite of the grass, Ash made no more noise than a faint breeze. He put one foot softly down in the lush, damp earth, waiting for it to absorb any sound before moving the other foot. The bamboo kept him hidden in deep shadow.

Ash blinked, drawing up his dark powers. He would use marma-adi to knock the person out. All he needed was to search the golden marks on the man for something nonfatal. But he couldn't see anything on the dark figure, and certainly no golden map of death.

What was wrong?

He stepped out of the bamboo, now less than ten feet away from the man. The guy hadn't moved.

Ash paused, digging deeper into the swirling energies within the pit of his soul. Raw, intense energy surged through him, but the glimmering lights did not appear.

It didn't matter. He'd punch the guy in the back of the head. Definitely knock him out and hopefully keep brain damage to a minimum.

Ash was right behind the man. He pulled back his fist and swung.

Then he screamed and hopped back, shaking his pulsing arm. He cradled his hand, groaning as pain filled it with fire.

John ran up. "What's wrong?"

Ash kicked the unmoving man. "It's a bloody statue!"

And not just any statue, but a life-sized copy of *The Thinker* by Rodin. He should have recognized it.

Now that Ash looked around, he noticed that there were dozens of statues scattered everywhere. Some were hidden by moss or entangled by vines and ivy; others just lay fallen on the ground. It looked like someone had emptied out an art gallery or a museum and dumped the statues here.

John pulled some loose vine off a rusty statue of Shiva. The statue's face and body were pockmarked by years in the rain.

"You crying?" asked John.

"So would you if you'd just punched solid bronze." Ash carefully unflexed his fingers, hoping he hadn't broken them. More tears sprang from his eyes. It really, *really* hurt.

They walked toward the first bungalow. Creepers reached from the trees to the roof like green flags, and large moths flitted in the night sky. The mustiness of the cantonment smothered Ash.

"Creepy, aren't they?" said John, poking one of the statues with a stick.

Yes, they are, Ash thought. They were from all parts of the world, some classical Greek, most Indian, some modern, many ancient. Most were copies of copies, a few sculpted with care and art, others crudely thrown together and misshapen. Ash couldn't shake the feeling that he was walking among the dead. Lifeless, empty eyes gazed at nothing, their forms frozen and slowly decaying. There were hundreds of them. It was worse than the graveyard.

The bungalow was uninhabitable. The wood was warped and rotten all the way through. The veranda seat creaked, and a couple of lizards scurried across the wicker chairs.

"Hasn't been used in decades," said Ash. He stopped at a notice board on the main street. There was a poster, yellow and streaked, advertising a hymn recital on March 13, 1941, with tea afterward, organized by Lady Middleton. There was also a small card referring to a missing cat called Gladstone and a list of the army's cricket fixtures for the summer.

This is time travel, Ash thought. Okay, not in a blue police box or through some wormhole in space, but he could feel what this place must have been like when the British had been here. They'd made the cantonment a small piece of England, with tea parties on the lawn and Sundays with the vicar. They came all the way here and brought all their Surrey entitlements with them. They'd made sure India was kept out, beyond the gates.

Now look at it. Moth-eaten furniture and rotten, crumbling bungalows, their prim English gardens turned into swampy jungle.

He and John moved farther into the compound. The statues filled the paths and lurked in the lush greenery, some so covered in vines they looked like they could have been dryads, tree spirits.

Ash, hands on hips, looked up and down the crossroads. More bungalows on either side, with a parade ground ahead. "Let's look over there." If they couldn't find anything, they'd head back before their ten minutes were up and the rickshaw driver left.

The parade ground was surrounded on two sides by office buildings, with a derelict but still magnificent hall at the head, a strange hybrid of English mansion and Indian palace with domes and battlements and towers. But the jungle surrounded it, a green giant stretching out its fingers of moss and bark, its many arms hugging the broken roof. Tall mangrove trees spilled their massive roots through windows and ran like monstrous tentacles over the walls.

Ash stepped onto the open parade ground.

What's wrong with this picture?

He bent down and inspected the grass along the edge. The stalks were ragged, but when he touched the edge, he felt a clean diagonal tip.

"Someone's cut the grass," he said.

It could be something, or it could be nothing. He looked at the statues gathered around the perimeter of the field. One, a replica of *David*, caught his attention. It had been made well, but something wasn't right. The grass all around it had been trodden on, he realized, great areas flattened as though an army had marched over it.

But where was the army? There was nothing here but statues.

"This is pointless," said Ash. "Let's go."

"No. Let's look around a bit more. Be sure."

"You really have changed, John. You weren't like this at the Lalgur."

"It took guts to help you escape." John turned his back on him. "And for what?"

"What do you mean?"

"You really don't remember, do you?" He spoke with cold rage. "We had a deal, Ash."

"But you escaped! You said you got out."

"Oh, yes. I did. I got out. I made a whole new bunch of . . . friends."

"Who, John?" A chill dread seeped into him.

"Friends who gave me money. Who helped me find my mother. Who still send her a thousand rupees every month."

"Tell me who these friends are."

John met his gaze. "What wouldn't you do to help your family?" He pushed Ash out of his way and retreated toward the line of statues. "I'm not sorry. I want you to know that. I'm not sorry."

Ash tensed, looking around as John disappeared into the darkness. But there was nothing. He was surrounded by lifeless stone. He glanced again at the statue of *David*.

Then, the stone grinding loudly in the still night air, *David* turned his head.

CHAPTER TWENTY-SEVEN

Another statue, fallen down and tied to the earth by thick vines, began to struggle against its bonds. The vines snapped as it pulled free a bronze arm. Its joints creaked as it stood.

One by one, the statues moved. Slowly, as though waking from a long, deep slumber, they shook free the tangling creepers and the rust of decades from their joints. Then they began moving faster. A Chinese stone lion jumped off its pedestal; the trees trembled as it landed. A heavy foot thumped behind Ash, and he tumbled sideways as a six-armed Shiva tried to grab him. Its hands clanged together.

Ash retreated back to the main street and stared as dozens of now-living statues lumbered toward him. Where did John go? What had he done?

The trees creaked. The ground shook violently and a cloud of leather-winged bats burst from their hidden perches within the foliage. Leaves tumbled down and the entire jungle came to life.

Ash looked up in mute horror.

Tree trunks bent, then splintered.

A groaning noise, then crashing, as the trees fell toward him.

And then something began to emerge. Something huge. As it stepped over the broken trunks, its footfalls made the ground buckle.

The statue towered over the forest, seventy feet tall, its gray body mottled with moss, weeds growing like veins across its stony flesh. It wore an embroidered and pitted skirt, and bracelets and necklaces were carved around its wrists and neck. The bare torso was sculpted with the lean muscles of a young man. Bats shrouded its head like a dark, chaotic halo. The head was as big as any of the bungalows. The statue raised a truck-sized fist, dust showering from its joints as it curled its huge fingers.

Ash started to run, not even conscious of having given the command to his legs. But he didn't seem to be getting any farther away. The shadow of the giant figure covered him, and the sound of rumbling stone drowned out his own panting breath and pounding heartbeat. His legs seemed sluggish, each step small, insect-like compared to the immense reach of the creature behind him. Was this how he was going to die? Swatted like a fly?

The wind roared as the fist swept down and Ash hurled himself forward. The ground shattered, throwing broken paving slabs, old rocks, and large chunks of soil into the air. The shock wave lifted Ash off his feet and he crashed into, and then through, the wall of one of the bungalows. Bits of plaster, wood, and moldy old thatch fell over him as he lay, coughing, head spinning, among the ruins.

Fear — empty, drowning fear — threatened to overwhelm him. The giant statue peered down through gaps in the roof; his fingers, as long and wide as building columns, ripped through the tiles and groped blindly within. Ash bit down hard to stop himself from screaming. The massive fingers broke apart the wooden frame as if it were made of balsa wood.

Run. Just get out of here. Nothing smart, nothing heroic, just run.

Ash shoved the chunks of plaster off and got up into a crouch. He felt sick, dizzy, frightened.

Outside, the feet of the hundreds of moving statues sounded like distant thunder, a constant rumbling, uneven and gross with threatening violence. The bungalow rocked on its brittle old beams.

A black shadow loomed over him, blocking out all light. The timbers over his head creaked and splintered, and in a long, thunderous wave of tearing and ripping, the roof came off.

The statue peered in, searching for him, his vast head blocking out the sky. It tossed the ragged roof away and reached down with its hand. Ash heaved himself to his feet and scrambled over the broken walls and fallen struts as the statue's palm, easily ten feet wide, flattened the room he'd been in, cracking through the floor and shaking the building's rotten foundation. The second hand crunched down in front of him, and he slipped over some mossy carpet to stop just before the fingers could grab him.

The bungalow couldn't take any more. Walls tottered and fell, and Ash turned just in time to see a support beam swing down. He ducked, but not fast enough. It struck him across the back and he was sent reeling into the corner.

He tried to get up, but a wall of stone encircled him. Ash pushed as trunk-thick fingers closed around him. He tried to scrabble out of the massive hand but was caught around the legs, waist, and chest.

Ash struggled, but what could he do? His powers were useless. This thing wasn't alive, so it didn't have glowing points of weakness. The giant statue lifted him out of the bungalow. Stone monkeys leaped upon the thing's arm and scurried up to perch on its shoulder. A little more pressure and Ash would burst like a grape. The statue straightened, lifting him higher and higher until it held him before its blank eyes. This close, Ash could see the weathered, cracked skin and the centuries of moss that covered its gray flesh. He could do nothing but glare and snarl, "Well? What are you waiting for?"

He'd been stupid and it had gotten him killed again. But this time there would be no coming back.

But the statue only held him. Why had it gone so quiet?

"Ash Mistry?" said a voice from below — a voice Ash recognized immediately. "Is that you up there?"

CHAPTER TWENTY-EIGHT

Ash had dreamed of what it would be like to hear that voice again. It was rich, proud, and arrogant, the voice of a man who thought he owned the world and everyone in it. Its deep, powerful timbre made him shiver with dread and anger. That voice had haunted his dreams and given birth to his darkest nightmares.

The statue lumbered side to side as it settled down into a kneeling position. Still holding Ash within its inescapable grip, it turned its hand so he was facing the gathered assembly below him. The vast crowd of statues — animal, human, and monstrous — stood immobile. But there were others among this field of stone and iron, and the closest was a figure in a white suit.

Lord Alexander Savage stood there, looking up, his hands resting on his tiger-headed cane. Ash stared, slack-jawed. Savage was not how he remembered him. The last time he'd seen him, Savage had been young, beautiful, and inhumanly perfect.

This man was anything but perfect. The suit hung off a skeletal frame with withered, parchment-thin skin that flapped upon the spindly limbs. Huge, dark liver spots covered the hairless scalp, and large yellow teeth dangled from shrunken gums. The lips were pale, thin, and cracked. He looked ready to collapse, and leaned heavily upon the cane.

But his eyes — his eyes shone with feverish power. Black upon black, they were the eyes of night, of pure darkness.

Beside him were Jackie and John. John trembled as the rakshasa put her clawed hand on his shoulder. Just at the edge of the moonlight, half-hidden in the jungle, were Savage's hyena rakshasas, cackling.

Ash looked at Savage, hate rising in his chest, churning in his guts. The distance between them wasn't great, but held as he was, it might as well have been a million miles. The Englishman's smile widened.

"So glad you could accept my invitation," said Savage.

Ash tried to move a little, but the statue only tightened its grip, crushing his chest until he was gasping for breath. It lowered him until he was just off the ground, eye level with his enemy.

"You look upset, Ash," said Savage.

"And you look like the Elephant Man's less handsome older brother."

"Very amusing, boy. Is that what passes for wit in this day and age?" He tutted and shuffled closer, bringing with him a putrid rotting odor. Not only did Savage look like a ten-day old corpse, he also smelled like one. "Ravana made me young again, as you well remember, but his magic failed the moment you killed him. And here I am, back where I started, thanks to you."

Yes, it was true. Savage had been a living skeleton when Ash had first met him. "Glad I did something right," he said.

Savage didn't appear to hear. He plucked at the shirt hanging loosely over his chest. "Now only my magic, such as it is, keeps the flesh and soul together. But it's falling apart. I can feel it."

"More good news."

Savage paused and looked at him, eyes filled with hate. Then he smiled and pointed up at the giant statue with his cane. "What do you think of my Jagannath?"

"What is it?" Ash asked.

"This one I found down south, at an abandoned temple near Bangalore. The Jagannath is the god Vishnu in his aspect as lord of the world. You will not believe how much trouble I had getting him here."

"And you got him — them — all to move?"

"Yes, my *loha-mukhas*." He tapped a nearby statue. "The Jews call them golems, but they must build their creatures from scratch. My magic can transform any inanimate object into some semblance of life. It's a trick I learned in China, near Xian."

Ash slumped in the thing's grip. Ujba had told him he needed to learn all the powers of the Kali-aastra but, in his arrogance, Ash had thought he had everything he needed.

"It took me a while to realize what had happened with the Kali-aastra," continued Savage. "It broke, didn't it? You had a part, the part that allowed you mastery over death, the ability to kill any living thing, didn't you?"

Ash said nothing.

"And when I used it, I got the part that allowed me to destroy — to smash things apart. That's how I was able to open the Iron Gates, you see. If you had tried, you would have failed. We both got what we wanted from the Kali-aastra."

Until now, thought Ash. What he would give to be able to destroy his stone trap.

"Where's the arrowhead now?" asked Ash.

Savage sighed. "Buried under a billion tons of sand out in Rajasthan. Like my dreams." His eyes flickered red for a moment before darkening to midnight. "I've been looking forward to meeting you again, Ash, and, I must admit, it turned out even better than I had hoped, thanks to your friend here."

John backed away. "I've done what you wanted. I've told you where the Koh-I-Noor is and brought him here."

Savage smiled slowly. "The English Cemetery, correct?"

John gulped. "Yes. The demon princess is there, with her followers."

"Hardly a concern." The Englishman gave Jackie the slightest nod. "Yes, I should reward you."

They're going to kill him.

For a second, just a second, Ash wanted John dead. He wouldn't be here, trapped and helpless, if it wasn't for him. Ujba had been right; John had lied to him. Even now it didn't seem possible. But, right or wrong, John had done it to help his mum. Would Ash have done any different? If Ash had thought more about John's needs, he would have helped him more to find his family. Instead he had let Savage do it. Could he really blame John?

But now Savage didn't need John anymore. Even from here, Ash saw the hungry look on Jackie's face, the saliva wetting her lips. She was waiting for the order, but Ash was not about to let another friend of his be killed by the jackal rakshasa. Begging them to let John go wouldn't help; they'd take delight in killing him while Ash watched. So he needed to do the opposite. Ash needed to demand they kill him.

"The best reward is death," Ash snarled. "The traitor deserves to die."

Savage twisted the cane top, a silver tiger head with ruby eyes, revealing a few inches of blade. The cane was a swordstick.

"My thoughts exactly," Savage said. He drew the narrow shining steel out and touched the tip against John's heart. "I have a rule to use traitors only once. If someone is happy to betray his best friend, how on earth can I trust him?"

Sweat dripped down Ash's brow and he flicked his damp hair out of his eyes. "Think I care?"

John yelled and turned to run, but Jackie leaped in his way. He ran to the side, but she was there. In the shadows beyond her, the hyena rakshasas prowled. Their bestial amber eyes were the only light in the otherwise complete darkness, and the trees shivered with their growls.

Jackie grabbed John and hurled him to the ground.

"Ash . . ." begged John.

"Your bed," said Ash. "Lie in it."

Savage's eyes narrowed. "You have changed, boy. There's a healthy ruthlessness there. You remind me of me when I was your age." He spun the sword in wide arcs. "It's such a shame we're on opposite sides. Ah, well."

Ash grinned as Savage raised the blade. His eyes met Jackie's and the grin broadened.

The sword flashed.

Then halted. Jackie held Savage's wrist, the tip of the sword a finger's width from John's eyeball.

"Wait," Jackie said. She glanced toward Ash. "He is the Kali-aastra."

Savage frowned. Then he stepped back and laughed. He waved the sword at Ash. "Good, very good. Very, very good."

They've fallen for it.

Savage lowered the blade. "What would happen if I killed this boy? His death energy would pass into you and make you stronger, would it not? And he's a friend, someone you cared about. Lord knows, it might even be a Great Death. We can't be having that, can we?"

Ash said nothing. But inside he sighed with relief. He'd saved John. Savage couldn't kill his friend if it risked Ash becoming stronger, perhaps strong enough to break free of the loha-mukhas.

Savage turned to John. "Run, boy. Run fast and run far and do not look back."

John got up and looked at Ash. Tears ran down his cheeks and he looked dead inside. Ash wanted to tell him it was okay, that he didn't blame John. But if he admitted to caring for him, Savage might use that against him. Better John think Ash hated him. It would keep him alive longer.

Ash glared at him. "Better start now. Once I'm free, I will find you."

John fled. Ash heard his sobs well after he'd vanished into the dark.

Savage gripped Ash's face, meeting his gaze. "I so want to kill you. But I did that once already, and look what happened? You came back. You killed Lord Ravana."

"This is just revenge?"

"Hardly. This is about the Koh-I-Noor. You were an unexpected bonus. I need the diamond, the Brahma-aastra. The Life Giver will repair all . . . this." He gestured to his hideous body.

"You know how to awaken it?"

"There is a way," said Savage.

Ash's heart leaped. Maybe he could save Gemma, like a true hero. He'd prove Parvati and Khan wrong. But before he could ask more, suddenly Savage hissed and panted, even emitting a brief, harsh scream as his body swelled and mutated. His spine stretched against the suit jacket and lumps grew on his skull. Then, chest heaving, the deformities reduced, and Savage's body reverted to its normal, frail shape. He stared up at Ash. "See what you've done? I have more power than ever, but my body cannot contain it. More magic than mortal flesh can bear."

"I don't feel bad about that at all." Ash met the Englishman's gaze. "So, the Koh-I-Noor will repair you. Then what?"

"And like a comic villain I will tell you everything?" Savage shook his head. "No, I want you to know just enough so all that follows will be because of your failure. In our last meeting the game went to you. That was beginner's luck."

"Luck was you getting away that night."

Savage bristled, but said nothing.

"So that's it? You're going to kill me? Skewer me with your sword?"

"Just stick you like a pig? After all we've been through together?" Savage waved the slim blade. "No, I've something far better in mind."

CHAPTER TWENTY-NINE

The Jagannath twisted its wrist and pressed Ash into the ground. As it opened its fingers, he squirmed, but it pressed harder, flattening him into the earth until he felt as if he were under a steamroller.

Then hard, unyielding hands gripped his arms and ankles. The Jagannath slowly released him, and two stone and marble monkeys, each the size of a man, lifted Ash and carried him through the cantonment. Branches and leaves brushed his face, and the monkeys' hold was every bit as firm as the Jagannath's. Twist as he might, Ash remained trapped in stone.

Engines revved and headlights came alive in the dark. After a few minutes a convoy of trucks emerged along the road. Savage glanced back as he stepped into the lead vehicle. "He's coming with us."

The trucks had high-sided wooden walls painted with garish scenes and designs — panoramic mountain views, the paint smeared with oily smoke and the wood chipped. A whole field of headlights shone from the front. The line of vehicles was less a convoy and more a parade. It might seem stupid to have such distinct vehicles, but here in India, the trucks and minivans were all the same, brightly and extravagantly painted and lit. These blended in perfectly.

The monkeys clambered into the back of the lead truck and

squatted down among wooden crates and trunks, Ash suspended between them. Then the engine shifted gears noisily and spewed out a cloud of black smoke, and they were on the move, rocking side to side as the truck bounced over the uneven ground and in and out of the potholes that punctured the old cantonment road. Ash winced with each jolt; it was like being on the rack, dangling by his ankles and wrists, the sockets stretched till they almost popped.

Where were they taking him? Ash twisted his head as they drove, but all he could see was the moonlight shimmering on the glossy black surface of the river.

The truck rumbled deeper into the countryside, past sleeping villages and the occasional herd of cattle resting by the road. Other trucks roared past with horns blaring and engines thundering. Ash glimpsed all this through the ill-fitting wooden panels on the side of his truck. He also caught a better look at the crates in the back with him. They were all large, at least five feet by five feet. As the truck's interior was briefly illuminated by the headlights of another passing car, Ash glimpsed a stamp on the side of one box.

INDIAN RAILWAYS ROUTE 2841.

Savage was taking a train ride. But where to?

Ash didn't have time to ponder as the truck jerked and the wheels rumbled upon the echoing frame of another bridge.

The brakes shrieked and one of the crates slid forward. It slammed into the first monkey and the stone beast tottered forward as there was a sharp crack. The corner of the crate had broken, and a stone face gazed out of the straw. It turned its head — that of a snarling demon with a leonine mane — then sank back down into the straw as if hibernating. More loha-mukhas.

The rear panel crashed down and the headlights from the vehicle behind filled the truck with harsh, blinding light.

"Bring him down. Just you," said Savage.

The two monkeys moved swiftly. One released Ash's ankles while the other wrapped its arms tightly around his chest, trapping his arms within its embrace. Even with his legs now freed, Ash could do nothing. The monkey had to weigh nearly a thousand pounds. It hopped down, its stone feet clanging on steel.

The entire convoy had halted on a bridge. Ash hoped that someone might be passing, but they were in the depths of the countryside, isolated and miles from anywhere. Savage gazed out at the river roaring between the supports beneath them. The bridge was another iron monstrosity, all vaulting beams and wide spans and fist-sized rivets. The iron bore patches of orange rust and the road itself was poorly tarmacked, cracked in places so the river could be seen, the headlights catching its flashing, foaming white spray as it collided with the vast, monolithic concrete supports.

A sudden, dull crash was followed by a sharp snap as a tree trunk collided against one of the plinths and shattered into a million slivers. The river was in full spate, swollen by the monsoon rains.

"Come here, Ash, close to the edge," said Savage.

"I'm perfectly fine here."

The monkey stepped forward. Ash pushed his feet against the railings, trying to stop it from getting to the edge, but the monkey was too strong, and he cried out as his feet slipped and the ragged edge of the iron beam scraped the back of his leg, ripping open his trousers.

Jackie laughed and joined Savage. She leaned over the edge and worked a bolt back and forth, the steel grinding against its socket. She gave it a hefty kick and the side fell away. It tumbled for a sickeningly long time before it splashed into the raging waters, more than seventy feet below.

"A bit closer — the view is rather splendid," said Savage.

Ash dangled over the black, churning waters. The monkey still held him to its chest, its own feet just barely on the bridge, its long toes curled around the rusty iron edge.

Savage let slip a low whistle. "I wonder how many thousands of gallons are flowing under this bridge every second. Look how high the river is; you can barely see the support plinths. Do you know, I remember when the only way across this river was a spindly old rope thing, like a cat's cradle?" He tapped the metal with his cane. "That was a hundred years ago. Wonder what's down there? You'd be surprised what gets washed up against the legs. Boats, cars, houses even, swept away in floods and trapped, too big to get between the foundations."

"Thank you for the history lesson, Savage. I'd like to get back in the truck now."

Savage turned to face him and smiled. "Good-bye, Ash."

Holding Ash tight, the monkey jumped.

CHAPTER THIRTY

They tumbled over and over as they fell. Ash froze. All he could do was stare at the kaleidoscope of blurring dark strips of the iron bridge and the headlights above and below him, reflecting off the raging waters as they crashed and surged between the massive concrete legs of the bridge. The wind howled as he cartwheeled through the air, ripping the tears from his eyes and the breath from his mouth. He took a single gasp and locked shut his teeth as —

— they slammed into the river and all went black.

Ash shook himself to consciousness a second after hitting the water. Water gurgled in his mouth and he almost swallowed again as the surface, glistening with moonlight, receded away. The monsoon-swollen current ripped him and his captor along as fast as they were sinking, and a second, bone-jarring jolt punched the air from his lungs as they crashed into one of the concrete plinths that the bridge stood upon. The monkey's grip slacked, loosening its hold on his left side, and Ash heaved hard, but then the water accelerated between them and Ash was scraped along a surface, scouring the skin off his body. He bit down ferociously to hold in his scream.

How long could he hold his breath? Not long enough. Even though he was far more powerful than a normal human, he had his limits, and being submerged under a million tons of water was one of them. Savage hadn't needed to kill him up close and risk Ash returning more powerful than ever, like the last time. He was going to die down here, and this time there would be no coming back.

While the marble monkey was heavy, the river was stronger, and they turned over and over like a pebble, bashing along with the flotsam and jetsam of garbage that lay at the foot of the bridge.

I can't hold on. Fire filled Ash, and he just wanted to breathe. Blood pounded in his skull as he fought the crushing weight of the water and the stone creature's embrace. Then, in the corner of his eye, he glimpsed light shining off metal. Instinctively he threw his weight toward it, kicking madly with his freed legs, desperate to shift direction, just a few inches.

He hit the river bottom and rolled in the mud upon the stones, some small and others the size of boulders. He blinked the mud from his eyes and saw the metal object ten feet away. It was the rusty skeleton of a motorized rickshaw, half-submerged in the bank. The cloth canopy had long since disintegrated and the front wheel had sheared off. It was this, half-buried in the mud, that Ash wanted.

Oh, God, he had to breathe! Lungs and chest aching, he could barely think; his head felt fat and swollen in agony. His jaw throbbed as he locked it shut.

He twisted his arms and something creaked. Even with his ears filled with the raging waters, he heard, he felt, the monkey's left arm give. The impact with the plinth must have cracked the loha-mukha's arm, weakening it. Driven insane with desperation, Ash pulled and shoved, not caring if he broke his own arm, just needing to get out. The stone groaned as he worked his entire torso side to side. The monkey's arm began to give way. It was a battle now, Ash's body both his savior and his enemy. If he could just hold his breath a few seconds longer . . . but the more he struggled, the more he wanted to open his mouth; instinct fought will.

The monkey's arm bent. It snapped.

Left arm free, Ash pushed and stretched toward the wheel rim jutting out of the mud. He leaned as far as he could, kicking the water with his heels to tilt him another couple of inches. If he could just reach it. . . .

His first two fingers scratched the rim, and that was enough.

Ash dragged the rim closer, pulling against the muddy grip. It was about a foot in diameter, a heavy steel circular disk weighting about fifteen pounds. The edge wasn't particularly sharp, but it was all he had.

Bubbles slipped from his lips. He couldn't hold on much longer.

Ash lifted it up with his left hand and swung it as hard as he could through the water against the monkey's right arm, aiming at the fingers.

The blow glanced off, barely chipping it.

Oh, God, he couldn't do it. More bubbles burst out, and Ash's arms and legs felt heavier than the monkey now. He struggled to lift the disk.

Concentrate. Concentrate. He glared at the thick fingers that held him trapped. His own tightened around the heavy steel disk.

Ash rammed the disk against the monkey's hand. Its fingers shattered as the last of Ash's breath tore free in a burst of bubbles. He dropped the disk and pushed. He pressed his heels against the inanimate stone, heaved with his left hand, and twisted his body as far as it would go. The jagged edges of the broken limb dug into his belly, tearing deeper into his flesh the harder he struggled. Blood, black and cloudy, swelled from the tears. He didn't care.

Ash spasmed as his body began to give up. His will, his heart raged, but he wasn't strong enough.

Savage wins.

No. That could never happen.

The thought pushed him harder, beyond the madness of this fight. Beyond the dark river and the mud and the bubbles disappearing above him.

Another inch. That was all there was between him and Savage. It came down to a distance shorter than a fingernail. If he couldn't get that much farther, Savage would win.

Not in this universe.

The monkey's fractured hand snapped, and Ash kicked free.

Thrashing upward, his neck stretched as far as it would go, Ash kicked and flailed toward the surging surface, eyes locked on the undulating patterns of moonlight above him. The current, still strong, carried him ten feet downstream for every one he rose. His arms felt like lead, and each stroke took double the effort of the last. His legs barely kicked now. The surface seemed miles away.

He gave up. His arms sank to his side, slowly, and his feet dangled loose and powerless in the flowing water.

Then someone touched his shoulder. Long, stiff fingers caressed his hand and Ash snapped hold. He locked his hands around the extended limb and pulled.

He gasped and swallowed as he rose free of the water. Then he looked for his rescuer. No, not someone, he realized — the branch of a tree, leaning over the water's surface, its tips submerged. It had been the twigs he'd felt on his back.

His heart pounded with joy and fear. He'd come so close, so close. Every part of him quivered with exhaustion, but Ash heaved himself up the branch until only his legs dangled in the river. Then, clumsy as a snail, he slid along on his belly, wincing as the twigs and stubs poked him. Eventually he dropped down along the marshy edge of the river. The bridge was a quarter of a mile away and dark. Savage was gone. Shivering, aching, bleeding, puking up river water, Ash waded the last few feet and crawled up the muddy bank.

C'mon, the hard bit's over.

Savage was on his way to get the Koh-I-Noor. Ash had to warn Parvati. Not only did she have no idea Savage was coming with an army of indestructible statues, but her deadly bite was useless against the loha-mukhas, and Khan's claws would snap on their impenetrable skin. If he didn't get going, Parvati and her rakshasas would be slaughtered. Ash couldn't let that happen, not when they'd parted the way they had.

I have to get back. Warn Parvati that Savage is coming with an army of stone.

But as he crawled through the long grass, Ash collapsed into the wet earth and knew no more.

CHAPTER THIRTY-ONE

He looked like one of the kids that clogged the streets of Kolkata, begging at traffic lights or waiting at hotels and posh restaurants for tourists. Ash didn't care. Covered in dirt and dressed in rags, he headed back to the city by hanging on to the back of a truck as it rattled along the road with the rickshaws and bullock carts.

How long had he been unconscious? He wasn't sure. A day at least. It was evening by the time he reached the outskirts of Kolkata. He'd managed to beg some bananas and a chapatti but still shivered with fever. His dip in the river had been almost too much. He closed his eyes.

I want to go home. There, he'd admitted it. He wanted to see his mum and dad, see Lucky. He'd thought he was tougher. He'd thought he couldn't be beaten, now that he was the Kali-aastra. Savage had shown him the error of his arrogance. Whatever move he made, Savage countered. Last night had almost been checkmate. And next time?

But he couldn't leave Parvati. He needed to see her, know she was okay, and make everything good between them.

Thunder rumbled overhead and the clouds, black and fat, hung over the city, ready to burst. The downpour hit just as Ash turned the corner into the English Cemetery.

Something was wrong. Police vans blocked the road and there were crowds gathered at the cemetery gates. People had gathered around a massive hole in the cemetery wall. Piles of rubble lay scattered on the street, over the tombs, and in the undergrowth. Khaki-uniformed policemen held the gawkers back with their long wooden staves, and a lemonade maker had set up his stall beside the broken masonry.

Ash pulled at a man's sleeve.

"Excuse me, but what happened?"

The man scowled as he looked down at Ash, who was filthy with mud and dust and his clothing in tatters. He brushed his sleeve off, and his hand went to protect his wallet in his pocket. "Begone, boy."

"What happened?" Ash said, with more than a little firmness, a little more anger.

The man looked down again and took a step back. He touched his neck, as if Ash was about to wrap his fingers around it, and swallowed. "No one knows. It happened last night. They say some beggars have been killed."

"Beggars?"

"Beggars who were using the graveyard for shelter. One of the big mausoleums has been vandalized."

"Whose?"

"The old Company president. Cornish or something."

"Cornwall?"

The man nodded.

Ash ran around the back of the graveyard and snuck over the wall. All around him were shattered gravestones, torn up trees, and demolished tombs. The mausoleum Parvati had used as her headquarters, and as the hiding place for the Koh-I-Noor, was nothing but rubble. The domed roof had been smashed in. The bronze doors themselves lay twisted and buckled in the grass twenty feet away. The surrounding trees were snapped in half, as if something huge, unyielding, and incredibly strong had just marched straight through them. The grass and earth were a mess of heavy footprints. Some were way too large and too deep for normal humans.

Savage and his loha-mukhas had struck hard.

Then, on the edge of his hearing, Ash picked up a quiet step. Someone else was hiding here. The bough of the branch above creaked with the weight of a body.

Ash jumped. Plowing through the branches and curtain of leaves, he grabbed the scruff of a neck and pulled the figure down with him, throwing him to the ground. Then he saw the frightened face.

"John?" Ash whispered. "What are you doing here?"

"Where else could I go?" The boy stared up at him. John was scared, but his big eyes hardened with defiance. "Are you going to kill me now?"

Something black and angry stirred inside Ash as he loomed over John. John had betrayed him and given Savage the Koh-I-Noor. What would Kali want? What would Ujba tell him to do?

That was easy. But that wasn't going to happen.

"You put your family first. Who can blame you for that?" said Ash.

"You're not going to kill me? What about what you said at the cantonment?"

"I had to call Savage's bluff. I needed him to believe I wanted you dead to absorb your death energies. Sorry if I scared you, but it was the only plan I had." He held out his hand. "Get up, mate."

"I *am* sorry."

"So am I, John." He really was. John had been desperate, and Ash knew what that was like. There'd been a breakfast, not so long ago, where Savage had promised Ash and his sister freedom in exchange for the Kali-aastra. Ash had given it to him almost immediately when Savage threatened to kill Lucky. He'd handed over the most dangerous weapon in the world to save his sister. John's crime was no bigger than his. Ash turned back to the broken mausoleum. "Savage and his loha-mukhas?"

"Yes. I got here just before them. I thought maybe I could warn Parvati, but it all happened so fast. Savage just . . . appeared."

"Appeared how? In his trucks?"

"No. Just like out of a cloud of smoke. Like a magician. He had his loha-mukhas with him."

"Then what?"

"A big fight. Savage hung back and got the stone monsters to do all his dirty work. But there was more." John tapped a fallen slab. "I saw him. He waved his hand and the tombstones just flew through the air. The big doors — he wasn't even near them and they tore themselves off of their hinges."

"What about Parvati? And Khan?"

"They knew they couldn't win. She went for the Koh-I-Noor, but Savage practically dropped a tree on top of her." John sighed. "My fault, Ash. I told Savage everything. Where you were, and where they'd hidden the diamond. It was all over in five minutes. He used his magic. It was unbelievable. He was all over the place."

"What do you mean?"

"I mean, just 'poof.'" John pointed at one corner. "One second he was there." He pointed at another. "Then in an eyeblink, over there. He had his statues doing the same. How can you beat someone like that?"

Teleporting. Savage had mastery over Space. That was a bad thing. "Do you know where Parvati is?"

"I don't know where any of them are. I've been here all day, but no one's come back." John glanced around. "What should we do? Wait here?"

"No, we go after Savage." He could wait for Parvati, but there was no guarantee she'd come back here; there was no reason to. Maybe she was chasing Savage already.

"We've no idea where he's gone."

"Maybe, maybe not. I saw a stamp on the crates he was using to carry some of his statues. It was for the Indian Railways and there was a number, 2841. You have any idea where that goes?"

"Easy to find out. But what difference will that make? He's got the rakshasas, the stone men, and now the Koh-I-Noor," said John. "There's no way we can beat Savage."

"There's always a way."

And Ash could think of one, but he didn't like it.

CHAPTER THIRTY-TWO

"I've been waiting," said Ujba.

Only the spluttering light of mismatched candles opposed the gloomy darkness of the temple. Weird shadows drifted back and forth across the uneven walls — creeping phantoms and ghosts of victims past, trapped where their lives washed the altar. The statue of Kali was glossy red. Blood dripped from her face, into her open mouth, and down her bare chest.

"A sacrifice?" said Ash. "Anyone I know?"

"Just a goat," said Ujba.

"Glad you could restrain yourself."

Ujba lit another candle. "So, you've failed. Again."

"You know what happened at the cemetery?"

"Of course. I have as many spies here as I do in Varanasi."

"Then why didn't you help find Savage? You could have stopped all this."

Ujba's lips turned into a fierce frown. "I offered you my help and you rejected it. Why should I offer more?"

"Is this where you say 'I told you so'? Let me save you the effort. You were right; I was a fool. I can't beat Savage, not as I am. I need more power."

"The Soma?"

"If that's what it takes."

Ash's heart trembled as he watched Ujba nod. He'd thought the guru might say something, maybe even object because he'd rejected him earlier. But the guru acted as if this was all part of his plan, like he always knew Ash was going to take the Soma.

"This will show me how to fight? How to destroy anything?" Ash asked. If it worked, then Savage's loha-mukhas would be no threat.

"Do you know what Kali is?"

"The goddess of death and destruction. What else is there?"

"Kali means black, but the word also comes from Kala, time. Kali is the essence of time. Time is the ultimate force of destruction. Even the universe, in time, will end."

"And that helps me how?"

"Parvati spoke to you about your past lives, I assume?"

"I've even met a few."

"Once you have taken the Soma, you may step out of time yourself, according to the priests, but the effects vary."

"I can time travel?" Ash said. If he could do that, then he could repair all his mistakes. He could fix everything. Just hop back and save Gemma.

"No. That is one of the sorceries, and that you will not be taught. No man should have that power. It is the path of fools. Even Ravana, though he knew how to travel back and forth through time, dared not use it. He understood that whichever path we take, it all leads to the same place."

"Then how will this Soma affect me?"

Ujba tapped his temple. "Inside here is all the wisdom, all the knowledge of all your past selves. Nothing is forgotten, as it is stored in the soul, and you, the Eternal Warrior, have only one soul. You may have been a hundred other people, a thousand, but that is just a suit of clothing upon your true self. Your *self* is unchanging. The soul remembers all those lives. If Kali is generous, and you devout, she will open the paths to all those memories and skills. If you are afraid, you will be able to draw on the courage of Rama. If you are confused, the wisdom of Ashoka. Think what it would be to know all the arts of war, every martial art, every weapon skill."

"I feel there's a massive 'but' coming."

For the first time ever, Ujba smiled. Ash couldn't believe it. It wasn't a nice smile — too wolfish to be warm — but the lips curled upward and some teeth showed, so technically, Ujba smiled. "Yes. But with so many lives, so many personalities, all advising, all demanding, all trying to control you, your own willpower will be your only defense. Let it waver, even for a moment, and your own personality will be washed away into the sea of all the others. Perhaps forever, and who knows who may take charge?"

"Oh joy."

"But the advantages outweigh the risks. Time stretches forward as well as back. You will see the threads of the future, see how one thing affects the other. Glimpses of what lies ahead. If you can understand them, you will be considered wise indeed."

See the future? Now that was something. "Then let's get this over and done with."

Ujba went to his medicine box. Over the next few minutes, in the dim candlelight, Ash watched him mix his ingredients. He ground leaves into a small silver bowl until all was a fine black powder. He worked in silence, whispering mantras as he worked. Ash tried to keep still, but he fidgeted impatiently. He just wanted the medicine and wanted to get out of there, after Savage.

Ujba stroked the razor around the rim of the bowl, making the metal hum. Then he faced Ash. "Blood," he said.

Ash held out his hand. A moment later there was a small cut, and Ash let a few drops drip into the bowl. Ujba stirred as Ash tied a cloth around the thin red line.

"What exactly goes into this Soma?" asked Ash.

"Best you not know."

"And what will happen to me, when I drink this?"

"It's poisonous, so you'll probably die. At least for a while."

Ash took the bowl and sniffed the contents. Putrid didn't begin to describe it. He wasn't sure he'd be able to swallow it, and if he did, there was good chance it would come straight back up, along with his supper of lentils, potatoes, and spinach. "Don't you have something of a less . . . fatal full-fat flavor? Y'know, diet Soma or something?"

"You are the Kali-aastra. It will protect you. The Soma will show you Kali."

"And what if Kali doesn't like me?"

"Then she will eat your soul."

"You're so not selling this," said Ash.

"Do you want to defeat Savage or not?" asked Ujba. "Did you think it would be easy? That Kali would just give you her blessing, merely because you asked? Gods want sacrifices. They want payment, like everyone else. There is nothing for free in this world or any other." He reached over to the Soma and drew it back. "I thought we had a deal. But I understand. Next time, when you're crying over the corpse of another friend, remember I could have helped you."

Ash looked at the man, then at the bowl. He didn't want to drink it. It was more than that it would probably kill him; after this, there was no going back. He didn't know what he might become after drinking the Soma, but he had a feeling the phrase "bloodthirsty monster" might be involved.

But then what if he did meet Savage again, and it was just as big a failure as it had been the last time? Would Savage kill Parvati? How many more of his friends would die?

"Give it to me," said Ash.

Ujba smiled and held out a small brown lump. "Eat this first."

"What is it?"

"*Goor.* The flesh of the tiger. It's consumed by Thugs before they go on their journeys. It's good luck."

"Not for the tiger, it isn't."

"Be at ease. It's only raw sugar." Ash put the lump on his tongue and swallowed. The sweetness might help him hold down the drink.

He raised the bowl to his lips. "How long will the Soma last?"

"If the Soma works properly, it will open a door here." Ujba tapped the center of his forehead. "The inner eye. There is no closing the door afterward."

"And if it doesn't work properly?"

"Death, if you are lucky. Insanity, if not. Perhaps your mind will crumble under the wisdom of Kali and you'll spend the rest of your life in a coma or as a drooling imbecile."

"Oh double joy."

Ash closed his eyes and gulped quickly, emptying the bowl in three swallows. The liquid burned as it went down, but as he lowered the bowl, he was thinking that it wasn't *that* bad.

"Bitter," he said. But that was all.

Only his mouth was dry, very dry.

Ujba leaned closer.

Ash shivered. He felt as if a cold winter wind were blowing.

The freezing air cut his skin. A sharp pang gripped his stomach, twisting it and screwing it into knots. He bent over, his muscles seizing up.

Ujba began to fade. Ash reached for him, but his hand moved sluggishly. The pain was increasing, spreading out from his belly to his limbs. It was as if his blood were boiling within him.

Ash spat and stared at the bloody spittle on the tiled floor. His eyes were hot and swollen, bloody tears forming a thin film over them.

"Help me," he whispered. Another spasm shook him, and he buckled under the agony. The pounding of his blood was deafening, and each heartbeat sent bone-breaking tremors through his body.

Ujba looked toward the statue. "Accept my offering, Kali."

Ash tried to breathe, but all that came out was a feeble hiss. He gazed at Ujba, his vision becoming dull. Then everything faded as his last breath escaped.

CHAPTER THIRTY-THREE

Ash walks silently toward the light flickering in the darkness. He passes vague, shadowy outlines of others, bodies that are mere cloaks for a single soul that returns again and again for battle. They touch him, phantom caresses both comforting and despairing. There ahead of him shines a figure, a being both human and something more. It is the light from this being that casts all the other shadows.

The Eternal Warrior.

He has no form: It is flesh that has form, and he has worn so many bodies over the endless eons. Ash is merely another.

Ash steps into the pool of light closest to the being. It senses him, and the flames stir and take on a vague human outline. It gazes down at him. It knows what Ash wants.

Ash looks about him. There are others there, ghosts of the past, stirring within the gray fog.

"Who are they?" Ash asks. Some are dressed in bronze armor, heavy scarlet cloaks draped over their shoulders. Some wear jewels and silks, others rags or unfamiliar clothes. They come from all lands and all epochs. They are African, Indian, Mongolian, Caucasian, male, female, young, old. The Eternal Warrior is of all nations, all ages. One man, old and wizened, has the round, flat features of an Inuit. He meets Ash's gaze with eyes of infinite sorrow.

"They are us," says the burning soul. "Here to welcome you."

All of them? The crowd stretches to the horizon, perhaps beyond. Ash hesitates. "I . . . didn't know there were so many."

"Many, but one."

"No. I can't do it."

"She comes."

Ash turns and faces the pyre. The blue flames roar silently. The touch of Agni, the god of fire, does not penetrate this world.

He sees there is a body lying on the flames. "No. It can't be."

"Your old self, to be burned away," says his soul.

He watches his skin blacken and crack. He sees his hair catch light and the fat dribble off his molten flesh. Bones break out from under the crisp, brittle skin.

A figure rises up out of the fire, tall and fierce.

"You are hers now, Ash."

She stands upon his burning corpse, and she is beautiful. Her long black limbs glisten with sweat and her chest rises and sinks with panting eagerness. The flames dance around her, shades of blue turning to white to the color of a midnight sea, licking her legs and caressing her taut belly.

Kali.

She glares down at him, her red tongue hanging with hunger and her eyes blazing with violence. The third eye, the destroying eye, opens the merest slit and the light from it blinds Ash. The heat is unbearable and he screams.

The fire of her eyes melts him to the core, stripping off skin and muscle and bone to what is beneath it all: his soul, exposed and raw beneath the devastating gaze of the goddess.

Then the pain ends.

Ash, curled up on the barren ground, slowly opens his eyes, expecting to see himself black and charred beyond any hope of life.

Instead, his fingers are clean and supple. His arms lean, dark, and strong. He stands and sees himself transformed, built of fast, lethal muscle and hard, merciless edges and angles. Not the smooth curves and softness of flesh, but the keenness of a blade.

Ash bows and claps his hands together. He performs the greeting ritual of kalaripayit. He sweeps his limbs in long, low blows and high kicks, and ends bowed before the goddess.

Kali's chest heaves with eagerness as she curls her long talons into a fist.

She shows Ash how to punch.

Kali raises her foot.

She shows Ash how to kick.

Her limbs dart, and blows and strikes come fast and furious until Kali is a hurricane of movement. Each action is of ethereal grace and beauty, fluid and elegant, like a tidal wave rolling over a mountain.

Ash follows. In her footsteps. In her shadow.

He mimics her movements, her attacks, her ferocity. Ash feels another pair of arms tear from his body. Another. Glistening with his blood, new limbs rip out of his torso, the flesh peeling away to reveal glossy, bloody bones. He stares at his hands, now claws, and runs his long tongue over his fangs. He dances in his own ashes.

He is now fully a thing of Kali.

CHAPTER THIRTY-FOUR

His mouth tasted of dust. Ash blinked and spat. He lay on the temple floor, the cold stone pressed against his skin. Dimly, he felt the vibrations of the city through the ground, and his ears pricked at the soft breeze moaning through the temple, the creaking of the old wood. Ash lifted himself up and settled down on his haunches. The temple was empty. Sunlight shone through the missing tiles in the roof. A large cockroach scuttled across the floor, pausing for a moment to look at him.

I'm alive. I think.

He touched his ribs, half-expecting to find a second — or third — pair of arms sticking out. Nope, no new body parts. On the outside, he was still the human Ash. Good news so far. He stood up, checking that all was normal. Nothing had changed. His muscles weren't any bigger, and as he ran his tongue over his teeth, he was pleased to find he hadn't grown fangs either.

He closed his eyes, recalling the many people he'd seen in his vision. Those guys in bronze armor and red cloaks. Ash knew enough of his history to recognize the most kick-butt warriors of the world, the Spartans. If Ujba was right, he should know ancient Greek. What about counting to ten?

"Er . . . er."

Hello, in Greek?

"Er."

Anything, in Greek?

"Er."

So the Soma had been a big fat fail. He wasn't any different.

A flutter of cloth caught his attention. A yellow scarf hung from a low beam, pinned in place with a katar. Ash took a firm grip and worked the punch dagger back and forth until it came loose. He took the scarf and wrapped the dagger within it.

Suddenly pain cramped his stomach, and Ash groaned as black spots danced in his eyes. He put his hand against a stone column, leaning on it as he steadied himself.

A series of cracks flowered out from his palm. Ash lifted his hand. The palm print was an inch deep. He followed the line of a crack down the white marble. The crack itself was only a hairsbreadth in width.

Ash put his finger against the minute line. And pushed.

The marble splintered. Ash pushed harder.

The column trembled and jagged tears ruptured along its length. The roof began to creak.

Ash stopped. He drew his hand back and then slammed his palm against the column. It exploded into a million white shards of marble, shooting out and riddling the wall like bullets. Ash glanced up as the ceiling bowed and the wooden beams splintered. He ran.

He was halfway down the alley before he turned and watched. The old temple groaned as the roof fell in. The wooden posts and beams within cracked and snapped; the old plaster shattered, tossing out white clouds of dust. Then the roof caved in with a dull boom.

The hazy morning sky had a hint of rose to it and there was not a single cloud. A light, chilly mist floated on the streets and down the alley. Birds chirped in the rooftops, stirred by the faint dawn light.

Ash looked around.

He felt the brittle bricks in the wall, the pattern of grain on the door and the cracks along the metal water pipes. A car passed, and Ash's body vibrated in harmony to the chugging, spluttering engine. He heard the hissing steam coming out of the minute hole in the radiator, and felt how the bald, worn-out tires bounced over the small stones.

He looked at the driver, smoking a cigarette and blowing the smoke out of the open window. Ash could taste the tar that coated the man's lungs from his breath.

These were all the signs of death and decay. Ash could feel the world rotting around him. And all he needed to make it collapse was to give it a little push. The wall. The door. The car. The man. Ash gazed at him and a sharp blossom of heat blossomed right in the middle of his forehead as he focused on the driver.

The driver takes a red packet of cigarettes from his shirt pocket and lights one. The man shifts gears and rolls forward, searching for a gap in the traffic. He cries out as ash from his cigarette burns his hand. He shakes it and doesn't see the yellow bus, its horn blaring a warning but the noise lost in the city's din. The man stares in horror —

Ash blinked. What had just happened? The taxi hadn't moved. He looked down the road and there was a yellow bus, but it was still half a mile away. The taxi driver wasn't even smoking.

Then the man reached into his pocket and took out a packet of cigarettes. The packet was red.

Ash's heart sped up. He knew *exactly* what was coming next. He was going to light it and drive into the middle of the road. The yellow bus got closer.

The man lit a cigarette and shifted the gears and with a

shudder and a cough of smoke, his taxi rolled forward into the junction. Rickshaws and cars and bicycles wove away, but the flow did not slow. The taxi driver, holding his cigarette loosely out of his side window, glanced up and down.

Ash waited. Any second now the ash would fall and burn the driver's hand.

The driver winced and shook his hand, dropping the cigarette. The car kept moving and was now in the center of the road.

Ash watched the bus; it wasn't far now. It was unwinding like an action replay. Each second was identical to what he'd seen in his mind only moments earlier. The future was unfolding before him.

The traffic parted and the bus, battered and yellow, its racks piled high with boxes and suitcases and crates and passengers, loomed out like a whale pushing through a school of fish. The sunlight shone off the dusty front windshield as the bus driver pushed hard on his horn.

The man, still blowing on his burned hand, did not notice.

Then the driver saw the bus. He stared in horror, then fumbled at his wheel and the gear stick. The bus began to brake, and a wall of dust rose up before it.

The taxi reversed six feet and the bus thundered past, missing the car by inches. The passengers waved and swore at the taxi as they shot by.

Ash shook his head. He'd seen it all seconds before it actually happened.

He'd glimpsed the future.

He rubbed his forehead, half-expecting to feel a third eye there, but found nothing. The Kali-aastra hummed louder than ever within every atom in his body. The Soma had done its work.

He was ready to face Savage.

CHAPTER THIRTY-FIVE

"You look different," said John.

John had salvaged some stuff from the cemetery, so at least Ash had a clean change of clothes: a pair of baggy trousers and a loose tunic. He'd washed off the dust and mud at a standpipe and got loaned a lump of soap for a rupee. "You mean more handsome?" Ash said.

"More something."

"I've been taking my vitamins."

"Just as long as that's all you've been taking."

Ash rolled up the katar and packed it in a backpack with a shawl and a few other traveling bits and pieces, like a compass, flashlight, and pair of binoculars. John had gone to the train station and found out that the 2841 train went down the eastern coast of India, all the way to Madras. Ash had no idea why Savage was heading south, but without Parvati around and with no better ideas, he was going to follow. He pulled the toggle of the backpack. "You know you don't have to come. There'll be trouble."

John packed up his own meager belongings. "I am responsible for getting you in this mess. Wouldn't be right if I didn't help fix it."

"We have a plan?"

John nodded. "Find Savage. Get the Koh-I-Noor back. You do what you do best."

"And what's that?"

John waved his arms in a kung fu–style flourish. "You know, like this."

Ash slipped the backpack on and looked around to see if he'd forgotten anything. "How are we getting to the airport?"

"We're not. Bad news. No Jimmy," John replied. "Engine failure."

"How bad?"

"The starboard one fell off halfway across the Indian Sea. He's sailing back."

The plan was falling apart and they'd not even started. Ash had hoped to save a day at least by flying down to Madras. He'd never been that far south and had no idea what to expect. Since Madras had been another of the main headquarters of the East India Company, it no doubt was familiar territory to Savage. They couldn't risk losing him again — though hiding an army of statues, including one seventy feet high, wouldn't be easy. "Then what are we going to do?"

John handed Ash a slip of paper. A ticket. "Take the train. There's one at dusk."

Ash threw down his backpack. The train was delayed by three hours, so there was nothing to do but wait on the platform. The world could be in total peril and he couldn't save it because of a herd of cows on the track. Harry Potter never had these problems.

So he sat there, waiting, in the Kolkata train station, a grand imperial building that had been the pride and joy of the British Raj. The grandeur was still evident, but like so much of the city, the structure was succumbing to a sort of benign decay.

Worn and crumbling, operating with ancient systems and a vast army of staff, the station had the feeling of a home. Life existed here; it was more than just a place to pass through.

Ash gazed across the tracks at a small single building called the Coolie House. A row of porters squatted in the shade, passing around a cigarette. Small children, orphans, runaways, those just lost, darted between the stacks of luggage, across the tracks, and through the stalls collecting trash — mainly empty plastic water bottles — or asking for handouts from the few Western travelers who had decided to see India by rail. A boy, younger than Lucky, balanced a battered tin tray on his head to deliver a dozen small glasses of milky tea to the khaki-uniformed staff at the signal box.

Where was Parvati? Her cell phone was dead. It wasn't just that he missed her and was worried about her — he *depended* on her. This was her territory, and he needed her around. The encounter with the Jagannath and Savage's loha-mukhas still haunted him, reminding him that this wasn't a game. The stakes were high, and he didn't know all the rules.

Simply put, he was afraid. Afraid Savage had more tricks up his sleeve. That the Soma hadn't worked properly, that he was out of his league. He'd left a message for Parvati at the cemetery, a letter tucked under the remains of the mausoleum. He had no idea if she'd ever find it, but what else could he do?

Dear Parvati,

Savage is taking his loha-mukhas on the 2841 train down to Madras, just in case you didn't know. I've no idea why he'd be going south, but I'm following with my trusty Padawan, John.

I'm sorry for what I said, and even more sorry for not listening to you. You were right and I was wrong. That will have to do as an apology as I've a train to catch and the world to save. Again.

Your friend,
Ash

Not the best letter ever. He'd wanted to put in more, about the injustice of Gemma's death, about trying to do something good and be more than just an instrument of Kali, about how, in spite of all his previous lives, this hero business was still new to him, and hey, who didn't make mistakes and he'd never said he was perfect, and frankly, Parvati could have done a better job explaining things to him instead of being all superior and stuck up, and while she was his closest friend and everything, she could be so pigheaded, and if she'd just dialed down her ego a little, she might have heard what Ash had been trying to say and they wouldn't be in this mess, which, when you really thought about it, was as much her fault as it was his, not that she'd ever admit it.

But Ash had decided not to write any of that.

When Ash had heard he'd be going on the sleeper train, he had entertained ideas of oak-paneled Pullman carriages; white-gloved attendants, and small, exquisitely furnished compartments with their own porcelain washbasins. Basically the Orient Express. Instead they approached a carriage that turned out to be nothing more than a big steel crate with bars on the windows. John checked the tickets. "This is us," he said.

"You're joking. This is for cattle, not people."

"I only had enough money for third class."

Ash sighed and climbed in. The carriage was comprised of open compartments along one side of a narrow corridor. Each compartment had a pair of triple-decked bunk beds facing each other. During the day, everyone sat on the lowest bunk, with the upper two folded against the wall. The attendant came around in the evening to unfold the top bunks, with a sheet and pillow for each passenger, and then it was lights-out.

Old women in fine saris sat while mustachioed business-men shouted into their cell phones and mothers wrestled with screaming kids and squalling babies. One boy, forefinger firmly fixed in his left nostril, watched Ash and John settle in.

Ash peered out the window as the train pulled out of the station. Passengers dashed across the tracks to climb in through the open doors, helped on board by the other commuters. The train ran through grand avenues of steel track lined with the pastel-colored government buildings. It wove through gleaming new towers and raced along through the shantytowns that encircled the city.

Then they were running smoothly on raised tracks along endless paddy fields, and Kolkata disappeared behind the wall of swaying palm trees.

That night, everyone slept except Ash. The carriage rumbled and the wheels screeched and rattled endlessly. The fans above him droned like a squadron of mosquitoes. Couldn't they afford to oil them? The noise put Ash's teeth on edge.

He thought about Ujba and what he'd said about Ash's past lives. He thought about all those people he'd seen, faces going back thousands of years from all over the world. Ashoka had been somewhere in that crowd, and Ash wanted to find him and learn more about the Koh-I-Noor, especially now that Savage had it. So, with the train rattling along, the fans buzzing, and the other passengers snoring, Ash closed his eyes.

He began to blank out the world around him. He let the rocking of the carriage pass through him so he felt as if he were floating, rather than resting on a shaking bunk. The noises around him faded and he lost touch with himself as he sank further inward.

He passed by gray-bearded men and women dressed in thick robes and wearing heavy jewels from ancient times. Ahead and around him there were others, some with swords or spears, some with scrolls and books or pots and quills, and he wondered what their lives had been like. Had they won their battles or lost? Parvati had told him once that the Eternal War-rior could fight for either side, for good or evil, but now as Ash looked further into his past lives, he realized it wasn't so simple. You could be hero and villain, often simultaneously. He'd been Brutus, the Roman who'd murdered Julius Caesar to save the Republic, but instead only brought about the reign of the emperors. By attempting good, his legacy had been tyranny and the era of Caligula and Nero.

Ash had ridden with the Mongols, slaughtering their way from the steppes to the very heart of Europe. But from the bones they'd built the first global empire and allowed the exchange of science, technology, and new ideas between the East and West. Such great evil leading to good.

What part would he play? Would he be a hero or a villain? He had no idea. But right now he needed one man, a conqueror who, more than most, had been both.

Ashoka. Where are you?

CHAPTER THIRTY-SIX

Ashoka looks down at the bodies of his dead soldiers. He raises the burning diamond high and the beams burst from the many faces of crystal, pushing back the darkness. The pure white light shines upon pale, bloodless limbs; on blank, empty eyes; on drawn, pale lips. Their bodies are scored with wounds and their clothes rent and encrusted with dried patches of blood. Limbs have been hacked off and others crushed under the blows of maces and clubs.

"Rise, brothers, rise," he urges them, thrusting the Koh-I-Noor ahead of him.

Behind him he hears the uneasy shuffling of his bodyguards, the sibilant hiss of warning from Parvati as she sees how much greater he is than her father.

"Rise!"

The diamond burns within his fist and shakes with power. A dull, deep drone vibrates from the rock and the light increases to a blinding intensity. Ashoka shields his eyes.

A harsh, desperate cry pierces the night. First one, then others. The diamond is almost unbearable now, but even as his skin burns, Ashoka holds fast.

He stares as the dead move. Groaning, they flex their limbs and drag themselves up from the bloodied earth of their graves. Then, one by one, they stand. Their eyes are dull and carry the light of Yama, and their mouths twist into savage, hungry leers. A deep, inhuman snarl rattles from the throat of the nearest, and he extends his arms, reaching out for Ashoka. His guards form a wall of spears between him and the risen dead.

"No," whispers Parvati. The four blades of her urumi, *her serpent sword, rattle free. She steps toward the men as they shuffle on ungainly, stiff limbs. A few, their legs broken or missing, crawl forward, clambering over one another with eager, monstrous bloodlust. One guard rams his spear through the torso of one, but the man, the creature, continues despite the injury, grabbing him and dragging him away from the line. The guard screams as they surround him, sinking their nails and teeth into his flesh. They pull and tear and devour.*

More and more of his bodyguards fall beneath the relentless mass until they can take no more and flee. Ashoka remains, the diamond still glowing in his hand. Parvati strikes, her urumi flickering, slicing, and ripping. But there are too many.

The living dead turn their hungry gaze toward him.

"No!" cries Ashoka.

"No," cried Ash, wiping the sweat off his face. He grabbed his water bottle and drained it in four gulps. Water spilled over him as he tried to stop his hand from shaking.

That was horrible, a nightmare. Ashoka had used the Brahma-aastra, but something had gone seriously wrong. By trying to return life to the dead, by trying to do good, he had only created a greater evil.

The ones who come back are never the ones who left. That's what Khan said. If Savage used the diamond the same way, he was likely to kick off a zombie apocalypse. Ash wouldn't need a punch dagger to face down the undead; he'd need a chainsaw.

If this was what would happen if anyone used the diamond, then Gemma was better dead and at peace.

Resurrecting Gemma. It was, always had been, a foolish hope. With that hope gone, all he had was despair. He'd go home and have to face the fact he'd failed. Josh and his other mates were afraid of him, and what about Lucky? She'd more or less said he'd become a monster.

Some hero.

He got up and walked to the end of the carriage. The door was wide open — no health and safety concerns here — and he watched the midnight landscape roll by.

The journey time was twenty-six hours, but John had told him that in India, that could mean thirty hours, or thirty-six. He'd checked the map at the station to get an idea of the route they were taking. Madras was way down south, almost at the tip of the subcontinent, a stone's throw from the island of Sri Lanka. The train followed the eastern coastline along the Bay of Bengal, and wove through mangrove swamps and jungle. Palm leaves brushed the tops of the carriages and the scent of lush vegetation, softly decaying in the damp heat, mixed with the smoky exhaust of the old diesel engine up front.

Occasionally the jungle fell away and Ash gazed out across the still sea. The sky, dazzling with diamond-light, shone upon the deep blues and greens of the water, stretching all the way to the horizon. Small black silhouettes — uninhabited islands — dotted the otherwise featureless ocean.

Stations came and went. At the bigger ones, tea sellers and porters sleeping on their carts stirred into languid life from under their threadbare blankets as the train clattered in. Hawkers sold drinks, ran errands, and handed snacks wrapped in palm leaves through the bars to yawning passengers.

John joined him as the night rolled on. "View's better up top," he said. He leaned out of the door, stood on tiptoe, grabbed the top of the door frame, and lifted himself out in a single, nimble move, as sprightly as a monkey.

The train was picking up speed and rocking from side to side. Getting up on the roof, at night, with low branches, sounded pretty damn stupid. Ash couldn't climb like John. The boy was small and light; Ash wasn't.

John leaned over the edge, his upside-down face quizzical. "Well?" he asked.

"What if I slip?"

"Make sure you don't."

"But what if I do?"

John frowned. "Then, I think, you'll be crushed to death under the wheels? Probably."

"Sod it," said Ash. "You only live once."

John smirked. "We both know that's not true."

Ash pulled himself up, fingers scrabbling for a second before John grabbed his arm and helped him onto the roof.

They weren't alone. A man lay asleep, his head resting on a small tucked-up package. Farther down, a trio of laborers passed around a steel dish and a bottle.

"I love trains," said Ash. "The feeling that you can go on and on, the world changing all around you, but you're just sitting still."

"Sounds lazy."

"Laziness is a vastly underrated quality. I used to be an expert in lazy."

"You and your decadent Western ways." John took a packet of Indian pastries from inside his shirt. "I lifted these at the last stop. Best while they're still warm."

More samosas? Fine by him. Ash nibbled at the corner of the deep-fried meal, wanting to make it last. "Where do you think you'll go, after this is over?"

"Get my mother and move. Go somewhere nice and quiet, like Kashmir. We've relatives up there." John held his hand under the pastry, trying to catch even the smallest of crumbs as the wind blew around them. He didn't waste anything. "Kashmir's very beautiful. There are lakes of pure blue and they're as still as mirrors, so the sky shines above and below. And you have beautiful boats, like floating palaces really. I had a postcard of one once. That's where I'd work."

"I'll make sure that happens. This time."

"Your father a rich man?"

"No. He's an engineer. Mum's an accountant. We get by, but we're not rich."

"That what you're going to be? Follow in your dad's footsteps?"

Ash shrugged. "Never thought much about it. I really wanted to be a computer game programmer. Trouble is, all that fantasy stuff doesn't feel quite the same now."

"Now that you've seen real monsters?"

"Something like that. Found out they're not that easy to beat."

"You're lucky you have a choice."

"Yes, I suppose." Parvati and Ujba didn't seem to think so. As far as they were concerned, he was the Kali-aastra, and that was that. "You know, I always wondered why Superman even bothered being Clark Kent."

"What?"

"Think about it. Why be a normal person? All that time he's working at the *Daily Planet*, there's an earthquake happening or volcano exploding somewhere in the world and he's not there to save people. He's in the office, watching dancing cats on YouTube like everyone else."

"Is there a point to this conversation, or are you just rambling?"

"He doesn't want the responsibility. Simple as that. He doesn't need a secret identity, he could be Superman twenty-four-seven, but he isn't. He has to be Clark or he'd go mad. You understand?"

"No. Not even a tiny bit." John looked worried. "Are you all right?"

"Forget it."

The two of them sat up on the roof as the train slowed down to a small station, alone in the middle of the jungle. There was a single small building and a long, crumbling platform. Huge flowers grew along the borders of the station, and the air was thick with musty pollen. A few small storerooms lined up behind the main building, such as it was, and there were several fenced-off vegetable gardens.

Ash pointed at one. "What happened there?"

The fence was broken, ripped out of the earth, and the entire vegetable patch trampled to paste. The trees beyond and the long grass had been just as thoroughly flattened.

"Elephants," said John. "Pain in the butt. Looks like a big herd got a taste of the station master's tomatoes."

"Yes, where is the station master?" There was usually a man with a lantern waving the train through, even in the smallest stations like this one.

"Ash?"

"What?"

"You're scratching your thumb."

He hadn't even noticed, but he was. He glanced at John. "I'll only be a minute."

Ash slid down the side of the carriage, using the window bars as footholds, and stepped onto the empty platform. After a few seconds John came down and joined him.

"Ash?" he asked, close behind.

Ash sniffed the air. His thumb was seriously itchy. He walked up to the flowerbed.

It wasn't just the vegetables that had been trampled. Lying in among the smashed tomatoes and clumps of coriander was a body. It had been a man — the station master, most likely — but now it was a pulped, red and pink smear.

John let out a small gasp as he saw the body. Ash continued searching. It took a second for his eyes to adjust to the night gloom, but then he made out a shape in the mud — a deep imprint depressed about three inches into the black soil. Whatever had made it had been incredibly heavy and large.

It was a footprint, but a size bigger than any human's.

Now he'd seen one, he saw others. Some human, some animal, some who-knew-what, but all heavy and sunk deep. All heading into the jungle.

"Not elephants," he said. "Loha-mukhas."

CHAPTER THIRTY-SEVEN

A few minutes later, the train was gone and the two of them stood on the empty platform. The only sound was the ticktock of the old station clock.

"What's out there?" asked Ash. As far as he could tell, there was just jungle. Why had Savage bailed out here?

"No idea. I've never been this far south."

The loha-mukhas had trampled a path through the foliage wide enough for a bus. Ash swatted at clouds of insects as they descended to feast on his blood. The high-pitched whine of mosquitoes echoed around his ears, and as they plowed through the swampy terrain, he was soon soaked from head to toe.

"Why are they picking on me?" He slapped the back of his neck as another mosquito took a quick snack. "They're eating me alive."

"It's your bland English blood," John answered. "Ours is too spicy."

Ash splashed waist deep in the murky water. Maybe if he put his head under? He took a deep breath and was about to sink under when John gasped.

"What?"

John pointed at a knobby log floating nearby.

The log blinked.

A pair of yellow crocodile eyes gazed from just above the surface.

"What should I do?" asked Ash.

"Just punch its nose," suggested John. "Isn't that, you know, a thing you do?"

"I thought that was sharks."

The crocodile swished its tail and floated closer. Ash thought about his katar, but it was stuffed deep in his backpack. He made a fist, ready to punch.

This is going to be the stupidest thing I've ever done. And I've done plenty.

"Just think of it as a handbag waiting to happen," said John from high up in a tree.

How did he get up there? Ash wondered. The guy was half-monkey. "Utterly unhelpful."

The crocodile stared at Ash, its ancient yellow eyes seeming to look deep into him. Then the giant reptile turned, and with a slow, languid swish, disappeared into the swamp.

Ash drained his third bottle of water. He must have lost half his body weight in sweat in just the last two hours. His clothes clung to him, and the air was so thick and heavy that breathing was like pulling air through a wet washcloth. The insects obviously had a taste for him and had told all their friends.

The trees were also full of monkeys. The creatures watched them from their shrouded perches. Big eyes in black furred faces, their long tails hooked around branches, some with wide-eyed babies hanging off them, others grooming each other or just sitting there, watching. The farther they went, the larger their audience grew. An army of monkeys.

John peered along the trampled path. "Can you smell it?"

Mixed in with the slimy odor of rot and damp decay was a crisper, cleaner scent. The air felt fresher than it had earlier. "The sea?"

On they marched. Despite the flattened foliage, the path they were following was slow going. The terrain rolled and dipped and dived through mangrove swamps, across deep streams and ravines of broken rocks. Ash's legs and back ached and John was falling farther behind.

They stopped, exhausted and hungry. Ash lay down on a slab of stone. Moss served as a thin, mushy mattress and the stone was flat. They'd rest for a while, get some strength back, then continue. He swallowed the last of the water. His super-strength and stamina were fading; the trek through the jungle had taken more out of him than he'd expected. He felt — almost — human.

He slid his fingertips over the edge of the stone. "Funny, these are chisel marks." He peeled off a patch of dark moss. The rock was scratched and grooved, but so heavily weathered the marks looked natural. Still, the dimensions of the slab were perfectly rectangular. No natural force would shape rock into a rectangle that neatly.

John inspected his own perch. "Look here." The boulder he'd been sitting on was actually three of the same slabs, stacked one upon the other.

"Paving stones," Ash said. "Big ones, and very old."

"But this only leads to the sea," said John.

Ash looked at the stones again. It was obvious they were man-made. But why and why here? "You sure there're no cities or towns this way?"

John frowned. "Doubt it. It's all just swamp."

The monkeys chattered frantically. They jumped up and down on their branches, some hopping from slab to slab, slapping their hands on the stone and crying out.

"What do they want?" John asked.

"If I spoke monkey, I'd ask."

Warily, they continued along the smashed-up path, the swamp filled with the howling of monkeys.

They hit the cliff top an hour later at twilight. *Just in time,* thought Ash. He hadn't been keen on groping around in the swamp in the dark and walking straight down the throat of a waiting crocodile. Their company of monkeys lingered, but they kept farther back, afraid to leave the safety of the trees.

An arch of grass-covered rock jutted out from the cliff. Ash peered over.

Vast house-sized boulders sat in the waters, their jagged corners rising out of the dark sea like the jaws of a leviathan as waves crashed and spewed upon them. A row of small islands stretched out toward the east. A wind was brewing on the sea, and storm clouds gathered on the horizon.

"Looks like Cornwall," Ash said. "That's an archipelago off the far western point of England. It looks as though it's stretching out to some distant island."

"Are those lights?" John pointed to one of the larger islands a mile or so away.

Ash took out his binoculars.

John was right. While Ash couldn't see any path leading up the tall cliffs of the island on this side, it was flat once you got to the top, and hidden among the palm trees were some small tents with lanterns. A wisp of smoke rose from a campfire.

Figures of all shapes and sizes, some human, some not, moved around the plateau. He saw a pair of overlarge stone monkeys lugging a large suitcase.

But no Jagannath. That was a relief. Ash may have knocked down a rickety temple to Kali, but he didn't feel ready to test himself against a thousand tons of solid stone. His guts tightened as he watched a white-suited figure move among the tents. Savage.

"There's a path down to the beach." John started down the slope. "Come with me."

The sea gently heaved upon the sandy beach. Once he'd climbed down, it didn't take long for Ash to spot the continuation of the stone path they'd followed all this way. Time and tide had broken it up, and the slabs tilted or sloped at odd angles, but Ash could see the path ran in a straight line into the water, disappearing into the waves after a few yards. A vast field of seaweed drifted from side to side across the shelter of rocks. Why a path into the sea?

"What's Savage doing out there? Waiting for a boat?"

"You don't have a plan?" asked John.

"Me? I'm the strong but silent type."

"You? Silent? I've never met anyone whose mouth was more disconnected from his brain."

"I'll take that as a compliment."

It was another eight hours till sunup, and judging by the campfires on the island, Savage was bedding down for the night.

"We'll wait a bit," said Ash. "Give Parvati time to find us."

"You think she'll come here? How?"

Ash prodded John's forehead. "She's smart. She'll have a plan. Several, most likely." He yawned and picked a dry patch of sand. It was cool and there was something soporific about the sound of waves lapping on the beach. "I'm having a little nap. We'll take turns. Give me a couple of hours, then wake me up, okay?"

John snored softly in the grassy verge at the foot of the cliff, while Ash sat on the shore, looking out at the dim thread of gray on the eastern horizon. He'd slept fitfully, his dreams still haunted by his memories of Ashoka and the twisted revenants he'd brought to life with the Koh-I-Noor. So he woke after a few hours and let John take the lion's share of rest, in spite of the bone-deep weariness that hung over him. The campfires on the far island were now just dim red glows, dying in their embers, and figures were moving about. It looked like Savage wanted an early start.

If they were going to do anything, it had to be sooner rather than later.

Savage was within easy reach. He had the Koh-I-Noor.

What would Parvati do? That was the question.

Whatever needs doing.

Ash kicked John's leg.

"Whuuh?" John rubbed his knuckles in his eyes and shook the sand from his hair.

Ash flicked off his sandals. "I'm going."

"You're joking. Aren't you?"

"Nope. I'm tired of waiting."

"Do you have any idea what you're doing?"

"Do I ever?" Ash wrapped his yellow scarf around his waist and tucked the katar into it. "I'm going after Savage. He's over there."

"Then what?"

"I'll get the Koh-I-Noor first and kill him second." That's what Parvati would do.

John looked at Ash. "You're really going to kill him?"

Ash nodded. He was the Kali-aastra; that was what he did, and no one deserved death more than Savage. "I've killed before. Ravana. Mayar. Even that vulture demon Jat."

"Oh, yeah, you're practically a serial killer, Ash."

"That's not funny."

"Murder *isn't* funny. You killed those others in war. I heard about them from your sister. You saved her life and that's why you did it. This is different. This is creeping up behind some-one and slitting his throat. You're not that sort of person. I hope you're not that sort of person."

"It's what Parvati would do."

"She's a demon, Ash."

Ash was waist deep in the ocean now. "I'm not saying it's what I want. It's just . . . what other choice do I have? How else am I going to stop him?"

"I'm just saying it's a bit extreme. Let's wait. If we've found this place, I bet Parvati can't be far behind."

That's what Ash wanted. He wanted Parvati to make the decision. If she told him to kill Savage, that would be different. It wouldn't be his choice. But then following orders wasn't an excuse for doing evil. "We've only got another couple of hours of darkness left. If I'm going to get over there, I need to go now."

"What about me?" said John.

"Head back to the old train station. If Parvati is on her way, she'll most likely come through there. You go and find her."

"And if I can't?"

"Then find someone else. Like the Avengers," said Ash as he waded into the sea.

CHAPTER THIRTY-EIGHT

He'd never swum in the dark before, and it was weird seeing the reflections of the stars and the light of the moon fragmented upon the dark waves. A strange green glow followed his limbs, fluorescent algae activated by his movements. He dipped his head under once or twice. The darkness beneath was endless. He felt like he was floating in eternity.

Was he halfway there? Maybe.

There was a thin strip of beach ahead, sheltered by the high cliffs. Ash, chin low in the bobbing waves, put a bit of effort in and headed for it.

His toes scraped the sand. Ash found his footing and waded the last few yards. He stared straight up the cliffs in front of him. They were grim and black, smeared with moss, and water trickled down crooked, narrow channels, collecting in rock pools at the cliff bottom. Ash shook his arms, trying to get some life back into them. But they hung heavily from his aching shoulders. He shuffled toward the high, rocky wall, desperate for a rest but knowing that if he stopped now, he'd never get started again. Dawn was approaching fast. Now was the time for sneaking.

He looked for a way up.

"Crap." The cliffs were a lot taller than they'd looked from the shore.

Why was nothing simple anymore?

No path up. No convenient rope dangling from the top. No escalator. Certainly no elevator. Just clumps of weeds and grass sticking out of cracks in the rock. Dripping wet, legs worn from the swim, Ash searched the cliff for a handhold. He grabbed an exposed root, wedged his toes into a long crack, and started to climb.

Ash crept up the dark cliff face like a spider, slowly, and planning each move. More than once his grip slipped, and he found himself dangling fifty yards over the rock by just his fingertips. His arms burned and his shoulders ached like this was his worst PE class times a hundred, times a thousand. He was definitely low on battery power.

Bad time to have second thoughts about all this, Ash.

He needed a death — for someone nearby to die and allow Ash to absorb those death energies. Then he could take on anyone.

That was sick, thinking about death so casually. The realization made him shiver, or was it just the night sea wind?

Savage was waiting at the top. His prize. He gritted his teeth and pushed on.

Eventually, with the eastern sky turning purple, Ash reached the top. He sat down to catch his breath and let his limbs recover.

Ash drew out his katar. It settled comfortably in his grip. The katar wasn't flashy; it didn't have gems or decorative carvings; it was as plain as could be.

It had one purpose, and he would use it for that: to end Savage's miserable life, once and forever.

Ash looked along the uneven cliff path. The sky was bloody now, dawn an hour away. Lights shone among the tents. They stood arranged in neat military rows, each of unblemished white canvas, like small houses. The island wasn't big; it was almost square and relatively flat, though overgrown and dotted with palm trees. Ash spotted a few more of the flagstones, mostly covered in grass. He crept closer to the tents and crouched, bare-footed and silent. He searched around, watching for anyone coming near. The darkness gathered around him. The shadows seemed thicker where he stood and the silence deeper.

The army of statues, the loha-mukhas, surrounded the edge of the camp. A pack of hyena rakshasas scouted the perimeter. One sniffed at the bush Ash hid behind, then wandered off.

Ash smiled to himself. His dip in the sea must have masked his scent.

He skirted around the edge of the encampment, heading toward the biggest tent. It was a plain thing, about fifteen feet square and tall enough for a man to stand up in. The flaps were closed but fluttered slightly in the wind. Up close, Ash saw the walls were embroidered with the crossed swords and poppies of the Savage coat of arms. There were two loha-mukhas standing guard outside, a six-armed Shiva made of bronze and a stone lion. Savage had to be in there.

At the back of the tent, Ash stopped and listened. Nothing. He scraped the edge of his katar into the heavy cloth, tearing a small hole. He peered in but couldn't see anything; it was too dark. His heart went into overdrive, and he wiped the sweat from his hands.

This is it.

Ash cut a line through the back wall. The cloth parted, the noise seeming as loud as a scream, but there was no response as he entered the tent.

Early morning light followed him through the tear and cast a soft glow over the sleeping figure of Savage. He lay on his back, shirt undone. Seven skulls marked his chest in a circle pattern, each one glowing softly with a pale, almost radioactive yellow. They were deep brands, and Ash, for a moment, wondered how much they had hurt. He knew they were a symbol of Savage's growing magical power, the number of sorceries he'd mastered. He'd only had five skulls when Ash had faced him in Rajasthan. Three more, and he'd be as powerful as Ravana.

Beside the bed was a low camp table. Savage's cane rested on it, next to a small leather satchel. Ash flicked it open. The Koh-I-Noor lay inside in its silk purse. He put the satchel over his shoulder.

Ash knelt down beside the bed and pressed the razor-sharp edge of the katar against Savage's throat.

CHAPTER THIRTY-NINE

The pale, almost translucent skin of the Englishman was reflected in the mirror-like steel. A thick blue vein stood out, running from behind his jaw to somewhere under his shoulder. It would take only a little pressure to open it.

Ash tightened his grip on the hilt. His palms were slippery. He stared at the passive, sleeping face, eyes gently closed and mouth just open.

Savage was pure evil. Ash would be doing the world a favor in killing him. It wouldn't even be hard; he was asleep and defenseless. This wasn't like fighting Ravana, or even any of the other rakshasas with their fangs and claws and totally negative attitudes. Ash had bathed in their blood, so why was his hand trembling now?

Just do it and feel guilty later.

But his arm wouldn't budge. He couldn't even get himself to lean over and sort-of-cut-Savage's-throat-by-accident.

Coward!

Would Savage hesitate? Would Parvati? It wouldn't even cross their minds. Ash was the Kali-aastra. Death was his job. But still he couldn't strike.

I can't kill a defenseless man.

"Difficult, isn't it?" whispered Savage, his eyes still closed.

"Don't move," warned Ash.

"I am completely at your mercy."

"I could kill you right now."

"Yes, you certainly could," said Savage. "But I doubt it. Heroes don't murder people in their beds."

"Just watch me." Ash leaned over Savage, the flat of the dagger on his skin.

"You do it and your friend will remain cold and dead in her grave."

"What do you mean?"

"The Brahma-aastra, of course. The Life Giver." Savage's eyes opened slowly. "I can bring your friend back."

"Yeah, as a zombie. No thanks."

"Listen to me, Ash. Do you think I'd waste all this time, money, and effort if I didn't know how to do it properly? I'm insulted you think so little of my abilities."

"How?"

"Let me get up and I'll show you."

Ash held the blade to Savage's throat. "You stay right there. Just tell me."

"Is that it? You expect me to talk?"

Savage was bluffing. He wanted to drag things out, hoping one of the rakshasas or loha-mukhas outside might come in and rescue him. Enough was enough. "No, Savage, I expect you to die."

Sweat shone on Savage's wrinkled face. "Listen," he said with rare desperation. "I've read the histories of Ashoka, how he tried to use it and all he awoke were monsters — zombies, as you call them — instead of living, breathing humans. Agreed?"

"The mantra, the spell, that activated the aastra was wrong," said Ash. "There's a mispronunciation in there, or some other error that's crept in over time. That mistake means that when you use the Brahma-aastra on the dead, they don't come back, not as they once were."

Now Savage smiled — sly, reptilian. "But there was one person who knew the correct, flawless mantra. He learned it from Brahma himself."

"Ravana."

"Yes. Lord Ravana knew the spell perfectly. But because he was a rakshasa, he couldn't use the aastra."

"And you know it? The proper mantra?"

"I know where it is. And with your help, I could get it and save your friend. I'm the only hope she has." Savage turned slowly so they faced each other. "The Brahma-aastra is no weapon. It cannot be employed for anything but healing. Used properly, it can repair any wound, cure any sickness, raise the dead. Look at me. I'm dying, boy. The diamond is my only hope. Do you honestly think I'd use it if there was a risk of being turned into some mindless, shambling monstrosity?"

"How do I know this isn't some plot to bring Ravana back? You did it before."

"You're the Kali-aastra, boy. When you killed Ravana, you killed him for good. And why would I bring him back now? I only freed him to regain my youth and learn more sorceries. I was going to destroy him myself afterward, using Kali's arrowhead."

"You're lying."

"Who would want to live in a world ruled by Ravana? Not me. I just wish you'd waited until I'd absorbed more of his magic, at least enough to stop me looking like this."

What should Ash do? Savage couldn't be trusted, but everything he said made sense.

And Gemma could be brought back to life. Hope surged through him again. Think what it would be like, having her back. All the damage, all the mistakes, would be undone. He could still save her.

"I'm no super-villain, Ash," said Savage. "I'm old, weak, and dying, trying to hang on to whatever life I have left. Would you deny a person, terminally ill, the chance to save themselves? Of course you wouldn't. Let me prove myself. If I am telling the truth, then think of the lives we'll save, starting with your friend. If I'm lying or can't awaken the Koh-I-Noor, then kill me. I won't stop you. I don't want to go on like this."

Ash lifted the dagger away. "One chance, Savage. That's all you've got."

"That's all I'll need." Savage swung his feet off the bed. He put his hand on the cane. "Shall we?"

"Wait." One hand still holding the katar point in Savage's back, Ash whipped his scarf around the old man's neck, so it became a leash. "I wouldn't want you running off." He pushed Savage out of the tent.

Ash kept close behind Savage, ready to use him as a shield if anyone tried to attack him. Everywhere he looked there were loha-mukhas and rakshasas. "Tell them to back way off."

"You heard him," said Savage.

The nearest, the Shiva statue and the stone lion, obeyed, their faces blank. The monkeys and the huge *David* watched, their joints creaking as they moved their heads to follow Ash and Savage's walk into the heart of the encampment. Seagulls cried overhead and the sea rustled below, but otherwise the only sound was Ash's galloping heart.

If Savage tried to double-cross him, it would be the last thing he ever did. Ash would skewer him and pray the death energies would be great enough for him to fight his way out.

"Looks like rain," Savage said, peering at the black clouds in the distance that just hid the dawning sun. "Morning, Jackie."

Jackie stood at the open tent, mouth agog and eyes saucer-sized on seeing Ash. She lunged forward but halted as Ash dug the katar in deep enough for Savage to cry out. "Stay where you are," Savage said.

"Let me kill him, Master," she snarled. "I want to eat his heart."

"I have other plans," replied Savage. "Ash and I are now . . . partners."

"But, Master —"

"No, Jackie." He met her gaze, and Jackie, growling deep in her throat, stepped back.

"Shall we get down to business?" Savage said.

The wind was picking up and lightning flashed on the horizon. Savage shuffled to the edge of the cliff, Ash close behind him. The wave tops frothed as the sea, so still and silent last night, churned far beneath them.

"This will do," said Savage. Ash realized they were on a square platform. Grass covered most of it, but bare stone could still be seen where the grass had been eroded. He looked back at the beach he'd swam from. Was this still part of that road that they'd found in the jungle? Then he turned back toward the storm, still so far away. Where did the road end? Somewhere out in the middle of the sea?

Savage touched the scarf around his neck. "You can loosen this."

The nearest henchman was Jackie, and she was just a pounce away. But Ash let the cloth slip free and wrapped it around his waist as a sash.

"Thank you," said Savage. "And now, to work." He raised his cane and peered far into the distance. His lips moving silently, his cane drew symbols in the air with sharp, swift cuts.

The ground around them trembled and shifted.

"What are you doing?" asked Ash.

"Things you wouldn't believe, boy." Savage pointed out to the sea with his cane. "You've heard of Lanka, I suppose?"

"Of course. Ravana's kingdom."

Savage grinned. Ash had seen that face before, frighteningly hungry and obsessed. "Out in the middle of the sea. And Rama's army, when he came for Ravana, was stuck on the land there, unable to cross."

Ash shook his head. "No. Rama's army attacked Lanka. Rama had them build a bridge stretching all the way across the sea. . . ."

His gaze fell upon the stone slabs under his feet.

"Not a bridge, but a causeway," said Savage. "That was four thousand years ago. The sea was lower then. Now the causeway's sunk under forty feet of water."

The waves rose and struck the island. Out in the distance the storm grew wilder. Great blinding flashes of lightning burst across the churning clouds. The wind howled around them, making Ash stagger.

"Lanka was a series of island kingdoms," continued Savage, "sustained by Ravana's magic. When he died, they disappeared, one by one, under the waves. They're still there, but many hundreds of fathoms deep. But that's where we'll find what we're looking for."

All around them, rocks and small stones rolled and bumped into one another. The earth beneath them surged and buckled, flexing like a springboard. One after the other, the loha-mukhas each turned to face the sea, watching the storm.

"I am master of the elemental sorceries, Ash," said Savage. "Air, Water, Fire, and Earth. I can make the very stones dance. And what else are these" — he spread out his hands to include the army of statues — "but stone, brought to life by me?"

Ash stared as slabs of stone rose out of the waves. Covered in seaweed and coral and dripping with barnacles, one after the other they broke the surface, creating a road across the water.

"You're raising the road to Lanka," whispered Ash.

"Yes," hissed Savage. His face was rigid with the effort. His skin peeled and flaked, and his body withered and reformed as the magic stole his life force. Ash watched as blue veins pulsed against his tissue-thin skin, and Savage bent double, as old and as frail as a skeleton. His white hair fell out in patches. "But not just the road."

By now the storm was in its full fury. Seventy-foot-high waves crashed against the rocks, followed by huge tidal waves and heralded by winds that caused the heavy statues to sway. Lightning dazzled the black sky and thunder roared like the screams of the gods.

Palace spires, ancient, twisted, black, and cruel, pierced the boiling waters from below. Ash watched tall towers, stout castles, and gardens made of coral rise out of the ocean depths. Water cascaded down paths and off roofs, rivers running from the heights of the palaces back into the sea.

Lanka, the capital of Ravana, rose out of the ocean.

CHAPTER FORTY

Savage screamed, his bones stretching and melting as the magic backlash hit him. The skull brands on his chest pulsed with light. His face melted like wax under a blowtorch, obscenely running and reforming, exposing raw muscle and bone as the body rearranged itself. His forehead bubbled and beads of blood dribbled from his eyes. Ugly blotches of pus and blood swelled under the skin and then sank away. He threw back his head and gave a hissing cry.

Ash watched with morbid fascination. This was more than just Savage's life force being robbed and fought over.

Savage groaned and stiffened. He clutched his head and pushed against the bloated lumps upon his skull. The magical energies within him twisted his limbs and marred his flesh with grotesque, cancerous growths. But Savage fought against them, and eventually he returned to his normal, though decrepit, shape.

Panting, saliva dribbling from his lips, he stared at Ash. "Now you understand why I need the Brahma-aastra. I cannot go on like this."

"I think you're mistaking me for someone who gives a damn, Savage." But briefly, Ash pitied the Englishman — and felt something akin to awe. Out where there had been nothing but sea, there now stood an island. If Savage could raise whole lands, then maybe he was telling the truth about the diamond. "I just want Gemma back, as she was."

"A promise is a promise." One of the loha-mukhas came up behind Savage and helped him slip on a fresh white linen shirt. "The secret to that lies in Lanka, upon the Black Mandala."

Mandala? Ash's dad had one at home. It was a religious painting, usually circular. Monks and other holy people used them to aid in their meditations. But he'd never heard of a black one. All the ones he'd seen blazed with colors.

"What is it?" Ash asked.

"Something Ravana created. In layman's terms, it is a scroll with the mantra of Brahma upon it. You give me an hour to study it, and I will awaken the aastra. I'll transport us to England, and you'll be holding hands with your friend before dusk."

Ash looked at the island. Water still cascaded down from the highest hills, and the entire place shimmered in the bright sunlight. The city of Ravana. He couldn't believe it. "What else is in there?"

"You tell me. You've been there before, as Rama."

Rama, one of Ash's past lives, and the human prince who had conquered Lanka. But nothing of the scene before him stirred any memories. Ash's focus was locked on to the first Ashoka. Maybe there wasn't any room for other memories right now.

"All I know are the myths," said Ash.

"Like me when I first came to India," Savage said wistfully. "Back in the eighteenth century, this country was a land of myths, as mysterious and as fantastic as that island over there. You have no idea how awe-inspiring it was to see my first elephant, to see the Himalayas. The wonder of it all."

"What happened?" The way Savage talked about India made Ash envious, almost. The marvel in Savage's voice was still there.

"I discovered many new things. I acquired great knowledge of an esoteric nature. I learned much, but understood little." Savage accepted a jacket from Jackie and adjusted a marigold in the buttonhole. "Look at Rishi. He was as powerful as I, but he restrained himself, avoided the traps I fell into. Magic's a drug: The more you use, the less effect it has, so the more you need to do even the smallest of spells. It is an endless downward spiral."

"Then why don't you stop? All the things you know, all the lives you've lived, couldn't you —"

"Use it for good? Is that what you're going to say?"

Ash blushed. It sounded so childish, but that was exactly what he meant.

Savage put on a pair of stout boots. "Don't you think I've tried? I taught others magic, hoping to create a society of wise men, but that failed. They competed against each other for power, wealth, and influence. Power corrupts."

"You had apprentices? Where are they?"

"In hell, I hope. It's as much as they deserve." Savage checked his cane, sliding out his sword and giving it a flourish in the shining sunlight before clicking it back in place. "But there is Lanka, and the day is passing. You and I, boy, are partners on a great adventure."

"That doesn't mean I trust you," said Ash.

A sly smile cracked over Savage's pale face. "Of course not."

Lanka lay before them, at the end of the wave-washed causeway. The storm had vanished as suddenly as it had arrived. Blue sky appeared through the patches of cloud, and the wind now just ruffled Ash's hair. Large waves broke on the beach, but they were half the height they'd been just five minutes ago.

Lanka glistened in the morning sun. The city looked like it had been made of coral and sculpted rock, not built, but grown. The spikes and edges of the buildings were ragged and sharp. It was a place where if you didn't watch your step, you'd be torn apart.

"Beautiful, isn't it?" said Savage.

"And dangerous," said Ash.

"Dangerous indeed." Savage's eyes, two black obsidian orbs, narrowed. "Are you afraid?"

"How can I be when you've got my back?"

Jackie growled, but Savage laughed and she backed down, her fur rippling across her shoulders. "Come, we are wasting time," said Savage.

Savage assembled his party: Jackie, of course; five of the hyena rakshasas; and five loha-mukhas. A pair of stone monkeys carried a set of heavy ironbound chests on their heads. Then came the six-armed Shiva and two winged gargoyles that looked as if they'd just come off the roof of Notre Dame Cathedral. It was like some bizarre expedition from the Victorian era, the brave white explorer and his native bearers. Ash wouldn't have been surprised if one of the trunks included a china dining set.

"We need all of that?" Ash asked.

"Lanka will be defended. Better we be cautious. I wouldn't want something unpleasant to happen to you."

"Sure you wouldn't."

The rakshasas led them down the steep path to the causeway, sniffing the route. Ash stayed close to Savage, his hand on the katar, the diamond in the satchel. The loha-mukhas trailed behind.

The road lay about a foot above the sea. Waves splashed across the weathered and seaweed-covered stone. Strange formations of coral had attached themselves to the causeway, decorating it with multicolored foliage. Bright greens, radiant yellows, blues, and golds all shone upon and within the rectangle slabs, as if they had been draped with gems.

Ash fell into step with Jackie. "Glad to be going home?" he asked.

"Lanka was the greatest city in the world, mortal. It is a holy place."

"Looks like it could do with a bit of paint."

Jackie glanced at him with a look of cold fury. "You killed my only two friends."

"And you killed Gemma," Ash replied, his voice low and threatening.

"A mortal? What was she?" Jackie snorted. "Mayar was a great, great rakshasa. He wore the skins of princes and feasted on the eyes of kings. Jat was a lord of birds; we ate the dead on countless battlefields. Carrion kings we were. And you killed them both. You, a small, pathetic child."

In spite of what he was, or was becoming, he didn't want to kill anything or anyone. But this close, it was as if he could smell Gemma's blood on Jackie's claws.

Jackie put her hand on Ash's chest, her claws just scratching his tunic. Two hyena rakshasas stood just behind her, and the other three, somehow, had slipped behind Ash. He glanced at Savage, but the Englishman was not paying attention in that "I know what's going on but I'm pretending I haven't seen anything" sort of way.

"Classic playground ambush," Ash said. His punch dagger sat tucked in his sash. "Really, Jackie? This the best you can do?"

Jackie knew how to grin, lots of teeth and bad attitude. "What's to stop me from just taking the Koh-I-Noor off you right now?"

Ash dropped his shoulder and the satchel slipped off. He caught it by the strap just before it fell into the water. "This?" He swung the satchel back and forth, higher and higher, holding the strap by a finger. "And what's to stop me from letting go and sending it to the bottom of the sea?"

Savage cleared his throat. "No more dawdling. We've still some miles to go."

"It's not over between us," said Ash as Jackie joined the other demons.

Where were Parvati and Khan? Ash constantly looked back, hoping to see them on the shore, but he was too far away.

He wished they could see what he saw. A bloody huge island with palaces and everything had just risen out of the sea. Even for Parvati, that had to be something special. And it was Lanka, her home.

Ash searched the chopping waves, wondering if there might be some boat out there bringing the two rakshasas to the island.

Instead he spotted the fins.

CHAPTER FORTY-ONE

Suddenly the causeway seemed terribly narrow and slippery. "Don't fall," warned Jackie. "I want to save you for myself."

"I can swim," snapped Ash.

Jackie pointed. "Won't make any difference to them."

A few of the dagger-cruel fins darted off to the side, and Ash saw a froth of water jet out. A curving, dark gray shape glided along the surface before submerging again. A whale.

The fins dipped under after it.

The other sharks changed direction and shot toward the commotion. The water churned and turned red as more and more of the deadly sea hunters attacked the whale. They slithered over one another and fought and gouged as great chunks of pink meat were torn off and shaken loose.

Ash stepped away from the edge as the waves lapped red over his toes. Even from here he sucked in the energy from the death, but it was sickeningly tainted, savage with mindless frenzy. The images of teeth and tearing and flesh slick with blood filled his mind, choking him. He wanted to stop it, but part of him craved more. A new strength surged through him. He licked his lips.

It went on for minutes, and all of Savage's party watched with mute horror or admiration. Savage, cane tucked under his arm, put a brass spyglass to his eye.

Finally the sharks broke away from their feast. A few smaller ones lurked and dived near the kill, but the bigger ones pushed their way back into the open sea. However, one pack swam toward the causeway. They were in formation, a tight, accelerating V with the biggest shark at the front.

They wanted dessert.

The sharks gained speed, and the waters rolled out in sharp waves. Black fins slipped parallel to the causeway, getting closer and . . . stopping.

"But sharks can't stop," whispered Ash. It was one of those freaky bits of useless information he knew.

Then slick, dark bodies with leathern skins and wide, long snouts clambered up onto the path ahead of them. Their beady black eyes were still fresh with desire and bloodlust, and in their grinning mouths Ash saw the serrated teeth of the ultimate predator. Their faces shrunk and narrowed as their tails split into legs, melding into human limbs. Their side flippers grew longer and thicker and were soon strong human arms. They resembled humans, and would have passed easily for them from a distance, but their eyes stayed the soulless black buttons of a shark, and their teeth remained ferociously wicked.

The leader of the sharks shook off the worst of the seawater. He picked a string of red flesh from his teeth and tossed it into the sea.

Savage stood his ground, immobile, as the rakshasa approached. Whatever else Savage was, he was not a coward.

The shark-man grinned, a smirk that could have fit Savage's head into it with space to spare.

"Looking good, Alex," said the shark-man.

"The same could be said about you, you old rascal," replied Savage. "Still chewing up Australian surfers?"

Then Savage and the shark rakshasa laughed and embraced.

After he greeted Savage and the other rakshasas, the shark-man came over to Ash. His gray skin shimmered with seawater, and Ash saw gill slits on either side of his neck. The rakshasa frowned and walked around Ash, inspecting him from all angles. "Tell me, how exactly did this piece of fish bait kill our king?"

"I agree, he's not much to look at," said Savage.

"Hey!" Ash said. What did they mean, "not much to look at"?

Half the pack remained in shark form, circling in the water. The other shark rakshasas waited ahead of the party. Of all the rakshasas Ash had seen, they were the least human, their skin thick and scaly. Two still had back fins, and all looked uncomfortable out of the water, moving unsteadily as they got used to having legs.

The lead shark-man, ignoring Ash, glanced back toward Lanka. "There are a lot of curses still in place. We've dismantled the outer ones, but beyond the walls, you'll have to tread carefully."

Savage smiled. "I would expect nothing less."

The sharks dived back into the sea, transforming before they'd even touched the water. Their fins sliced through the green waters and were soon lost among the waves.

"Let's move," said Savage.

Ash searched around him. There was sea in every direction. Even if Parvati and Khan were out there somewhere, with the loha-mukhas guarding the causeway and the sharks patrolling the ocean, the chances of them getting to Lanka without being torn limb from limb were pretty negligible.

And — *what curses?*

This was Ravana's capital. This was the heart of the demon nations. There would be treasure, for sure. Magic? Yeah, pretty likely. And none of it would be lying around in easy-to-access locations. The word *deadly* sprang to mind. So did *lethal, fatal,* and *extremely hazardous to your health.*

How did he keep ending up in these situations? Ash was going to have a serious talk with his career adviser when he got home.

It took almost half a day to reach Lanka. The sun passed over its zenith and began its descent over the land behind them. The causeway bore signs of extensive damage the closer they got. Great chunks had been broken off and turned to rubble.

With the city walls a mile ahead, the party paused.

"Battle stations," ordered Savage. One of the loha-mukhas, a monkey, lowered the trunk it had been carrying. Savage took out a leather gun belt and a bandolier that went over his left shoulder and clipped on to the belt just over his right hip. An old German Mauser "Broomhandle" pistol went into the holster across his belly. He jiggled the belt and bandolier, shifting his shoulders until the gear sat comfortably, and then he put on a pair of thin leather gloves, his tiger cane tucked under his arm. The leather creaked as he flexed his fingers and made a fist. Savage caught Ash watching him.

"What did you expect?" Savage asked. "A whip and fedora?"

"Why do you need them? Can't you just lightning-bolt everyone? Or just teleport us to where we need to go?"

"I could, but I prefer to save my magic for when it's truly necessary. You've seen what happens when I use it." He gestured to the satchel. "You want to save some of the power in that for Gemma, don't you?" He peered at the city walls. "And I can't teleport because I don't know where to teleport to. I've no idea of the layout. The last thing you want is to jump into a wall, half-in and half-out. Human and brick atoms are not very compatible."

Savage continued his preparations, checking and loading his pistol, then counting the rounds on his bandolier and spare ammo in the pouches on the belt. He double-knotted the laces of his boots and gave them a tug. "You won't believe the number of men I've seen die on a battlefield because they tripped over their laces."

Ash scratched his thumb. "It's the little things that make all the difference, right?"

Savage tapped the cane against his heel. "It's a shame we're not on the same side, boy."

"Yeah, like, together we could rule the galaxy."

"So sad. In my day we would quote Shakespeare or Homer."

"I can quote Homer. I've memorized entire episodes of *The Simpsons*."

"Master, we are ready." Jackie stood a few yards away, dressed for a fight. Her arms were protected with stiff steel plates with blades projecting from the forearms. Under her T-shirt, her body was covered in a light tawny fur, revealing her muscles across her shoulders and back. Her thick mane rippled in the wind and long fangs filled her elongated jaw. She'd taken off her shoes so her toes, long and tipped with sharp claws, clicked on the stone. Steel plates covered her thighs and shins.

The five hyena rakshasas were similarly armed, protected on the arms and legs, but not over the torso. Ash realized the armor they wore allowed them to transform safely: Wearing something over the body would have either prevented it from working or been excruciatingly painful, as their animal shapes were very different from their human ones.

"Let's move," ordered Savage. The monkeys hoisted the trunk back up and the party continued toward the city, with Ash walking alongside Savage.

"What are you expecting?" asked Ash. The island ahead of them had been sunk under the seas for thousands of years. What could possibly be alive in there that required all this?

"I'm expecting the worst. I always do. Helps me stay alive," said Savage.

"What are these curses that shark went on about?"

"After Ravana was killed, his brother, Vibheeshana, took the crown. He was almost as great a magician, but without the passion, without the ambition."

"What happened?"

"The rakshasas left. Soon the city was empty but for Vibheeshana and his court — noble rakshasas holding on to their faded glory. All rather sad and somewhat pathetic. Then on one fateful night there was a terrible storm. Waves, dozens of feet high, crashed onto the shore, and the land shook with violence. By the time the storm broke, Lanka had vanished."

"Just like that? It seems very . . . convenient."

Savage looked toward the island. "Some say it had only been sustained by Ravana's magic. With him gone, the island just collapsed. Others believe Vibheeshana himself destroyed it. Who wants to rule an empty kingdom? He was frightened that people would come and try to discover Ravana's secrets or search for treasure among the ruined palaces. So he lay curses and traps all over the island to deter the greedy, and then as a final precaution sent the entire thing to the bottom of the sea."

"Sounds like this Vibheeshana was a clever guy."

The walls of Lanka rose straight from the ocean. The causeway had been reduced to rubble for the last hundred yards, and Ash moved step-by-step, occasionally having to crawl over the broken slabs, slick with seaweed and covered in sharp coral and shells.

He almost didn't see that the rest of the party had stopped.

"This is it," said Savage.

Pearly white walls shimmered in the sunlight. When Ash looked deeper into them, there were a myriad of other colors swirling within, reds, pinks, greens, blues, and others, fractured and crystalline, sending multicolored beams deeper into the infinite space within the strange stone. The twisting rose-hued stones formed strange, glorious tree-like structures along the battlements, their branches made of coral and their trunks encrusted with barnacles. The city looked like it had become overgrown, but with petrified foliage.

Ash gazed up and up. "Those walls must be a hundred and fifty feet high at least." He put his hand against them. Perfectly slick; a total nightmare to climb. "You sure you don't want to teleport?"

"Please, Ash, assume I've planned for this." Savage turned and faced the sea. "I'd stand back too if I were you."

The sea looked perfectly calm.

"Any minute now," said Savage.

"Right. Any minute."

There were a few waves.

"Impressive," said Ash. "Not."

Then the waves rose and tumbled, white foam spraying along the tops. A huge mass moved under the water, rising. Ash pressed back along the wall, fast.

Yard by yard, a vast head appeared. Seaweed hung off it like green dreadlocks and water ran from its brow. Ash groped for handholds as a ten-foot wave fell over everyone on the causeway. Everyone, that is, but Savage.

Ash spat out the salty water. "So that's what you did with the Jagannath."

The giant stone creature rose until the water came up to its waist. Up close, in the daylight, it was still utterly awe-inspiring. The head creaked as it gazed down at Savage.

"Please give me a door," said Savage. He pointed at a spot in the wall. "Just there."

A massive fist pounded the walls, over and over again. First tiny lines burst like spiderwebs over the surface. Then chips shot off in all directions, and long, splintering cracks radiated out from the pummeled surface. The sudden, sharp blows echoed well beyond the other side of the city walls. The smaller loha-mukhas buried their fingers in the broken wall and tore out great chunks of the pearly stone, hurling them into the sea. It took no more than a few minutes before a hole had been made, roughly ten feet wide and seven feet high. The Jagannath stopped and stood still as seagulls circled around its head.

One of the hyena rakshasas crept near. He shook his mottled black fur as he inspected the hole, wrinkled his snout, and growled. He turned to Savage. "Smells bad."

"I'm not interested in the smell."

The hyena growled once more and leaped in through the opening. His claws skittered across the rubble, and then there was silence.

A sudden, petrified howl made Ash's hair stand on end. There was a bark and snapping of jaws, followed by another noise — a faint, mournful keening, or shriek. The hyena yelped, the sound of it fading as though it had fallen down a long deep well. Then nothing.

Savage peered in the hole. "Hmm," he said. "That's not a good sign."

CHAPTER FORTY-TWO

"After you," said Savage.

"Now why would I want to do anything that stupid?" asked Ash.

"I thought you were a hero, Ash. Heroes go first." Savage touched the wall. "You're the Kali-aastra, destroyer of demons, remember? And this is their city."

Ash met the cold, arrogant gaze of the Englishman. In the complete blackness of Savage's eyes, there was a thin circle of deep red where the edge of the iris would have been. Subtle hues lurked within — sometimes deep, like looking into the endless night sky, other times shallow, like black paint across glass.

"Well, if you're too chicken," said Ash, "I'll take a peek."

The rubble half-filled the hole the loha-mukhas had made. Light moved and played on the other side, strange shadows and colors sliding over the broken wall. Ash stepped in, breathing lightly, every muscle and nerve on hyperalert.

No sign of the hyena rakshasa.

Ash took control of his breathing, letting his supernatural abilities rise up out of the depths to stir the Kali-aastra into action.

The passage through the wall went on for hundreds of yards, even though the wall itself couldn't be more than fifteen or twenty feet thick. As he crouched in the opening, the exit was just a small bead of light at the far end of the crooked tunnel. It looked like reality was being left behind.

Lights danced within the translucent stone. Some of the lights formed almost complete shapes, humanoid and not; others drifted like jellyfish.

Ash shuffled a few yards in, fingers tight around his katar. There was no sign of the hyena rakshasa, except for a red stain within the wall that faded away the closer he got to it. The tunnel forced him into an uncomfortable crouch, moving crab-like, eyes and ears alert to any danger. He kept low to avoid the rough edges and sharp corners of the broken coral. Small spikes of stone jutted out from the walls, and water dribbled from the cracks, forming small sparkling pools.

"Ouch." Ash winced as he splashed into one. He hopped out and sat down, inspecting his sole.

A small spine of coral stuck out of the flesh. Not deep, and —

He pulls the spine out easily.

A spot of blood falls.

Coral spines grow out from the place the blood lands. They thicken every second, and from each branch more sprout, each covered with slim, needle-pointed thorns. Nails of stone mutate into knives, their edges serrated and designed for carving flesh. Within seconds the tunnel is blocked by a wall of deadly thorns, both ahead and behind him. Ash grabs hold, but more spikes erupt from the barriers, piercing his palms. Trapped, unable to go forward or back, he watches in helpless horror as long skewers rise from beneath him and sink down from above. He screams as they bury themselves in his limbs and torso. Blood sprays from his wounds, feeding more of the bloodthirsty stalks. Two narrow needles, their points glistening, push out from the walls and stretch toward his eyes. . . .

Ash rubbed his forehead and inspected his foot and the nail of stone sticking out of it. He had been seeing the future: Blood activated the trap. The hyena rakshasa must have stood on a spike or sliced a little skin on one of the edges, all easily done. And the more blood poured out, the faster the deadly stalks grew. He pulled out the small spike and wrapped his scarf around his foot. He'd have to tread carefully and stay out of the puddles.

So he moved slowly along, shuffling forward step-by-step and giving any edge or spine wide berth. Sweat dripped from his forehead, fat and hot, running down his tunic and limbs as he focused on the path ahead. It didn't look like he was getting any closer to the end. How long had he been in here? Minutes? Hours?

The sweat coated his palms and soles. The dampness soaked through the scarf, and when Ash picked his foot up, he saw the faint outline of a red circle on the shining stone.

Move, Ash, move!

Forearms crossed in front, he charged ahead as twigs of sharp coral burst out of the tunnel's inner walls. He barged through the branches, shattering them before they grew too thick, but he was scored with dozens of cuts. Spear-tipped stalactites sprang out above him. One tore a patch of skin off his back, and more stalagmites shot up, catching his heels with their slim, sharp tips.

Ash roared and dived forward as the tunnel filled with hundreds of teeth, a vast serpent closing its mouth, trapping him within. The exit was right before him, a bright shining light that stood for life and freedom, but if one more hook caught him, he was dead.

Ash tumbled out as the tunnel sealed behind him. He fell flat on his face on warm, sunlit stone. His clothing hung raggedly off his scratched and bleeding body, each cut stinging. "Mega-ouch." He rolled onto his back and gazed up, happy to see the sun and the sky and the clouds. Happy to be breathing and not completely holey, like a sieve.

The spears and nails of coral scraped against each other as they retreated back into the walls. The tunnel reopened, and within seconds there was no sign of the danger. It appeared temptingly safe.

He looked around. The street running along the inside of the perimeter wall was neat with wide marble paving slabs. Large bundles of green seaweed lay against the walls, with long strands crisscrossing the ground like a cat's cradle, or a web. The buildings here were just tumbled-down wrecks. Weird, twisted trees of coral and limestone rose out of the ground and wrapped themselves around the ruins.

But it was the shifting lights that caught Ash's attention. Shadows flickered across the ground, but there was nothing or no one to cast them. Black shapes slid in and out of the hidden corners, figures made up of the void, with no physical substance beyond the thickness of darkness.

And they whispered to Ash in languages long faded from the world, but full of urging. Cold fingers caressed him; shivers ran down into his soul.

"What do you want?" Ash asked.

Mumbling groans and pitiful moans. He felt the stone-heavy despair, the weariness.

"Well? Are you all right?" shouted Savage from the far side of the tunnel.

"I'm peachy. Come on through," said Ash. "Just don't cut yourself."

The creeping black shapes began to retreat, slowly, warily,

their dark thoughts still attending him. The whispers were cruel, angry, but Ash felt their trembling fear too.

Savage, Jackie, and the remaining four hyena rakshasas clambered through the tunnel, weapons drawn and eyes searching for danger. Next lumbered in the ten-foot-tall statue of Shiva, then came the two stone monkeys, one carrying Savage's trunk on its head, and finally the two gargoyles.

Jackie gazed about, mouth open in awe. "It's changed so much."

Of course. This had been Jackie's home, many lifetimes ago. For the first time Ash looked at the rakshasa with some sort of understanding. Eternal exiles, that was what rakshasas were; an outcast race. Jackie tenderly put her hand on a nearby door.

"Which way to the palace?" asked Savage.

Jackie bit her lip as she checked the path. Then she pointed northward.

Savage drew his pistol. "Let's go."

Ash had never been anywhere so alien. Towers formed of pure coral rose up beside jagged spires of crystal and metal. Streets shimmered with marble, and the squares were decorated with grotesque and monstrous statues of pocked and corroded bronze. Winged fiends with serpentine tongues and leonine bodies sat perched on the rooftops, their bodies covered with multicolored coral. Many of the buildings had been destroyed, and there was rubble and demolished remains everywhere. War had come to Lanka. Ash crossed a large crater, where the heat of some long-ago blast had turned the entire square to glass. He touched the smooth, curved pit edge.

"Aastras," said Jackie. "Rama and his army sent down fire from the skies. Lanka burned for many days."

"You started it," said Ash. "Ravana kidnapped Rama's wife."

Jackie laughed bitterly. "And you think that justified all this? The utter annihilation of a civilization?"

They walked on, doubling back where the streets had been destroyed by fallen rubble or transformed by coral and other growth that had crept over the city during the millennia it had lain at the bottom of the ocean. The sky darkened and the clouds shifted from pink to purple.

They entered a large square dominated by what looked like a giant swimming pool, easily over three hundred feet long and almost the same wide. Steps led down seven feet to the bottom. It was empty but for algae.

Ash noticed Jackie beside the pool, head bowed and palms pressed together. She was praying. As she finished, she met his gaze and started. There were tears in her eyes. Embarrassed, she abruptly wiped them away, then stormed off to speak with the hyena rakshasas.

A rakshasa crying? Ash hadn't thought it possible.

"The rakshasas are a warrior race," said Savage, standing beside him at the pool's edge. "They value their honor more than their lives."

"Like the Rajputs," said Ash. The Rajputs were a clan of ancient Indian warriors, and there were plenty of tales of their battles and wars. They would rather die than admit defeat.

"Yes. Very much like the Rajputs."

"Why was she crying?"

"What do you see, Ash?"

Ash looked at the pool. It was made of huge blocks of sandstone, fitted together so neatly there wasn't a gap wide enough for a slip of paper. It was clearly for water storage. "It's a tank, isn't it? This was how the city's water supply was distributed.

Some tanks would be for washing and bathing, some purely for drinking."

"Very good. What else?"

Ash walked along the pool. He spotted cracks and black smudges along the stone. "There's been a fire here."

"A huge bonfire, in fact. I imagine the sky must have been filled with smoke. Or flame."

"What did they burn?"

"When the Rajputs face certain defeat, do you know what they do?"

Ash nodded. "The men put on their finest clothes and jewelry and charge the enemy. They fight until every one of them is killed. A 'death or victory' sort of thing."

"You think that heroic?"

He frowned. This sounded like a trap. "Of course."

"Do you know what happens to the women and children? The old folk left behind?"

Ash shook his head. His eyes fell on the scorch marks and an uneasy dread crept over him.

Savage walked down into the vast pit. "The Rajputs would break up their furniture, their doors, everything and anything that burned. They piled it all in here. Then they poured ghee all over it. Ghee burns hot and fast."

Ghee. The thick, high-fat butter used in all Indian cooking. And it was also used to accelerate . . .

"They built a funeral pyre," said Ash. "This is one giant funeral pyre, isn't it?"

"The children they drugged, so they wouldn't know what was happening," said Savage. "Then, with their babies in their arms, the women leaped into the flames. The old folk followed so the conquerors would find nothing but ash."

"I . . . that's horrific."

"That is a warrior's honor. Jackie's people did this to themselves rather than face the humans' vengeance."

Ash stepped back. He didn't believe it. He didn't want to believe it. "But Rama. Rama was a good man. He would never let such a thing happen."

Savage laughed contemptuously. "Rama, perhaps. But he had hundreds of generals under him. They in turn had thousands of soldiers beneath each of them. Men who had suffered years of war, men who'd seen their cities destroyed and families massacred. Men who had nothing left in their hearts but hate and bitterness. Do you think they would be *restrained* when they conquered Lanka? That they would not take revenge?"

Ash said nothing. What could he say? Savage was right.

Savage continued, "I've seen slaughters like you couldn't imagine. There's not a war in the last two hundred years I've not been a part of. I've witnessed what man does to his fellow man, the things he'll do just because the other fellow's skin is a bit different in shade or he follows this god and not that one. If there's one thing we humans have always been good at, it's genocide."

Ash looked toward Savage. "Is that what's kept you going all these years? War?"

"You wound me, boy. Look at us. I am here to uncover the secrets of the Koh-I-Noor. Secrets your friend Parvati wanted kept hidden. How is she, by the way?"

"Still desperate to kill you."

Savage sighed. "Rakshasas know how to hold on to a grudge."

"You tricked and betrayed her, Savage. You took her father's scrolls of magic from her. But I think she hates you because you once promised to make her human. She'll never forgive you for that."

"Parvati's pure poison, boy."

"No, you just don't get her." Ash knew that, trapped between two races, Parvati suffered the worst of both — the immortality of her rakshasa heritage and the human desire for companionship, for love, with the loneliness of thousands of years of seeing loved ones and people she cared about die. The world moved on, but she didn't. "Perhaps you wouldn't be so keen for immortality if you really knew what it was like. It's a curse."

"A curse? Who doesn't want to live forever? You and I are the same, Ash. We've both cheated death once, and now we know it's possible; why settle for less? You want your friend back, and I want to see what lies ahead."

"We're not the same." The idea made him sick.

"Perhaps you are right. Once I discover how to fully awaken the Koh-I-Noor, I will be able to heal any sickness, cure any disease. I will be able to resurrect the dead. Tell me, is there any parent in the world who has lost a child who would not want me to succeed?

"Now, let us consider you, Ash Mistry. Your touch brings death to the guilty and innocent alike. It is a power you barely control. You worship a goddess who revels in death, and you are here for nothing more than revenge. Not to better the world, not to redress some wrong, just for revenge and to satisfy your own pride. I wield the Koh-I-Noor, the bringer of life. You are the Kali-aastra, and bring only death. Am I wrong?"

"That's not how it is. I'm not the bad guy here," said Ash.

Savage just smiled. But he was wrong. Wasn't he?

CHAPTER FORTY-THREE

"The greatest treasures will be in Ravana's palace," said Savage.

"And I suppose they'll be well guarded?" asked Ash.

"Exceedingly well guarded."

"By who? Or what?"

Savage looked up toward the buildings on the hills overlooking them. "By the most powerful spells. The most deadly traps and terrifying guards."

"What a surprise. Another suicide mission. And this is going to work because . . . ?"

"Because this time you and I are working together."

"Yeah, I'm not quite clear how that happened." Ash still couldn't pinpoint the moment he and Savage had gone from being mortal enemies to Best Friends Forever. "You'd better be right about this," he said.

"If I'm wrong, then I'm dead," said Savage. "But I'm not wrong."

The streets and buildings changed. The paths were wider, the buildings grander, and the atmosphere more . . . anxious.

The dull gray sky returned and spread a gloomy shadow over the city. The wind whispered, sad and cruel things just at the edge of hearing. It whirled down the streets and moaned through broken windows and empty doorways. Shadows continued to move of their own accord, not driven by any light Ash could see. No one spoke, and Ash's nerves were as tight as violin strings. He almost wanted some attack, some action. The waiting and the searching was exhausting, never knowing if a trap or some threat might be in the next doorway or around the next corner.

Ash touched the pale, shimmering marble wall and traced his fingers over the softly undulating curves. He winced at a sudden sting and drew his hand away sharply. Four red fingerprints remained on the surface before they were sucked into the depths of the marble.

"My fingers," said Ash, holding them up. "They're bleeding. I think the wall just bit me."

"We're in Lanka, boy," replied Savage. "An impossible realm."

Jackie halted. She held her breath and stared.

Savage joined her. "At last."

A wide avenue stretched out before them. The air rippled and parted. Ash peered at it closely, but it was as if he were trying to see something on the other side of a waterfall. The air was transparent, but fractured and disruptive.

"Ravana's palace," said Savage.

With those words, the view ahead crystallized into reality. The fragmented patterns of light, a view through a broken mirror, assembled into a single whole. Needle-like towers protected by a curtain of spikes. Walls of glass with passages of nails and spears. Long ribbons of shell lining the paths, their edges as keen as razors. The stones bore tormented faces, forever frozen in the ecstasy of torture. All Indian temples were decorated with apsaras, divine maidens of extraordinary beauty, heavenly houris. Here the apsaras were cruel and harpy-like, with talons and mouths filled with broken and jagged teeth, eyes glaring with fierce hatred. They clung to the columns and stalked along the upper balconies, immobile yet alert.

Icy fear stroked Ash's heart and shivered in his soul. The others clearly felt it too, and Jackie swallowed loudly.

A cloud of despair drifted off the tallest towers and spread across the city, shutting them off from any warmth or sunlight. This was a realm separate from the world of life and color, the gloomy, dead kingdom of a race that abhorred nature: demon-kind. Standing at its very heart, Ash sensed how the world recoiled from it. Every element of his body wanted to retreat.

Steps, cracked and tumbled, led up to a smashed, open gate. The rubble was oily from thousands of years of being submerged, encrusted with barnacles and littered with the flotsam of the deep ocean, with bones of ancient creatures and weapons rusted to almost nothing.

Jackie touched the ground reverently. "This is where we made our last stand." She gazed out across the city. "We'd heard rumors that Ravana was dead, but we'd sworn to defend his palace no matter what. You could see the banners of Rama's armies all the way to the city's edge. Mayar led Ravana's royal guard and I was there, by the outer courtyard. We'd all prepared for a glorious death."

"But that never happened, did it?" said Ash.

Jackie spat on the step. "No. Our new king surrendered. Vibheeshana, Ravana's own brother. He was as mighty as Ravana, but a coward. He knelt before Rama and handed over his scepter. A rakshasa, kneeling before a mortal. Even now I feel the bile in my throat. So instead of honorable death, we became exiles. Vagabonds. Thus ended the reign of Ravana."

Ash looked about him, at this ancient battlefield where a whole race was wiped out. He almost, *almost* felt pity for the rakshasas.

Here in this immense plaza, they had become a near-extinct species. In one day they had been toppled from their golden thrones to become refugees, hated and hunted by their conquerors.

Jackie looked out from a broken lump of rock. "The sky was on fire and you could hear the cries of the gods themselves. The universe trembled when Ravana died."

"I know. I was the one who killed him, twice."

"You have no idea what you did." The bitterness was still acid sharp, yet tempered with weary acceptance. The story of Ravana had finally ended in Rajasthan, and it had been Ash who'd written the last line.

Savage snapped his fingers and pointed at two of the hyena rakshasas. "Sniff it out."

They nodded and swept up the steps to the vast entrance of the palace. They nuzzled along the stones and snarled at the dark, open mouth of the doorway, and then both went in.

Savage looked back at the loha-mukhas. "Come on, then."

The statues remained stationary. The Shiva statue was still and the monkeys frozen with their tails high loops in the air. The gargoyles both had a foot in the air, midstep.

Savage glared and raised his cane. "I gave you an order."

They remained as still — *well, as still as statues*, Ash thought.

"Your spell's worn off," he said.

"No, it's been nullified," said Savage. He peered into the doorway, twisting the cane in his hands. If Ash didn't know better, he'd have thought Savage was looking a bit anxious. Maybe a little afraid.

What was in there? Something more powerful than Savage?

Ash was halfway up the steps already. Despite the dread radiating from the palace, he couldn't help himself. His curiosity was too great. How could he not want to look? Being in Ravana's palace was like being at the heart of time, at the greatest moment in humankind's existence. It was here that humanity had inherited the earth. All that had followed, the thousands of years of human civilization, its domination, was decided on this spot. What was inside?

Ash paused, still forty feet from the doors. He couldn't penetrate the gloom beyond the palace opening, but he felt —

From within, one of the hyena rakshasas howled. Then there was a hiss and sudden silence.

A moment later the rakshasa's head rolled out. It tripped down the steps, slowly at first, then tumbling faster as it built up speed, splashing wild patterns of blood over the marble with each bounce, until Savage stopped it with his boot.

"What a shame," he said, looking down at the dead eyes. "I rather liked him." He kicked it down the last few steps.

Ash breathed in the vanishing spirit of the rakshasa. This was death, and it was sweet. Power surged along his limbs and his heart swelled. He grinned hungrily at the perfume of spilled blood and drew the katar.

So, treading through the puddle of blood, Ash crept into Ravana's palace.

CHAPTER FORTY-FOUR

"Hello?" said Ash.

Hello. Hello. Hello.

"Anyone home?"

Home. Home. Home.

His voice echoed down and down into the palace. He sensed a yawning vastness before him. Cold air drifted around him and moaned in the space above him. Who knew how high the ceiling was? Columns wound their way upward, each one unique, disappearing into the infinite darkness. Some were stout, others slim, some carved with delicate designs and images, others faceless but threaded with veins of color in the marble.

Ash stepped farther in, a chill wrapping itself over him like a cloak of ice. Goose bumps rose up over his bare skin and clouds of frosty breath spread out as if he were exhaling his soul.

Savage and Jackie came in a few paces behind. The remaining two hyena rakshasas entered last, sniffing at the bloody trail left by their dead fellow. Savage had his pistol in his left hand, his cane in his right. Jackie prowled in semibeast form, still lumbering along on two legs, but hunched over with a huge muscular torso and thick, fur-covered arms. The click of her long toenails on the marble floor echoed through the palace.

Long spears of hazy, pearly light fell from hidden windows high in the walls. Glittering dust motes drifted in the cool wind and the slanting darkness, stirred as the trio passed by. Savage paused by Ash and silently handed him a flashlight. They stopped at the headless body of one of the hyenas. Blood soaked its fur and flesh, and the spine had been neatly, almost surgically, severed.

"Where's the other one?" asked Ash.

"Look," said Jackie.

Claw marks ran across the floor into a dark doorway. It looked as though something had been dragged away . . . something like a hyena rakshasa. The two left whined pitifully, and their tails hung low between their legs.

Voices moaned. The walls splintered like cracked ice, and Ash saw swirling images forming within. The stone began to bulge and grow as faces pushed themselves against the surface. Fingers, crooked and hooked, reached out desperately; mouths widened and long, eager tongues lashed out. Ash backed away, but Savage wasn't quick enough. One bony claw locked around his arm and pulled.

Savage put the pistol against the stony limb, and the hall thundered with bullets. They sparked as they ricocheted off the marble, and Ash ducked as one nearly clipped his ear. Savage struggled frantically, the sleeve of his jacket tearing free, and the pistol clicked on empty. But he was dragged closer, more hands and talons rising from the wall, embracing him.

Ash shoved the tip of his katar into a crack and twisted it sharply. The hand holding Savage shattered as if made of ice. Ash swept his blade into a pair of long claws, focused on the minute points of weakness he could see shining upon them, and they erupted into a thousand pieces. Jackie hauled Savage away as the limbs, snarling faces, and clutching fingers vanished back into the stone, denied their prize.

Savage wiped his forehead. He inspected his jacket with the sleeve dangling loose and pulled it off. "I must have words with my tailor. Such poor stitching." His voice shook, unable to hide the fear beneath the pithy remark. He shook Ash's hand. "Thank you."

I saved Savage's life, Ash realized. *I'm such an idiot.*

They descended a series of disjointed stairs. Some were wide with handrails of silver, studded with precious gems; others were of creaking rotten wood, and one was made of pale bone. Savage paused at each of them, inspecting faded symbols and writings that had been carved at various points and junctions. More than once he stopped to let the others get a few steps ahead before catching up. Eventually the party reached a narrow corridor. Unlike the rest of the palace, this one was mathematically square, the walls, floor, and ceiling each of identical length. Ash pointed his flashlight down it and saw that each surface was covered with tiles.

Savage wiped the slime off the nearest tile. "Interesting," he said. "Harappan pictograms."

Ash's blood went cold. Uncle Vik had been an expert on the ancient language of Harappa. It was the reason Savage had employed him. "Can you read it?" he asked.

"They're too badly worn away. This entire building has been submerged for thousands of years, so it's not surprising so much is damaged." He nodded to one of the hyena rakshasas. "Off you go."

The rakshasa sniffed the floor, then took a few steps. His paws brushed the algae covering the tiles.

A low, grinding noise shivered down the corridor. The long, rectangular path began to rotate. Sections twisted as if the corridor had been made up of five open boxes connected together.

One box turned clockwise, the other counterclockwise, the walls becoming the floor and the ceiling becoming the walls. The hyena rakshasa tumbled sideways, around and around as the corridor turned, not fast, but unevenly. He scrambled to the second section but failed to find his balance as the box turned in the opposite direction at a different speed. He left a trail of smeared green slime where he'd fallen and slid.

The grinding stopped and the corridor settled back into place. The floor on which the rakshasa had first stood was now the ceiling. His paw prints were up there, but then he'd slid down the side, across, back up to the ceiling, and down the floor and wall of the second section. He was covered in green, snot-like filth, but, shaking himself, otherwise unharmed.

"That doesn't seem too bad," Ash said. Sure, they'd get knocked about a bit, but as death traps went, he'd faced worse at the local summer fair. He took a step and —

Savage stopped him. The Englishman was staring at the hyena.

The rakshasa barked as tufts of hair shed off of him. He tried to get back to the group, but after a few wobbly steps, he slumped to the ground. His fur turned gray and his body began to decay. The fur sunk away until his pelt hung on mere bones, before the skin likewise thinned and crumbled. Within seconds there was just a skeleton, and then even that cracked, eroded to dust, and blew away.

"We need to get from here to the far end without touching the wrong tiles," said Savage. "Remarkably simple, if you know the right sequence of tiles."

"Do you?"

"Haven't a clue." He looked at the floor. "Fifty tiles on each face, four faces, five sections. A thousand tiles exactly, and probably only a handful safe to stand upon. And the corridor will start turning once you enter, so you must time your steps perfectly, otherwise you'll be tilted off, hit the wrong tile, and disintegrate."

Ash blew out a long whistle. "I've come across this before."

Savage looked surprised. Then he smiled. "Ah, in one of your past lives, yes?"

"No. In an old *Dungeons and Dragons* scenario, 'The Clockwork Maze.' A nightmare it was, with the map constantly changing and the traps moving positions. I lost my tenth-level paladin in that maze."

Savage said nothing, but just looked at Ash as if he were a lot less than sane. A lot less. But he'd survived the maze, thanks to Josh's wizard. And, as luck would have it, they had a real live one here.

"Can't you teleport to the other side?" Ash asked. "That's how we beat the maze."

Savage frowned. "Whatever blocked my control of the loha-mukhas is also stopping me from using my mastery over Space."

So, scrap the *Dungeons and Dragons* solution. Ash smiled at the last hyena rakshasa. "Good luck."

The demon whimpered and retreated, tail well and truly between his legs.

Savage watched him, tapping his heel with his cane. Ash didn't like it. "What?"

"You've changed, Ash. You've acquired an interesting disregard toward the suffering of others. I've seen it before, mainly in psychopathic killers, but rarely in a child. I really am most impressed."

"That's not true," he snapped back. "I care about a lot of people."

"You've just seen a living, sentient creature die quite horribly. You passed a headless hyena rakshasa earlier without batting an eyelid. Are you remotely concerned? No, you joke. I wonder: Why is it you're here?"

"To awaken the Koh-I-Noor. To bring Gemma back."

"Really? What were your feelings toward her? Do you really care for her, or do you merely want to assuage your guilt? You can't stand that you failed, and *that's* what hurts you, not Gemma's death. You just want to make yourself feel better. You don't care about her."

"That is not true." Savage was just trying to get under his skin. But Ash glimpsed the cowering hyena and there was a sharp rush of heat, shame, in his heart. The demon was afraid, and Ash had made a joke of it. What had Ujba said? That he should purge himself of weaknesses like compassion. He glared at Savage, chilled that the Englishman might be right.

Savage smiled. "And you call me a monster?"

CHAPTER FORTY-FIVE

Ash dried his palms on his trousers for the third time in as many minutes. He looked down the long, dark corridor and listened to the faint, melancholy whispers of the wind as it blew toward him. The flashlights lit the first ten yards; beyond were just glints of light on the ancient, slimy stone. He glanced over his shoulder. Savage, Jackie, and the remaining hyena rakshasa watched him intently. "See you on the other side," he said and stepped onto the first tile.

So far so good. He narrowed his gaze and channeled the power of the Kali-aastra to see ahead, just a second or two into the future. Visible to no one but himself, a soft, faint trail of golden motes stretched out in front of him. The lights shone and burned out, marking the routes that would kill him. He saw shadowy images of himself, his futures, explore the way ahead. Flickering and pale, like mirages, they stepped on tiles and worked their way along the ever-changing tunnel. Some faded away, destroyed by the traps; others grew stronger, more solid the farther they got, moving from one safe tile to the next. It was in his own footsteps Ash followed.

As he reached the halfway point in the first section, the ground started to tremble. It shifted clockwise and the terrible groaning of stone upon stone grew louder as he jumped to the next tile, already at an angle to the horizontal. He slipped on the wet green algae, tottering on the edge of the tile before leaping to the next, focused on the square some ten feet ahead.

Farther away, two of his future selves stepped into the last segment. One took a wrong step and vanished.

Ash landed as the floor became the wall and he searched for the next tile; he had only a second to jump. Which tile was it? What had been the wall was now the ceiling and the golden path to it was fading, while another was glowing brighter as it became the floor. Ash jumped, bouncing off one tile and onto another. His toes just touched the edge before he stopped. The next section of corridor was turning the opposite direction and faster. The golden paths were blinking on and off like strobes at a disco. No route was safe except for a second.

This was impossible. But he had to move; the ground was rotating. He sprang forward, ricocheted off one tile on the wall, and used it to launch himself another seventeen feet to a bright golden landing point in the corner of a floor.

Halfway there, almost over.

Idiot. You're only halfway. It can still go wrong if you start acting cocky.

Sweat dripped off him and his chest felt as if it were on fire. Every sense tingled and power surged through him. Ash catapulted forward, drawing on everything he had as all five sections of the corridor rotated, the first, third, and fifth clockwise, the others counterclockwise. He was unstoppable, hitting one tile and then another, his toes barely touching the stone slabs as he chased the golden path shining brightly ahead.

Ash slammed down on the hard marble on the other side of the corridor with both feet and skidded a few yards before turning back. God, his lungs burned! He stood there, taking huge breaths, but immensely relieved. He'd done it! He'd used his inner eye, as Ujba had called it, to see the future and plan out the safest route. Back down at the far end was the bright dot of Savage's flashlight. Ash just needed to explain which tiles were safe.

The flashlight blinked off.

The air hummed and Ash stepped back as a sudden draft rose from a rent in the air — a tear in space. Ash glimpsed endless night, a fathomless darkness decorated by minute shining points. The air turned blizzard cold, and then Savage was standing there, right in front of him. The tear vanished, leaving Jackie and the hyena rakshasa shivering where the rip had been.

"You said you couldn't use your magic," Ash snarled.

Savage shrugged. "I might have misled you a little, but I wanted to see what you were capable of. And may I say, I'm very impressed. You really are very good."

"You lied to me."

"Come now, Ash. Don't tell me you aren't a little pleased with yourself for having made it? Think of my trick as empowering you to new heights."

Ash wasn't having any of it. "Let's move."

CHAPTER FORTY-SIX

Down, down, and down they went. Sometimes they wandered in the darkness, guided only by the beams of their flashlights and Jackie's memories. Other times they would enter halls lit by strange glowing ghosts, ethereal bodies that haunted the ruins. But always down.

The ceiling of the latest room curved over them, making Ash feel as if he were descending into the throat of a monster. The support beams arched like a beast's ribs. The upper ridge of keystones could have been the joints of a spine.

Broken mirror frames lined the walls. The glass lay shattered upon the floor. The light in here, rather than being reflected in the glass, rose out of it.

Ash took a few more paces in before he spotted something on the floor among the debris. He picked it up.

A pair of reading glasses. The lens of one was broken and flecked with blood. The frame, thin and bent, had two large hooks behind the ears so they'd sit firmly in place no matter what happened. Ash straightened out the kink. The glasses looked familiar. He looked into the lenses.

*   *   *

Ash stumbles down the slope toward the Mercedes. The car lies crumpled, the tires torn and the roof caved in. His uncle and aunt are in there.

The smell of gasoline clouds the air as he approaches. Broken glass is scattered over the dusty, furrowed earth. There is a constant tapping sound. His heart quickens.

"Uncle Vik?"

Ash?

Ash runs forward and crawls into the car. He waves an object in his hand. "I found your glasses."

His uncle sits in the driver's seat. His head is distorted and blood seeps from a hole in his forehead. The tapping sound comes from the wiper hitting the bent frame of the windshield.

Ash takes his uncle's hand. "Are you hurt?" he asks.

We're dead, Ash.

Ash looks to the rear. His aunt lies there, her neck broken. "Why?"

Because of you, Ash.

He wants to deny it, but it's true. They would be alive, but for him. "I . . . I didn't mean to."

You are the Kali-aastra. You kill everything you touch.

"No, it was an accident."

Aunt Anita sits up, and her hideously twisted neck creaks as she turns her lifeless gaze toward him. Her fingers, broken and black, touch his neck softly, but firmly.

Uncle Vik faces him. He smiles and blood swells in his mouth, dripping down his upturned face. We miss you, Ash.

"I miss you too."

Stay with us. That way we won't be so lonely.

"Okay."

Aunt Anita's fingers tighten around Ash's neck, but he doesn't fight back. He killed them both and should be with them. He deserves this.

His breathing is hoarse and his head pounding as his air is cut off. His vision goes murky and dark. He's dimly aware of a white shadow in front of him, one of bright silver steel.

The fingers drop their grip and Ash gasps. He stares around, bewildered, as Aunt Anita screams.

Savage drags his aunt out of the car, pulling her out by her hair. She flails at him, but Savage is young, strong, and utterly ruthless. He throws her to the ground and drags the blade from his cane.

"No!" Ash cries out.

Savage pushes the sword into Anita's heart. Blood spurts as she screams, washing his white suit in crimson. He tugs the blade free and approaches Ash's uncle.

"No!" Ash hurls himself between Savage and Uncle Vik, but Savage knocks him aside without breaking his step.

Uncle Vik hisses, eyes red with rage and unholy bloodlust, but Savage, gaze cold, flicks the tip of the blade across his throat. Uncle Vik covers the wound, but the blood washes through his fingers and he sinks to the ground.

Ash, knees in the dirt, stares up at the Englishman.

"You killed them," he accuses.

"No, Ash. You did." Then Savage twists the glasses from Ash's grip and tosses them away.

Ash gasped. He gulped big, lung-swelling quantities of air as if he'd been drowning and just broken the water's surface.

"What . . . happened?" It had been just like he'd remembered — his uncle and aunt dead from the car crash. The stink of gasoline lingered even now.

"Mastery of the humors. A combination of Black Bile and Phlegm, which control the emotions and mind, and used to manipulate your dreams," said Savage. "We're up against someone very, very good."

"And you were there too." Savage had gone into his mind. The thought made him sick.

"I had to come in to save you." Savage brushed the dirt from his clothes. "You entered a nightmare and it almost got you. Someone looked into your heart and found what you feared most."

"Death? Being killed?"

"Hardly. No, you fear failure. You feel you should have saved your uncle and aunt, and the guilt of failure almost killed you, Ash. The same as with Gemma." Savage slipped his sword back into his cane. "You want to be this superhero who always succeeds. The sort who always does the right thing and goes the right path. I sympathize. I was just the same, once."

"You, a hero?" Ash scoffed. "That'll be the day."

He heard a deep, distant rumble, and the roof above them creaked. A light sprinkle of dust fell over them. He looked up and saw thin cracks along the stone. "How far underground are we?"

"Many fathoms," said Jackie. "Ravana's private chambers were deep under the sea, inaccessible but for this route."

"What else is down here?" asked Ash.

"Let's go find out." Savage pushed Ash, not softly, ahead. "Let's not linger here. We don't want you having another nightmare."

CHAPTER FORTY-SEVEN

The hall's roof rose over two hundred feet above their heads, supported by a forest of columns. Broken statues lay scattered across the floor as if they'd entered the lair of Medusa. Some were stone, others bronze or strange metals that glowed with golden light, casting weird shadows across the shimmering water that rippled ankle deep across the floor, which was itself one unimaginably huge mosaic. Ash couldn't take it all in — it was too big — but he could see what it was. A map.

Upon the map, awesome dragons flew across sapphire skies and creatures strode across mountains and shining cities, where courtiers sat among soft cushions, their attention captivated by jewel-clad dancing girls. At the summit of a snow-clad mountain, wreathed in swirling clouds, sat Ravana, lord of all. Beneath him, wrapped in chains and kneeling in humble homage, were the gods. There was war, there was love, death, and birth, and the lives of maharajahs and peasants, of gods and demons. Ash followed a line of blue rivers as they crossed empires that were now less than dust.

"Ravana's kingdom," said Jackie with soft awe. "He was the first Alamgir."

Ash recognized that word from one of his books about the Moghuls, the ancient emperors of India. It meant "Universe conqueror." But if anyone had the right to be called Alamgir, it was the demon king.

Water dripped down from the ceiling. The groaning from without was louder now, and it sounded like the sea was pounding against the building's shell. The remaining hyena rakshasa sniffed at the nearest column, then relieved himself on it.

"Are we totally lost or what?" said Ash.

"No, we're very near." Savage scrutinized his surroundings. "Though being near isn't good enough. It's the last step that's the most slippery." He checked his pistol, drawing back the slide and letting it slam sharply back in place. The abrupt metallic rap sounded like a gunshot in the vast space.

"We expecting trouble?" Ash asked.

Savage shook his head. "No. Trouble's already come."

A splash brought Ash's attention to the wavering shadows ahead. One after the other, long-dead lamps rose into the hall, casting a chaotic battle of swaying and entangled images across the columns, across the water. The flames multiplied a thousand times, a million, on every wave and droplet.

The air in front of them shimmered and the lights around it spiraled with dazzling colors. Ash shaded his eyes as a dark outline began to form within the white heart of the blaze. A gale suddenly screamed to almost ear-piercing heights, forcing them back. The wind bit Ash's bare skin so hard it burned. Then it calmed and the light died. Ash blinked the white spots out of his sight.

A man stood before them. Ten feet tall and naked but for an elegant white and gold loincloth, he was young and slim, and his dark skin was covered with occult symbols. Ash realized the figure was standing on the water's surface, only his soles getting wet. The symbols slid and mutated over him, merging and rewriting themselves constantly. Upon his forehead, like a third eye, was a glowing brand. Even from this distance Ash counted nine skulls.

Nine sorceries. Savage knew only seven, and he was the greatest sorcerer in the world.

Ash had a bad feeling about this. Really bad feeling.

The man's black-on-black eyes gazed over the party.

Savage tucked his cane under his arm and bowed. "My lord Vibheeshana."

CHAPTER FORTY-EIGHT

The demon lord, Ravana's brother, kept his distance, but even from here Ash sensed the power surging within the immortal's spirit.

"You must turn back," he said simply.

"I served your great brother, my lord." Savage stood up now, coolly appraising the rakshasa prince.

"You serve only yourself, Savage." Vibheeshana's voice sank low and the threat within it was unmistakable. "And do not take me for a fool. I know why you are here."

"I also know of the vow you made to Rama." Savage smiled contemptuously. "The deal you made so that you could take Ravana's throne when he died."

"Deal?" asked Ash. "What deal?"

Savage continued, his eyes never leaving the demon lord's. "It's well-known that Vibheeshana sided against his own kind, that he served Rama and betrayed his brother."

"My brother was on the path of destruction. If he had only listened, he would not have brought doom upon himself and his people."

"He died honorably, as a warrior should," snarled Jackie. "Not cowering behind the skirts of a mortal, begging for his life."

"You forget your place, dog," said Vibheeshana. His eyes glowed and the air hummed electric around him, momentarily wrapping him in a haze of heat and power. The water under his feet bubbled and hissed. The demon lord hadn't made a move, but those glowing brands, the cool confidence, the utter lack of fear couldn't have been a clearer warning.

Do not mess with me.

Savage, Jackie, one rather petrified hyena rakshasa, and Ash. Against a demon lord. They should quit now. He could wipe the floor with them. But then Gemma would stay dead. Ash had come so far, but Vibheeshana had powers that were off the scale. Ash tried to use his marma-adi to search for some weakness, but the golden spots never settled on the rakshasa; they just flickered and drifted away. It was all too unclear.

Vibheeshana shook his head. "I saved our race, our existence. Do you not understand? There were those in Rama's army who wished our total annihilation. For what Ravana had done, can you truly blame them?"

Savage straightened. "You swore to serve Rama, and in exchange he gave you the throne of Lanka."

"Even when it sank beneath the waves, I did my duty. There are treasures here that must never leave." Vibheeshana met Savage's gaze. "Treasures you cannot begin to comprehend."

"Look, sir," said Ash. "We want to awaken this." He held out the Koh-I-Noor. "We just want the Black Mandala."

"Child, you have no idea what you ask."

Ash shoved the diamond back in the satchel. "It's the only way I can save my friend."

"Stand aside, lord," said Savage.

For a guy facing a demon lord who was master of nine of the sorceries, Savage seemed incredibly sure of himself. Ash hadn't moved and, he noticed, neither had Jackie.

Savage joined Ash. "You are my ace of spades, Ash."

"He's already tried to kill me with the dream," said Ash.

"No," answered Savage. "He used your own guilt against you. That's subtle, but once you know the trick, easily beaten." Fire sparked within Savage's black eyes. "Remember your oath, Lord Vibheeshana? Your oath to your master and king, Rama?"

"I remember."

"You swore to serve him *forever*."

The demon lord's gaze faltered. "I did."

What was going on?

Savage put his hand on Ash's shoulder. "Just ask him for the Black Mandala. He'll give it to you."

"Why would he give *me* it? I'm just . . ."

Ash Mistry. Yes. But you've also been Ashoka, first emperor of India. And a Trojan noble. And a Spartan warrior.

And, once, a prince of Ayodhya. Rama.

Ash looked at Vibheeshana. "Give me the Black Mandala, my lord."

Vibheeshana raised his hand. "Sire, please reconsider. Come no farther."

Savage pointed his cane at him. "And who's going to stop us?"

The sound of metal sliding across metal, the sound of razors caressing each other, was unmistakable. A figure stepped out from behind a nearby column, lithe, clad in green scales, and emerald eyed. Her long black hair had been swept up and tied in a compact braid. In her hand twitched the urumi, the serpent sword. The four whip-like blades hissed with anticipation.

"I am," said Parvati.

CHAPTER FORTY-NINE

"You took your time, Ash," said Parvati, her eyes never leaving Savage's.

The hyena rakshasa cackled and Jackie dropped to all fours beside it, now more beast than woman, all except for her deformed head, which was a grotesque amalgam of both. Jackie and the hyena spread out to either side like stalking predators, wary but searching for an opening in Parvati's defenses.

The hyena sniffed the air. It paused, eyes widening as the hall echoed with a deep-chested growl. A huge tiger appeared from between the thickset columns, his golden eyes glistening with pending violence. Khan had joined the party.

Wow. This gathering was about to go cataclysmically bad any second now. Ash came closer to the tense trio of Parvati, Vibheeshana, and Savage. He needed to calm things way, way down.

"Listen, Parvati, I need Savage alive," he said. "He can help me."

"Stand aside, Ash."

"Listen! He can resurrect Gemma with the Brahma-aastra. I know he can."

Parvati showed absolutely no emotion. "There are bigger things at stake than a single girl." She raised her fist and the urumi blades began to weave in the air as though they possessed life of their own. "This has been a long time coming, Savage."

Parvati flicked the urumi and the blades whipped out, four silver tongues of lightning, any one capable of decapitating a man. Ash leaped between Parvati and Savage, his katar ready. With one hand he shoved Savage aside, and with the dagger he knocked one, then two of the blades off their path. The third shot across his leg and the fourth sliced his face, drawing a thin, stinging line across his cheek. A few inches lower and it would have opened his throat.

"Step aside, Ash." Parvati drew the urumi in, slowly circling to get a shot at Savage.

Ash touched his stinging cheek. "What was that?"

"A warning. There won't be another."

"You're my friend, Parvati, have you forgotten?"

"You're mine, Ash." Her steps barely stirred the water. "But if you don't get out of the way, I will kill you."

Jackie, aided by the remaining hyena rakshasa, circled Khan. Her bristles were up and stiff, and she slavered and snapped angrily at the silent, bright-eyed tiger rakshasa.

Ash had a chance to save Gemma, and Parvati wasn't going to let him. What did one more death mean to the demon princess? Nothing, less than nothing.

But she was his friend. Ash lowered his katar. She deserved one more chance.

"Please, Parvati. Let me save Gemma."

Parvati paused and the four steel whips fell silent beside her. Then her lips thinned with harsh conviction and she replied grimly, "No."

Fire rose in his veins and intense heat flooded his heart, accelerating it and opening floodgates of adrenaline and more.

The Soma. He shivered with the growing power, the brightest pain focused in the center of his forehead.

Golden lights spread over Parvati, lights only Ash could see. Not only did he spy the golden death points, but he glimpsed glittering lines, paths, through the space between them. They ran from her to him and back again, ever-changing patterns of attack and defense. Moves and feints exposed themselves so he could see the fight spread out before him. He watched a weaving path that would mean his death, and he watched new snaking lines shine bright, showing him how to turn defeat into lethal victory.

Ash closed his eyes. He breathed deeply, feeling the Soma possess him. Then, eyes narrowed so as not to be blinded by the bright, shining paths all around him, he surrendered himself to the dance of Kali.

CHAPTER FIFTY

Parvati shot past Ash, intent on killing Savage. Ash ducked under the screaming steel whips and knocked her arm aside, spoiling the attack. She stared at him for a fraction of a second, bewildered, then retaliated with a shockwave of jabs and kicks that slid and slipped between his defenses, forcing him back. The paths exploded in all directions and Ash reacted like lightning, parrying a finger strike to his throat, untangling himself from a choke hold, and launching his own counterattacks against half a dozen bone-breaking strikes, any one of which would have crippled him.

Without the Kali-aastra, without the Soma, he would have been dead ten times over in just a few seconds. He somersaulted high over Parvati, bouncing off the nearby column to land forty feet away.

Elsewhere, Savage fought Vibheeshana. Fire and shimmering walls of heat burst all around the Englishman as the demon lord threw a wave of ice daggers at him. The hall thundered with the sound of the supernatural forces the two men summoned. Walls creaked and columns buckled and shook.

Ash's body ached and he was panting already. He rested, crouching, trying to get his breath back, trying to get some cool air into his burning and bruised lungs.

She's trying to kill me.

Parvati stepped backward on unsteady legs, sweat dripping over her pale face. She put her palm against a red swelling on her cheek.

"That . . . hurt." There was a hint of a cold smile as she said it. "Not bad, Ash."

Had he done that? He hadn't even realized.

"It doesn't have to be like this, Parvati."

"Then stand aside and let me kill Savage."

The air dropped ten degrees and the water drained away from around Ash's ankles. He felt the air rush around him, a freezing wind that accelerated and became a scream.

Savage drew up a wall of water, first thirty, then fifty, then seventy feet high. The wave shivered and undulated, held in magical stasis as frost and then ice spread across the surface, creating a solid wall. The ice creaked and groaned. Splinters, long dagger-shaped shards of frozen water, sheared off and multiplied.

Ash dived behind a fallen column as Savage sent wave after wave of razor-sharp spikes across the hall toward Vibheeshana. Small skin-slicing splinters, others large enough to skewer a horse, and still others the size of boulders, exploded as they smashed into the stone columns and punched craters into the mosaic, hurling up more shrapnel. The ceiling shook and quivered as the columns that supported it and the sea above began to weaken. Vibheeshana stumbled back as the minute blades cut his skin, and then he whipped his hands in front of him so the ice evaporated into a bellowing cloud of steam, filling the hall with hot mist.

Howls and roars echoed from the spreading fog as Khan and Jackie fought. The hyena rakshasa lay dead on the floor, its throat torn out, head still on by a strip of fur.

And Ash stalked Parvati.

CHAPTER FIFTY-ONE

She's my friend.

> *But she's a demon.*

> *She saved my life.*

> *But she has killed thousands.*

The confusion flooded Ash's head. He couldn't think clearly. The Soma? Was it affecting him? Making him see Parvati as something that had to be destroyed?

She is good. She's just doing her duty.

And you are the Kali-aastra. Do yours. Kill the rakshasa.

The punch came out of nowhere and almost took Ash's head off. He fell head over heels and sprang up, dazed, but on automatic. A cross-arm block stopped the kick and he avoided the body slam with a sudden handspring. Still, as he shifted into a battle stance, his senses swam. The mist hid everything beyond a few yards away.

"You're trying to kill me," said Ash.

Silence and fog. Parvati was an assassin, and would use both to take him out.

All around him lay rubble: huge chunks of floor smashed apart, leaving craters and fallen columns. The roof above groaned ominously as somewhere in the distance another huge column crashed down, sundered by the magic swirling between Savage and Vibheeshana. Both were using their command over the elements, Savage now brutally raising fires and winds and ripping open the stone while Vibheeshana deflected and quashed the attacks just as rapidly. The air itself hummed with electric currents, and sparks buzzed and flew across the fog. Elsewhere, Khan roared and Jackie howled as they fought each other.

How did I end up on the "bad guy" side of the fence?

Ash stepped across a wide, jagged crack in the floor. The mosaic, once filled with dark beauty, was in ruins. The small tiles had been scattered in all directions and large chunks were nothing but powder now.

There was only one way to end this. Ash wanted Gemma back, but what was the price? He peered into the haze and caught a glimpse of silvery steel and a vague figure stepping closer.

Did she want him dead? Really?

Parvati could have bitten him. Her poison guaranteed death. But she hadn't. She'd tried to disable him; that was what these attacks were.

They'd been through so much together. Fighting each other was utterly wrong.

But it came down to Gemma. He knew Parvati: The only way through her was to kill her.

It was her or Gemma.

Ash thought of Gemma taking his coat. The way she smiled at him in class. They'd been friends since primary school. They'd played that stupid board game every day, all summer.

She was dead.

"Parvati, please. I just want to save my friend."

"I am sorry, Ash." The voice whispered out of the fog, from a direction unknown. "But Gemma is gone. If Savage tried, what you'd have is a monster."

"Not if he recited the proper mantra. From the Black Mandala."

Parvati laughed. The sound was cruel and sad. "The Black Mandala is the ultimate source of my father's power. Savage wants it not only to awaken the Brahma-aastra, but to learn the remaining sorceries. He'd be as great, as terrible as Ravana, the master of all reality. He's been using you, Ash. Now do you understand?"

He felt lost. "But Gemma . . ."

Parvati appeared. The fog rippled around her as she approached. The urumi dangled in her loose grip. "The Black Mandala should stay here." She dropped the weapon. "But the choice is yours." Parvati touched his cheek. "Let her go, Ash. For both your sakes."

"I . . ."

The sound of breaking stone was as loud and sharp as a cannon shot. Chunks of marble shot through the air and knocked Ash off his feet. He crashed down, shaken to his bones. Blood, hot and sticky, dribbled down his back as he tried to get up. His spine screamed and he fell back on his face.

The column above him groaned as the supports cracked, then shattered. With an awful slowness, it began to topple. Dust showered down as blue electric sparks jumped and burst across it, breaking off chunks and slivers that tumbled like the beginning of an avalanche.

Ash stared, paralyzed, as the pillar collapsed. He struggled to his knees, but the dark mass of the falling column covered him, and all he could do was watch it accelerate toward him. He wasn't going to make it.

Parvati grabbed him and twisted hard, spinning Ash out of the path of the crumbling tower. The impact threw him off his feet and the sound almost burst his eardrums. He couldn't even hear his own screams.

Ash lay on the floor, gasping in the dust. Thin trickles of blood ran down his torso and limbs from dozens of cuts. He put a hand against his back and pulled at a blood-slicked marble shard, fighting the sickening agony as the edges cut along his spine. Then it came free and Ash gasped with relief. Slowly he got to his feet. He wasn't dead yet. Biting down on his lip, he wrenched out the splinters in his arms. Blood dripped from the gaping holes, and Ash stumbled with dizziness.

All around him columns began to bow and crack. Great tears rent the ceiling as jets of seawater poured through the fractures, each one expanding moment by moment as lumps of stone tumbled down. The hall was collapsing in on itself. Already the water was splashing around his knees.

Ash approached the fallen column, sweeping the dust from his face. "Parvati?"

Blocks the size of a car lay within a cloud of dust. The floor beneath them was cracked and thrown up like the frozen surface of a wave.

Ash spotted a glimmer of metal and picked up the urumi. Two of the blades had been sheared off and the remaining pair were pitted and scored by the stone. He dropped to his knees, gazing hopelessly at the immovable rubble. "Parvati?"

CHAPTER FIFTY-TWO

Ash heard footsteps rapidly approaching him. The dust and fog parted as Vibheeshana appeared. He stared at Ash, then at the weapon in his hand. Ash dropped the urumi.

"She's trapped," he said as he tried to shift a huge boulder. She had to be trapped. The alternative was too horrible to think about. He sweated and strained, but it didn't move a fraction of an inch. "Help me."

"Step away." Vibheeshana's skin shone with sweat, and he was cut and bruised all over. He moved slowly, and his breath was ragged. Savage had hurt him badly. But he gathered himself, straightened, and pressed his fingers together, weaving and locking them in weird bone-flexing patterns. The nine skulls pulsed with a stark, golden light.

The rubble began to rise — delicately at first, so as not to cause any of it to fall on top of another piece and crush Parvati. Small brick-sized lumps floated away, trailing pebbles behind them. Vibheeshana closed his eyes as his lips moved with silent spells.

The larger rocks began to float impossibly and drift off.

"Come on," Ash whispered.

They would save her. Vibheeshana would lift the rubble away and they'd save her.

A giant rock rose over him. Ash blinked as grit fell into his eyes. Then, the shadow of the rock having just passed over him, it smashed to the ground.

"Vibheeshana?" Ash said. That almost crushed him!

Vibheeshana groaned, arching his back. He jerked again, staring wildly at Ash. His lips reddened and parted, and blood dribbled down his chin. A narrow steel sword blade tore through his chest in a sudden burst of scarlet. He went up on his toes as the blade, pushed from behind, stuck out farther and farther. He reached out to Ash, asking him to help, to do something. Ash took the demon lord's hands, and Vibheeshana crushed his with desperate strength. The sword began to draw itself out, sinking into the dark flesh, where the sigils thrashed and squirmed as blood covered them.

Vibheeshana collapsed, Ash holding on to him as they both sank to the ground.

"Sometimes it's worth getting your hands dirty," said Savage, stepping over the dead Vibheeshana with sword in hand. He wiped the blade clean on his sleeve, marking the white cloth with long strips of crimson, and slid it back into the cane. He smiled at Ash, a grotesque leer through blackened teeth and shriveled gums. "Thanks for distracting him. I couldn't have done it without you."

Ash stared at the bleeding corpse. His fault. His fault. Oh, God, what had he done? Vibheeshana dead and Parvati under tons of rock. He couldn't save either.

Savage must have seen the confusion and misery on his face, because he laughed. "Still such a child, aren't you? Didn't I warn you once not to get involved in grown-up plans?"

Ash spun around, but Savage raised his cane, and a rock shot out from the pile and hit Ash square in the forehead, knocking him off his feet.

Savage stood over him. Ash could make out three blurred images, melding and splitting each time he blinked. Waves of nausea rolled over him as the pain in his head swelled and rolled, overwhelming him. Savage flicked his narrow sword so the point was above Ash's shoulder. He pushed the point in.

Ash cried out as the Englishman twisted the blade. Then, with a second flick of his weapon, he cut open Ash's satchel.

The Koh-I-Noor fell out. Savage put it in his jacket pocket.

"I don't need to kill you," he said. "But you'll never know why."

Then he blew some dust off his cane, rubbed the tiger head clean, and tapped it against his forehead in salute. "Good-bye, Ash Mistry. It's been a pleasure."

Savage left. His laughter echoed long after he'd gone.

CHAPTER FIFTY-THREE

"Rama . . ."

Ash groaned. The pain throbbed in the center of his skull as if someone had put a jackhammer in his brain. He got up and gasped as the agony multiplied. His head weighed about a million tons. He clutched it with both hands, afraid it was going to break apart.

"Rama . . ."

Ash opened his eyes and let his vision clear. Out of the fading blurriness he saw Vibheeshana. His fingers twitched and his mouth moved.

"Rama . . ." said the demon lord. "Hurry."

Ash crawled to him, ignoring the blood staining his hands and knees. He lifted the demon lord so his head rested on Ash's lap. Vibheeshana looked up at him. "My lord Rama. I tried. Forgive me."

He's delirious. He thinks I'm the prince.

"What can I do?" Ash asked. "Tell me how to save you."

"Not important," said Vibheeshana. "You must stop Savage from getting the Black Mandala. Ravana wrote the secrets of all ten sorceries upon it. Savage aspires to be as great as my brother."

"But how? No human can contain all that magic. Savage would be torn apart." He could barely handle the seven sorceries he had already mastered, twisting into hideous shapes each time he cast a spell.

"That's why he wants the Brahma-aastra. It would counter-act any changes, prevent the colossal energies from destroying him." Vibheeshana sighed as he sank into Ash's arms, then a humorless smile spread across his bloody lips. "But he's twice the fool. Ravana cursed the diamond. He told me that if he couldn't use its powers, then no one could."

"No . . ."

Ash stopped himself, and there in the flooded hall, cradling the demon lord, he knew Gemma was never coming back. That he'd failed as completely as anyone could. It wasn't fair, it wasn't fair. A sob caught in his throat and he tightened his grip on Vibheeshana, as if he could squeeze another answer, a better one, out of the dying rakshasa prince.

He could picture her in the cafeteria, looking at him with her hazel eyes. Her shivering in her thin jumper on Bonfire Night. Her standing in his hall.

Her smile.

All that was gone, and forever. "It's my fault. All of it."

Vibheeshana looked at Ash with immeasurable sadness and put his bloodstained hands on Ash's cheeks. "No. Never think that. Parvati told me why you were here. You wanted to save your friend."

"But Parvati said . . . I should have listened." He looked hopelessly at the mountain of rubble. She was still there, some-where. Had he lost her too? "I should never have come."

"You came because you hoped, and few things are as power-ful as hope. That is how the world changes. Now let her go. Give her, and yourself, peace."

Ash should have known Savage was lying. Deep down, didn't he know that? His own desires had blinded him. He'd only heard what he'd wanted to hear. Now the terrible truth came to him. There was one mastery Savage wanted above all others. The sorcerer had talked about fixing his past mistakes. "He wants to go back in time."

"Savage is insane; he doesn't understand," Vibheeshana whispered, his strength fading. "To change the past destroys the future. That is why Ravana never used his mastery over Time. My brother was wise enough to know that, at least."

"Where is the Black Mandala?"

Vibheeshana pointed to the opposite doorway. "Quickly now. Lanka will not last long without my magic to maintain it."

"But what about Parvati?"

The demon lord smiled. "My niece has escaped more deadly traps than this. Please, there is little time. You must stop him."

Ash gritted his teeth and hissed. "Savage is a dead man."

Vibheeshana didn't reply. A last breath whispered out as the demon lord, the brother of Ravana and the last king of Lanka, died.

CHAPTER FIFTY-FOUR

"SAVAGE!" Ash ran through the hall. "SAVAGE!"

There was just one exit. Ash barreled toward the crooked archway as the lintel bent and split and the roof above him cracked. Jets of seawater sprayed down. A huge crack rent the wall above him and a waterfall burst through, creating a mighty roaring wall of water seventy feet high. Foam fizzed and sprayed everywhere, soaking Ash as he raced through it. Vibheeshana's death had revived him, closing up his wounds and adding power to his rage.

"Savage!"

The corridor was lit by spluttering lamps. The floor shifted to the side and Ash grabbed hold of the wall. There was a sharp hiss and a sudden shot of water as another fracture appeared in the ceiling.

We're all going to drown.

But he would kill Savage first. His uncle and aunt. Gemma and Vibheeshana, dead, all because of Savage.

And him. He'd led them down the path of destruction.

Why fight destiny? You are the Kali-aastra. You are the death-bringer.

His fingers tightened around Parvati's urumi. Unable to find his katar, he'd grabbed her weapon instead. Two blades were missing, but it was lethal enough with the remaining pair.

A light shone ahead of him — not the flickering flames of a lamp, but a bright, clear, steady glow of pale blue. Ash slowed down. He carefully wrapped the two remaining blades of the urumi into a loose loop. He didn't want the metal to scrape together and alert Savage.

The door in front of him was open just wide enough for Ash to look into the room beyond. Ravana's treasury. The light reflected off the extravagant bronze paneling, engraved with glorious scenes of beautiful nymphs and mighty demon lords. It was studded with precious gems, each one glittering. Ash, as silent and as certain as death, slipped in through the narrow gap.

The entire ceiling was made up of millions of small crystals. It was like being inside a diamond. Gold coins, jewelry, and gems lay scattered across the carpeted floor. There were statues of silver with eyes of sapphire. Crowns lay gathering dust, discarded in the corners and now home to spiders. Here were Egyptian statues, Mesopotamian engravings on golden plates, and cups wrought with swirling Chinese dragons. Ash recognized some of the styles and designs. His bare toes sank into the moldy, algae-covered carpet, smothering whatever sound his footsteps might have made. The thunder of the collapsing hall behind him and the encroaching sea seemed dull and distant.

The glow of pale blue still came from around the corner. Ash stepped toward it and peered ahead.

The air crackled and sparks jolted out of thin vapors that seemed to be emerging from a black surface on the far wall. A vast circular scroll hung there, suspended in a frame of iron.

The Black Mandala.

It was glossy black and decorated with shimmering patterns, also in black. Concentric circles seemed to turn and spiral in and out, trapping Ash's gaze. Minute figures guarded each ring, demons and things yet more hideous, so that his eyes burned with pain looking upon them. The painting gave off a low, powerful hum, something soul deep, and it drew Ash irresistibly toward it. He struggled to breathe, captivated as he was by the Mandala. The painting sucked in everything, an abysmal void as all-consuming as any black hole. In the patterns he saw galaxies, stars, the endless depths of the universe, as if the Mandala held it all within it. But even deeper within that infinite darkness, Ash sensed a lurking presence, something beyond the boundaries of existence.

Savage sat facing the Mandala. His back to Ash, his ankles up on his knees, he meditated in the classic yoga lotus position, his attention completely consumed by the painting. The Koh-I-Noor blazed in his left palm, casting a blue light out in all directions.

Ash swayed, unable to take his eyes off the blackness. It was as though he were tottering on the edge of a fathomless pit, some unknown power tempting him to jump. There would be no pain, because the fall would never end. He would tumble through all time, over and over. How long? It would have no meaning. Time wouldn't exist if he fell.

His heart pumped harder and harder in desperation. He grabbed hold of the table beside him and knocked over a pile of stacked jewels. Plates and bowls and countless jewels chimed and rang as the treasures fell upon each other. But the ringing noises distracted him from the hypnotic patterns on the painting. Distracted him — and Savage.

Savage was on his feet, tiger cane in one hand and the Koh-I-Noor in the other. "You're becoming quite annoying, boy." Already his flesh was firm and strong, his skin smooth and unblemished.

Ash released the urumi. The two blades unraveled and lay along the floor. He flexed his wrist and the steel rattled with anticipation. Ash peered through his death senses, using marma-adi to find the way to kill Savage.

But all the golden points dimmed on Savage. Rather, paths of power radiated from the Mandala, strengthening him. Through his shirt glowed the outline of a new skull, the eighth, which had begun to take shape upon his chest. Soon he'd be as powerful as Ravana ever was. And as invulnerable.

The skulls on Savage's chest burned, first a brilliant, bloody red, then brighter, turning yellow, and finally blinding white. The air buzzed and the table shook. The weapons hanging from the wall clattered against each other. The hairs on the nape of Ash's neck rose, and the air around him thickened, making it hard to breathe.

The paths of power between Savage and the Mandala multiplied. The eighth skull was almost complete. Two more were appearing as faint outlines.

Then the colors of the Koh-I-Noor changed. The brilliant azure light dulled and turned foul with sickly greens and vile browns, pulsing in the sorcerer's hand. The hand began to melt. The flesh bubbled as Savage's fingers fused together.

"What's happening?" Savage stared at the hand as the arm twisted, the muscles flexing unnaturally. His bones distorted under the skin, and Savage howled as his neck twisted sharply, almost turning his head backward. His skull inflated on one side as the other sank, his cheekbones collapsing. Teeth tumbled from his slack jaw.

"Ravana cursed the diamond, Savage. You should have known better than to trust a demon king."

"No, it can't be." Crackling sparks jumped over Savage's body and his eyes filled with lightning. "This is your doing. Time to die, boy."

CHAPTER FIFTY-FIVE

Savage swept up the cane, and the air burst as a lightning bolt erupted from the tiger's eyes.

The urumi screamed as Ash flicked out the two blades.

Electrical sparks from Savage's magical attack shot off in all directions, shattering mirrors and punching holes in the walls and ceiling. Ash shimmered with blue light, uncontrollable energy screaming along his nerves. But he gritted his teeth, sweat evaporating off him, his skin tingling as the sparks danced across him, leaping from his fingertips onto the rattling metal around him. The shock waves hit him again and again as the very air burned. His flesh blackened under the scorching heat and he thought he'd burst apart, but something held him, an iron core of strength that protected him from incineration.

He almost collapsed the moment the lightning ended. He groaned as the smoke rose off his skin and the stench of his own burning flesh filled his nostrils. But, slowly, strength returned, and the wounds covering him began to heal. The blistered flesh cooled and turned back into a healthy, firm brown. He stood in a smoldering crater of molten rock, but he was fine, when he should have been a pile of ash.

Vibheeshana. That was why he was alive. He'd been with the demon lord as he died and had absorbed his magical powers.

And a master of nine sorceries always trumped a master of eight. Instead of being fried by the lightning, Ash had survived.

Ash gazed at the urumi. The metal had completely rusted. The hilt crumbled as he closed his fist. The carpet under his feet was burned away and smoking, and the wall had a big dent in it. The only sound was the *chink chink chink* of gold coins falling off a broken table.

"No . . ." Savage said.

Ash looked at the Black Mandala. It was powerless now. One tip of the urumi had ripped it in two, destroying its magic. The ragged paper flapped in the breeze.

"No . . ." Savage stumbled over, cradling his left arm, which now ended in a bloody stump. He moaned with impotent rage and slumped down to his knees. "It's too much . . ."

Savage's massive, deformed head now rested upon a stick-thin neck. The skull was so huge that the skin across it was stretched to a tearing point. The flesh, yellow, cancerous, and flaky, hung upon a twisted, mutated skeleton, the legs different lengths, one with a huge foot twisted backward. The fingers of his remaining hand had melded together as well and were more like a flipper, the nails curled and thick. Any resemblance to a human being was purely incidental.

But his eyes — his eyes shone with feverish power. Black upon black, they were the eyes of night, or pure darkness. One was swollen, a bulbous growth stricken with yellow pus that dripped from sores across his brow.

Savage's severed left hand lay near Ash's feet, its fingers still curled around the Koh-I-Noor. The second blade of the serpent sword had cut his hand off his wrist.

Ash pressed his foot onto the severed appendage and the fingers opened. He took the bloody diamond and put it firmly in his waist sash. He looked down at Savage, moaning on the floor, pale and deformed, blood pumping out of the stump.

The room shook and the walls bowed, cracks burst along them and the columns began to splinter. Ash sat down.

He'd stopped Savage. Destroyed the Black Mandala once and for all. He'd done it.

But there was no escaping. They were deep under the Indian Ocean, and water was already spilling into the room. Outside he could hear the dull roar of the sea flooding the corridors and hall. The route back to the surface would be underwater by now. What he would give to just magically appear at the shore.

Hold on . . .

Ash grabbed his shirt and lifted Savage to his feet. "Get us out of here," Ash snarled. "Teleport us back to land."

"Do it yourself," Savage snarled back. "You've absorbed Vibheeshana's powers, haven't you?"

He could be right, but Ash had no idea how to make use of the demon lord's energies. He could end up on the moon or send different parts of his body in a dozen different directions. He pulled out Savage's belt and buckled it as tight as he could around the man's forearm. The blood flow decreased. He needed Savage alive, just a bit longer.

"We had a deal, Savage." Million to one shot, but things were desperate.

"Look at me. One more spell and I'll explode."

Ash grinned. "Now that I'd like to see. But at least you'll die trying."

"I can't do it. I've never moved that far. And I don't know where to go. I need coordinates, a sense of the target arrival area. I need —"

"Just get up!" Ash dragged Savage to the door. If they could get nearer to the surface, Savage might stand a better chance. Better than no chance at all.

Water flooded the corridor, and they had to fight against the rapidly swelling current. The hallway rocked and fractured, and with each shudder more water burst out from between the cracks.

The roaring sea deafened him as it was amplified by the narrow confines of the corridor. The water was waist deep by the time they got to the entrance to the hall.

The waterfall that had erupted from the wall slammed down over them as they entered. Ash disappeared under the water but never let go of Savage. He came up coughing and spluttering, shaking the water from his ears.

"Come on!" Ash shouted.

Savage struggled to escape, but he was too weak from blood loss. One foot was now so enlarged that the toes had torn through the leather boot.

Then Ash heard something above the roaring water.

Perched on one of the broken columns was a tiger, its fur gleaming and soaked. The waters swirled around it as it flicked its tail back and forth. Around its neck hung a girl in green-scaled armor. Her cobra eyes met Ash's, and there was something that looked like a smile.

Ash pointed at them. "We're bringing them with us."

Savage stared in horror. "I can't! I can barely take the two of us."

"Then let's hope you can hold your breath for a really, really long time," said Ash as he waded across to them.

Parvati and Khan leaped into the water and joined them.

Parvati hugged Ash very hard like she was never going to let go. Then she peered at him and gave him a light slap.

"Ouch," said Ash. "What's that for?"

"Being suicidal," she said. She stared up at the mighty wall of water descending down from on high. "You should have got out while you still could."

"Where's Jackie?"

"She fled. Should have followed her. Now it's too late. The exit corridor's collapsed. We're not leaving here, Ash. I'm sorry."

Ash dragged Savage forward. "That's why I brought him."

Parvati frowned. "What?"

"He's getting us out of here, aren't you?"

Savage stared at Ash with pure, volcanic hate. His veins throbbed in his forehead. "I do this, I go."

Ash met the man's gaze. "Get us out, Savage."

Parvati grabbed Ash's hand. "Are you totally sure about —"

CHAPTER FIFTY-SIX

Sunlight shimmered above him, fragmented upon the waves, and long beams shone down into the deep blue depths of the sea. The water surged, and Ash swam upward through it, kicking hard toward the light. Bubbles slipped out from between his lips. He fought the water, pulling himself higher.

He gasped as he broke the surface. He stared around frantically and saw Parvati burst out of the sea nearby. The sun was bright, warm, and oh so welcoming. He felt like he'd been underground forever.

Khan, back in human form, had Savage around the waist. He pointed beyond Ash's shoulder. "The shore."

They swam and spluttered the last four hundred feet until Ash felt sand under his toes. Waves rose over his head and he was knocked over twice before he decided to just crawl back to the beach. Even on his hands and knees, he barely had enough strength to do so, and he was embarrassingly glad when Khan dragged him the last few yards and dropped him onto the sand.

Ash lay there, on his back. "I thought cats hated water."

Khan grinned, his canines still long. "Not tigers. We love it."

Parvati gazed back at the sea and raised her hand in farewell.

Ash struggled up to see what she was looking at. Great waves were pounding the cliffs and walls of Lanka as it slowly sank beneath the swell. The earth shook as the walls protecting it crumbled, gigantic slabs of pearly marble tumbling down as towers toppled into them. Palaces slipped into the foam, hills disappeared back into the depths. The Jagannath swayed as the waves crashed against it again and again. The giant statue fought back, bracing itself as the waves grew higher and more powerful. Finally one towering wall of water engulfed it. The waters frothed and great jets shot up high into the sky as the last of the towers descended into the abyss. Then the churning sea settled, finally at peace.

Lanka was gone.

Savage groaned as he rolled over. His arms and legs jutted out from his bloated body at odd angles, forming strange shapes. His eyes were almost hidden under a huge swollen brow, a cliff of bone under a cancerous strip of yellow skin. There was no way he should be alive, not like this. The Brahma-aastra had stopped the magic from destroying him, keeping him alive, but in this cursed, monstrous shape. Savage was broken in every way possible.

Parvati, Khan, and Ash gathered in a loose circle around him as he lay cringing in the sand.

Savage raised his arms, crossing them in front of his face, hoping perhaps that those two bony limbs might hold off the killing blow. In spite of everything, even like this, he still wanted to live.

"Why, Savage?" Ash asked. "Is this 'living'? Are you that afraid to die?"

"You have no idea what waits for me on the other side of death." His voice, feeble and weak, was little more than a faint croak.

"So tell me."

Savage lowered his arms a fraction. "Would that make any difference?"

"You need to ask?"

Ash saw the golden map fall and spread over Savage, a dazzling constellation of lights so bright and dense it seemed as though the old man's body was a single glowing mass. He just needed to touch him, and Savage was dead.

The old man tried to wet his lips, but there was no saliva in his mouth. He closed his eyes, but not before a tear slipped out, a small, single crystal of sadness that slowly rolled down his cheek, weaving its way through the wrinkles and old scars, rising over the bony cheekbone and down the other side, hanging on his jaw before dripping off.

Ash touched the Koh-I-Noor, warm against his belly. They'd said it was cursed from the very beginning. There had been so much death because of Savage. If Ash killed him, would it be revenge for his uncle Vik, his aunt Anita, for Vibheeshana and Gemma? Innocent lives destroyed because they crossed paths with Savage?

Ash shuddered. They'd all crossed Ash's path too.

"Ash . . ." said Parvati. "I could —"

"No. He's mine." Ash raised his fist. Death would be instant and very permanent. "Good-bye, Savage."

"Good-bye, boy."

And in an explosion of light, Savage vanished.

CHAPTER FIFTY-SEVEN

"How could I have been so stupid?" said Ash. "He still had his magic!" They stood on the beach, staring at the empty spot where Savage had been lying just moments ago, the sand still indented with his shape.

Parvati nodded. "But that spell will have cost him. He so much as pulls a rabbit out of a hat, it'll kill him now."

"You sure?"

"No."

Could he be nearby? "Come on, let's look around. Khan, you head down the beach and I'll go that way —"

"Easy, Ash," said Parvati. "Savage isn't stupid. He'll have gone somewhere familiar to him, and I doubt it'll be within a thousand miles of here."

Ash kicked the sand. "So we've lost him again." He looked out at the now-calm sea. It was as if Lanka had never existed.

"What are you going to do with that?" asked Parvati.

The Koh-I-Noor. It wasn't glowing anymore. It settled in his hand, cold and heavy. Just a shiny stone. "I don't know."

"Who's hungry? I smell breakfast," said Khan. He turned his head and sniffed the air. Then he pointed to the top of the cliff. A weak stream of smoke drifted like a smudge against the morning sky.

"How did you find me?" Ash asked Parvati as they clambered up the slope.

"I had a few spies in the English Cemetery even after Savage's attack. They brought me your letter. Once I knew Savage was heading down south, it was obvious he was making for Lanka."

"There was a lot more I wanted to say in that letter."

"Tell me now."

Where to begin? "I was blind, Parvati. All I could think about was fixing my mistakes and bringing Gemma back, no matter what. I almost let Savage win — I *trusted* him, how stupid was that? I almost let him gain all of Ravana's powers, just so I could cheat death."

Parvati held his hand. "I trusted Savage once, so I know how cunning he can be. He promises you things and you want to believe him. It's easy to do. But you did it for the right reasons, Ash."

That was what Vibheeshana had said, before telling Ash to let Gemma go.

"How do you do it, Parvati? Cope with losing people you care about?"

"Remember what was best about them. Take joy in having known them. Strive to be the person they wanted you to be. That's how you honor the dead."

Ash nodded. He'd try. He cleared his throat and gestured toward the ocean. "How did you get out to the island? The route was guarded by sharks and all sorts of magic."

Parvati smiled and there was devilish amusement in those big eyes of hers. "Ash, Lanka was my home. There isn't a secret passage or hidden chamber I don't know about. And my uncle was there to greet me." She sighed. "It was good to see him again."

"I'm sorry I couldn't save him."

"No, I think he deserves his rest. You destroyed the Black Mandala; no one will ever be able to learn Ravana's magic."

"And you knew I'd make it through?"

"You've taken the Soma, haven't you?" She looked at him as if trying to see behind his eyes. She didn't wait for an answer. "Of course you have. How else could you have survived both Savage and Vibheeshana's magical traps? There's no stopping you now."

"You make it sound like it's a bad thing. We beat Savage, didn't we? Stopped him from getting the Mandala or the Brahma-aastra."

"At what price, Ash?" There was a long pause and her tongue flicked between her lips, her big pupils dilated. Ash heard, ever so quietly, a threatening hiss. "You are the Kali-aastra and the weapon rakshasas fear above all else. And I am a rakshasa. Where will it end between us?"

Ash wanted to laugh, but it died in his throat. He wanted to tell Parvati to not be silly, that they were friends and nothing would ever get between them, that she had nothing to fear from him. But that would all be lies. She should be afraid. The things Savage had said made Ash afraid himself. Maybe, maybe some time far away in the future, or maybe someday soon, Ash would become the monster Kali wanted him to be. A remorseless killer, more of a monster than the things he fought.

"Being a superhero's not half as much fun as I thought it would be," he said.

Parvati touched a fang with the tip of her tongue and smiled mischievously. "I'll keep an eye on you. You're not so tough."

"As if! You think you can take me on? You and whose army?"

"That army," said Parvati as they approached the top of the cliff and saw some of her rakshasa followers mingling around a campfire. "And this is just the beginning, Ash."

Mahout stood as they approached and gave Parvati a huge hug. John sat hunched over the flame, turning a small crude spit with a trio of fish skewered on it. He grinned as Ash reached the camp, then handed over the first skewer. "Consider yourself saved."

Ash sat down and peeled off the cooked meat with his fingers. The other rakshasas gathered around Parvati and Khan, leaving them alone. John gave him a skin of lukewarm water. "Well?"

"Savage got away again."

"How?"

Ash slumped down on a rock, exhausted. "Later, John."

"What about the diamond?"

He patted the rock in his sash. "Safe."

"What now, Ash?"

Ash finished his meal. He watched Parvati smile and laugh with her followers. She accepted their bows, and they in turn accepted her command. There was something different about Parvati now, and seeing her surrounded brought both a pang to Ash's heart and a sense of unease. But she seemed happy, and why shouldn't she be? She was with her people. There were people he wanted to see too, and he was weary.

"I'm going home," he said.

CHAPTER FIFTY-EIGHT

Ashoka sits, bone-weary, upon his horse. The snow falls heavily, and his eyelashes are encrusted with ice. Great white clouds billow out from his horse's nostrils as it heaves steadily through the dense, snow-filled path.

He is the emperor Ashoka. His name means "without sorrow." He would laugh, but his chest aches. Without sorrow. He has much to be sorrowful about. Even now, weeks later, his dreams are haunted. Haunted by unliving creatures that snarl and claw and try to drag him into darker realms. They are the faces of friends and allies, but in their eyes blaze a hellfire, and all around them is a miasma of putrescence. They creep from each shadow, alive, yet dead. The fighting had been hard and close, but eventually the monsters had been destroyed, their bodies piled high on a pyre and their ashes scattered to the winds.

He turns as he hears the jangle of a bridle and watches dully as Parvati urges her own steed beside his. She peers up the mountain slope. "There. Look."

Through the curtain of snow, Ashoka glimpses a building, a temple. The path is guarded by ferocious statues of warriors, and the roof, a dome, is surmounted by the trident symbol of Shiva. Beyond rises the crystalline peaks of Mount Kailash, the god's home.

"I cannot go farther," says Parvati.

Ashoka stops, fear cloaking him. "No, just see me to the door. I beg you."

Parvati says nothing, but stays where she is.

How can he go there? He gazes at the terrifying statues and sees in their cool gaze judgment. Judgment for the things he's done. Every night he is haunted by the spirits of the dead — and there are so many. Men, women, children. Some are covered in sword wounds, others black and still aflame, others with crushed skulls and limbs.

A priest appears through the white. He wears a thin orange cloth about his waist, but otherwise he is naked to the elements. Ashoka wears furs upon furs and is still chilled to the bone. This man's feet are bare as they step lightly through the drifts. He carries a straight bamboo staff and has a cloth bag slung over a bony shoulder.

Ashoka dismounts his horse.

Then he, an emperor, prostrates himself before a spindly old man dressed in rags.

"Rise, Ashoka," says the priest.

The emperor gazes into deep azure eyes, full of warmth and wisdom. The man's gray dreadlocks are piled high upon his head, and he touches the sandalwood beads about his neck, smiling at Ashoka. "We are pleased that you have taken the pilgrimage."

"I have much to atone for, guru."

"Call me Rishi."

Ashoka fumbles in his pocket and pulls out the diamond. Eagerly he holds it out. "A gift. Please, it is yours."

Rishi's eyes narrow as if he senses the dangers within its flawless surface. Ashoka stops breathing. What if Rishi doesn't take it? What if he has to bear it, cursed thing that it is? How much more horror will it bring him?

But Rishi nods, and then it is safe within his bag. "Come, my emperor. We have much work to do."

Emperor and holy man vanish into the swirling snow.

Ash switched on the side light in his bedroom. Four in the morning. He passed his hands through his hair. God, he was exhausted. Even when he had okay dreams like that one, the broken nights were taking their toll.

He had been back in London for three weeks now. As glad as he had been to see his parents and Lucky, the return had been difficult. His first adventure had been out in India, and that had been easy to leave behind. This time around, the horror had been on his doorstep, and the consequences and reminders of it were here as well. Some days he'd pass by Gemma's house on the way to school. He'd slow down, even stop, half-expecting the door to open and see her come out, school bag over her shoulder, smiling. But the door never opened. Now he took another route to school and avoided her place entirely. He hadn't slept a full night since he'd been home.

The first day back at school had been a nightmare. If he'd thought being away a few weeks would have helped people get over Gemma's death, he was sorely mistaken. The memorial display at the school entrance hall had grown, with lots of new photos from friends joining the main school one, and the wall was covered with messages.

And they still blamed Ash. Why had he gone? Where had he gone? The rumor mill went into overtime while he was away. Some said he'd been arrested by the police, or that he was on the run for Gemma's murder, or he was in hiding to avoid reprisals. Jack had done his best to stir it all up until the whole school, even if they didn't say it to his face, thought Ash was a killer.

They had no idea, Ash thought.

Josh, Akbar, and Sean were making a bit of an effort to bring him back into the fold, but even Josh, his oldest mate, had taken almost a week before he'd spoken to him. He still looked at Ash as if he didn't really know him, or trust him.

Ash got up and went to his closet. He reached up to the back and drew out an old book, *The Story of India*. He opened it and lifted out the Koh-I-Noor from the cavity he'd cut through the pages.

What should he do with it? He couldn't just turn up at a police station and say he'd found one of the Crown Jewels on the street. The thing still weighed more than it should: It felt lead-hearted.

Footsteps whispered on the carpet outside.

"You might as well come in, Lucks."

Ash's sister opened the door, and then, with a quick look up and down the corridor to make sure their parents were still asleep, snuck in. She saw the diamond in his palm. "More bad dreams?"

"Ashoka's not letting me go." He held out the diamond. "It's this. He wants me to do something with it."

"Like what?"

"Maybe I should have left it in Lanka. Too late now." He closed his fingers around it and squeezed the rock, wondering if he could crush it if he wanted to. Maybe, but maybe not, and all he'd get was a shard of it stuck in his skin. He knew what had happened the last time he mishandled an aastra.

"What about Parvati? Did she have any ideas?"

Yes, what about Parvati? Things had been awkward after Lanka. Khan had stayed just long enough to gather lots of praise and then he'd left without saying good-bye. That was just the tiger's way. Ash and John had returned to Kolkata while flights were arranged, Ash to London and John to Kashmir.

Then Parvati had said good-bye, and that was it. She'd continue the hunt for Savage, and there'd been an unspoken offer for him to stay and help, but in all honesty, Ash was sick of it all. Nothing good had come out of anything, except maybe for Parvati. He had watched uneasily as more rakshasas gathered around her. They looked at her with an awe bordering on worship — the same way they'd once looked at her father. Ash didn't need to be reminded of that.

"We didn't talk much about the diamond," he said to Lucky now. "I think she was happy to see the back of it."

Lucky frowned. He could see she was worried. And Ash knew exactly why. He looked like death — dark-eyed, gaunt. Something was eating him up from the inside.

"What else?" asked Lucky.

"It's Gemma. What I tried to do."

"Ash . . ."

"Yeah, I know." Ash bounced the gem in his hand. "I betrayed my friends and helped Savage, and all because I thought I could cheat death. If I hadn't been stopped, I would have brought Gemma back, and she'd have been a monster."

"But you were stopped."

"Only at the very end, when it was almost too late." Ash gazed into the diamond, seeing himself distorted in the crystalline faces. "I can't undo the past. I look at Savage and see what I might become. That's the path of blind obsession, and I think Ashoka's trying to show me another way, but I just don't get it."

Lucky peered around the room. "Could you talk to Dad about Ashoka? He and Uncle Vik were always crazy about history."

"And Dad chose to name me after a man who spent his career burning and slaughtering. Gee, thanks, Dad."

"That's not all Ashoka was." Lucky got up and yawned. "You know he turned his back on war. He became a pacifist, embraced religion. His name was even changed, wasn't it? To Devan something something." She took the diamond from his hand. "If you don't do something with this soon, I'm going to use it to buy a pony."

Hold on. Devan . . . what? Something shot through Ash, something unfamiliar but bright. Something like hope. "Lucks, you know what? You're smarter than you look." He sprang up and went to his shelves. "It's got to be here somewhere."

Lucky yawned. "That's me, Lucky, the girl genius, and don't you forget it. Good night."

Ash searched his books. He found one about the rulers of India. On the front was a painting of Shah Jahan, the Moghul emperor who built India's most famous monument, the Taj Mahal.

Ash flicked through the pages until he got to Ashoka. There was the meaning of the name he knew so well: without sorrow.

But as Lucky said, he also had another name, a title.

• *Devanampiya.*

Beloved of the gods.

Devanampiya created monasteries, went on pilgrimages, studied with the Brahmins and monks of all sects. Some histories believed he converted to Buddhism, others that he became a sadhu, a holy man.

Beloved of the gods.

Ashoka's first step had been to get rid of the Koh-I-Noor. Suddenly Ash knew exactly who should have it.

CHAPTER FIFTY-NINE

I am going to prison. That or the loony bin.

Shining frost covered the grave. The flowers and tributes around the headstone sparkled as if made from jewels. Ash took hold of his shovel.

His breath came in big white clouds as he dug into the frozen earth. It was early December and painfully cold. A single dark cloud covered the sky like a shroud, and flakes of snow descended lightly, drifting down in the still night.

Onto Gemma's grave.

He thought of her smiling at him in the dining hall, of how her hair shone, of the kind way she treated him. She was his friend and always would be.

Ash threw great black showers of dirt, digging down and down. He worked steadily, stopping only for a drink of water and a quick look around the graveyard to make sure he was alone.

This is insane, but what else can I do?

The shovel edge cracked against wood. The sharp, abrupt sound shocked Ash to a halt. He'd broken the coffin lid.

Moonlight shone upon golden hair.

Ash chucked the shovel out and dug the rest of the dirt off the lid. He got out a screwdriver, but soon gave up trying to open the lid that way. Instead he dug his fingernails into the side of the lid and tore it off.

Gemma lay upon the silk lining, clumps of soil on her white, lifeless skin. She held a bunch of withered flowers in her fingers.

"I'm sorry, Gemma," he said. There should be more. He should tell her how much he hated himself, how he'd failed everyone because he'd thought he was better than they were. How he'd trusted Savage. How he missed her.

Ash bent down and took her hand, noticing its coldness and the papery skin that wrinkled around her slim fingers. He cleared a few strands of hair out of her face. The brittle threads cracked.

Gemma didn't feel like a person, someone who'd once breathed and laughed. She felt utterly alien, as cold as the earth. Whatever had made her human — her life, her soul — had gone.

But in spite of the scent of decay, he could still smell her perfume. It lingered on her skin, the delicate aura of flowers and the soft hint of summer rain on the grass.

"Rishi told me we always come back," he said to her. "I believe him, but that doesn't make this any easier. It hurts, Gemma, and that's good. It means you took a part of me when you died. I wish I could give you more, but I hope you'll be happy with this."

Ash took out the Koh-I-Noor. He put it softly among the dried rose petals that covered her chest. The diamond glinted and a faint silver hue spread over Gemma, and for a second, a mad desperate second, Ash thought she might awaken. But she was dead, and the color was just the moonlight coming out from behind a cloud.

"Good-bye, Gemma. Rest well."

Ash closed the lid, pushing it firmly back in place.

It didn't take him long to fill the grave. He worked steadily, sweating hard, but did not draw on his powers. Gemma deserved more, his human effort. He was the Kali-aastra, but he was more than that. Ashoka had gone from warrior to man of peace. *Be what you want to be; be better than you are.* That was Ashoka's message. The Kali-aastra didn't have to define Ash.

His arms ached and his back was a single mass of agony as he finally patted down the last of the soil. The snow was falling heavily now and would cover the grave soon enough, and there'd be no sign that it had been disturbed. He arranged the flowers around the headstone and climbed over the high iron railings that surrounded West Norwood Cemetery.

CHAPTER SIXTY

Ash brushed the dirt off his tracksuit as best he could and checked the time. Just gone half-six. Mum and Dad would be up now. He'd sneak in, get changed, and be off to school.

He dug his hands into his pockets and lifted his hood over his head. The snow smothered the high street and a truck was off-loading fresh bread to the local supermarket. The shops had their Christmas decorations up, and there was a thirty-foot Christmas tree in front of the church, lights sparkling on its green needles.

Ash took a deep breath as he glanced back at the graveyard. He could barely see past the railings as the snowfall began to increase, fat flakes drifting in the still, freezing air. He couldn't see Gemma's grave.

A new start. That's what he needed. Enough saving the world; he needed to just get back to being a fourteen-year-old. That was hard enough.

SAVING THE WORLD.

The words were on a billboard, huge and epic, spanning the entire roof of the supermarket. Ash grinned. *Yeah, let someone else do it for once.* He adjusted his hood and —

Stopped and stared at the billboard.

The left side showed a small African child, malnourished and crying, face covered in flies, lying in her mother's arms as a doctor gave her an injection. The right side was the same girl, smiling and healthy and standing in a field of wheat. Her eyes were bright and she wore a beautiful printed dress. SAVING THE WORLD. ONE CHILD AT A TIME ran over the whole image.

But what made Ash's blood freeze was the logo at the bottom corner. Poppies with a pair of crossed swords.

Savage's coat of arms.

It was nothing to worry about, surely. The Savage Foundation was a big multinational business; sooner or later, Ash would come across it. It employed thousands around the world, people who had nothing to do with Lord Alexander Savage.

But as Ash continued home, he couldn't shake a creeping unease. Why hadn't he ever noticed the poster before? It must have been up there for days. He would have walked past it on his way to school.

Five minutes later, he turned the corner to his house. He pushed open the gate and saw a brand-new Range Rover parked in the driveway.

He closed the gate. The snow was confusing him and he'd gone to his neighbor's house. His dad drove a ten-year-old Ford C-Max.

Weird. This was his gate. This was his driveway.

But whose car was that? His gaze fell on the license plate. M1STRY 1.

Something caught in his throat. His dad had always wanted a personalized license plate, but Mum had always vetoed the expense. And the Range Rover was brand-new. No way they could afford something like that. Some new company car scheme his dad hadn't told him about? Yes, that had to be it. Or maybe he'd been promoted. The directors all had flashy cars.

Ash unlocked the door. The kettle whistled and the radio

murmured in the kitchen as his parents chatted and got break-fast ready. He kicked off his All Stars and rushed to his room. It was already seven.

He threw his clothes on the bathroom floor and showered, then dried off.

"Ashoka! Breakfast!" shouted Mum.

Crap. She only called him that when she was angry with him. He must have left muddy tracks on the carpet.

Ash opened up his closet and grabbed a shirt. He shook the water off his head as he buttoned up, only to discover the shirt didn't fit. He pulled it off. It was one of his old ones, back when he'd been big and blubbery, before his Kali-inspired diet and fitness regime. Mum must have got it mixed up. He looked for another. That was the big size too. He picked up a T-shirt, but it was his old baggy Nike shirt that he'd sent to the charity shop three months ago.

What was going on?

Ash put the T-shirt on and a spare pair of track pants, then went downstairs.

Breakfast lay on the table as usual. The newspapers and a few magazines were neatly piled in the center. Mum had a cof-fee in one hand while adjusting her earrings with the other. "Wasn't sure if you were still here."

"I went out for a run." He looked at her. "When did you get the new haircut?"

Mum laughed. "You've only noticed it now? Ashoka, I've had this style for months."

Dad came in. "Has anyone seen my watch?" He ruffled Ash's hair without really looking at him. "Morning, son."

"Look on top of the fridge," said Mum.

Dad did. "Ah. Here we go." It was big, gold, and shiny.

Ash's eyes narrowed. "And since when have you had a Rolex, Dad?"

Dad clipped it around his wrist and gave it a quick polish. "You know how long. And no, you cannot have one until you're eighteen. We discussed it, remember?"

Lucky came in and looked around the kitchen. "Mum, I can't find my hat anywhere."

Mum waved back toward the hall. "It's where you left it after your last lesson, with your riding boots."

"So when did you start riding lessons?" Ash asked. "Last couple of weeks?"

"Since we came back from India, dur-brain."

This wasn't right. None of it. Ash stared at his family. There was something different, but what, exactly?

Then he noticed the wall behind Lucky. "Where's the photo?"

Mum poured out some tea. "Hmm?"

"The photo of Uncle Vik and Aunt Anita. It used to be right there." Instead of their old wedding photo, which had hung in that space since their deaths, there was a picture of Lucky sitting on a black-and-white pony, looking very pleased with herself. Ash stood up, heart racing. How could they take down the photo?

"Are you all right, Ash?"

"This isn't funny," he said. "Where is the photo?"

Dad looked at Ash, frowning. He shook his head. "You look different, Ashoka."

"Why are you calling me 'Ashoka,' Dad?"

Dad looked at Mum and she shrugged. He picked up a piece of toast, though he still watched Ash with an odd expression. "We thought that's what you wanted. When you came back from India, you said you wanted us to use your proper Indian name."

"No. No, I didn't."

Lucky rolled her eyes. "He's gone mental. I knew it would happen sooner or later."

"Where is the photo?" Ash insisted.

Dad smiled. "We have plenty of you and your uncle and aunt. We could put one of them up. You know, from your holiday."

"But they're dead, Dad." Savage had killed them. Mum and Dad knew that!

Dad frowned. "Who's dead?"

"Vik and Anita? No, you know they're fine," replied his mum, confused. "Are you sure you're all right? You do look a bit pale."

The world had gone mad.

Mum smiled. "Wait, I've got something to show you. You know how you're always going on about Lord Savage?" She flicked through the newspapers and took out *Time* magazine. "Here. It's their annual 'Man of the Year' issue."

Lord Alexander Savage.

He stared at Ash from the photo: young, beautiful, smiling benevolently. They'd given the cover a metallic sheen so he looked less than a human and more like a golden god. His skin was porcelain and perfect, unmarked by wrinkle or blemish. His eyes were hidden behind his shades, but the smile chilled Ash to his soul. That was a smile of a man who'd won everything.

Dad clicked his tongue. "They'll be making him Prime Minister next."

No. No. NO. Ash gripped the magazine. "This isn't right." Dad put his hand on Ash's arm, but Ash shoved him off. He backed up against the door, staring at them. "Who are you?"

Mum looked worried. "Ashoka . . ."

"Stop calling me that!" Ash grabbed Lucky's arm. "What happened in India? You *know* what happened."

"Ow, Ashoka, you're hurting me!"

"I said stop calling me that!"

Lucky stared at him, pale and eyes wide. Tears dripped down her cheeks and Ash's fingers sprang open. He wouldn't hurt his sister, not ever.

But was this Lucky?

"Son, you look sick," said Dad. He reached out, but Ash pushed back through the door, away from them. He stumbled into the hall and, just wearing his socks, out the door.

He had to get away.

Heart racing, he ran along the road, with no idea where he was going. He bumped into a man coming out of the newsagent, knocking the paper out of his hands.

Ash reached down instinctively to get it. "Sorry, I didn't see you . . ."

Prince William was on the front page of the *Independent*. Then Ash read the headline.

KING WILLIAM CELEBRATES A YEAR ON THE THRONE.

Knees in the snow, Ash stared at the newspaper, hoping against hope this was some joke. He checked the date. Today. It was today.

"My paper, please?" said the man.

Dumbly Ash handed it back and stood up. It was all different. Everything. Something had changed. Not with a bang or a thunderbolt or with storms. But something had changed, and it was all different.

Ash couldn't breathe. His chest felt like a massive weight was pressing down on it. Kids walked past him on their way to school. A dog yapped at him, but Ash, eyes blurred with tears, just stood there, utterly lost.

What had happened? Last night, he'd left home after talking with Lucky, *his* Lucky. He'd gone to the graveyard and everything had been the same until he got home. His parents, his sister, were different people.

It had to be Savage. Savage had changed the past. He had mastered Time and done it, just like he said he would.

And because Savage changed the past, Ash's family had developed in different ways, their lives taking other paths. Things had happened, and hadn't happened.

He blinked. His uncle and aunt were alive. They'd never had the car crash. That was a good thing, wasn't it? But what else was different that he didn't know about?

"Ash!"

He wiped his face. Who was that?

"Ash!"

A group of West Dulwich High students were on the opposite side of the road. He peered through the curtain of snow, just able to make out someone waving at him. He stepped toward the person, raising his hand instinctively.

It was Josh, wrapped up for an Arctic expedition, his eyes and nose just visible between the collar of his coat and his low-drawn hat. He raised his gloved hand. "Ash!"

A boy bumped Ash's shoulder as he passed him from behind. "Sorry," said the boy, waving back to Josh. "Hey!"

The ground tilted and Ash grabbed a lamppost, his legs suddenly jelly. This boy was the same height and build as Ash, just a bit plumper, with the same hairstyle, maybe a little bit shorter. He wore a pair of Converse All Stars and carried a backpack just like the one Ash owned. He was wearing Ash's greatcoat, his Sherlock Special. He crossed the road and joined Josh.

Ash wandered into the middle of the road, following the boy. Dazed, he just stood there, watching. A car beeped its horn, but he didn't move. He couldn't. He was frozen in time and space.

The boy slapped Josh's well-padded shoulder. "I thought I told you, Josh. I'm not Ash Mistry. . . ."

The boy smiled. He had Ash's smile. He had his eyes, his nose, his face.

". . . I'm Ashoka."

This book was edited by Cheryl Klein of Arthur A. Levine Books/Scholastic and Nicholas Lake of HarperCollins UK. The book design is by Phil Falco, with art by Jason Chan. The text was set in Garamond, with display type set in Martin Gothic. This book was printed and bound by R. R. Donnelley in Crawfordsville, Indiana. The production was supervised by Starr Baer. The manufacturing was supervised by Angelique Browne.